DEATH
OF A
TRAITOR

The Hamish Macbeth Series

DEATH OF A TRAITOR

TRAITOR

M.C. Beaton

with R.W. Green

GCP

GRAND
CENTRAL

NEW YORK   BOSTON

Copyright © 2023 by Marion Chesney
Excerpt from *Death of a Spy* copyright © 2024 by Marion Chesney

Cover copyright © 2024 by Hachette Book Group, Inc.

Grand Central Publishing
Hachette Book Group
1290 Avenue of the Americas, New York, NY 10104
grandcentralpublishing.com
twitter.com/grandcentralpub

Published in the United States in hardcover by
Grand Central Publishing in February 2023

First U.S. Mass Market Edition: January 2024

Grand Central Publishing is a division of Hachette Book Group, Inc. The Grand Central Publishing name and logo is a trademark of Hachette Book Group, Inc.

The publisher is not responsible for websites (or their content) that are not owned by the publisher.

The Hachette Speakers Bureau provides a wide range of authors for speaking events. To find out more, go to hachettespeakersbureau.com or email HachetteSpeakers@hbgusa.com.

Grand Central Publishing books may be purchased in bulk for business, educational, or promotional use. For information, please contact your local bookseller or the Hachette Book Group Special Markets Department at special.markets@hbgusa.com.

Library of Congress Cataloging-in-Publication Data has been applied for.

ISBNs: 978-1-5387-4677-6 (mass market), 978-1-5387-46752 (ebook)

Printed in the United States of America

OPM

10 9 8 7 6 5 4 3 2 1

Foreword by R. W. Green

Sergeant Hamish Macbeth knows far more than most about secrets and lies. If someone told you that they had no secrets and never told lies, Hamish would tell you that they were clearly lying to cover up their secrets. Everyone, after all, has a secret or two, and we've all told the odd fib at some time, haven't we? What—not you? Hamish would have a hard time believing you...

No one, you see, knows more about how secrets and lies work than Lochdubh's police sergeant. He deals with them on a day-to-day basis and, like the village's twin paragons of virtue, the Currie sisters, who manage to waylay him and lambast him for his laziness or some perceived dereliction of duty whenever he leaves his police station, Hamish knows that the twin demons of secrets and lies forever walk shoulder to shoulder. If you see them coming, like the Currie twins, they're best avoided.

For Hamish, of course, avoiding them really isn't an option. His beat covers a vast swathe of rural Sutherland in the far north of Scotland. Here he deals with all sorts of problems, from rowdiness and burglaries to stolen bicycles and—on occasion—murder. Whatever crime or misdemeanour he's investigating, the culprit will certainly tell desperate lies to avoid the wrath of the law—and hiding in the shadow of desperate lies lurk dark secrets. Fortunately, Hamish has a Highlander's unerring instinct for recognising a lie when he hears one and the dogged determination to root out its twin secret.

When M. C. Beaton—Marion—first devised her Highland policeman character almost forty years ago, she endowed him with all of the talents, traits and foibles she believed she saw in the people of the Highlands. Having lived there, she loved Sutherland and its inhabitants, admiring the strength and fortitude it takes to live and work in one of the most remote areas of the United Kingdom. She also regarded them as intuitive and astute, well able to bend the truth themselves when it suited their needs. Hamish is certainly capable of bending not only the truth but also the law when he sees it as a means to an end. That's not to say that Marion based Hamish on any one particular person. She cherry-picked ingredients for her Hamish recipe as she thought fit—a little from someone she'd met in a shop, a smidgen from someone she'd seen in the street, a pinch from someone she'd overheard talking in the post office, and a huge portion from her own imagination.

So did Marion regard Hamish as a typical Highlander? Is there even such a thing as a typical Highlander? Just like everywhere else, the Highlands are populated—albeit far more sparsely than most other places in the UK—by a wide variety of people, many of whom come from outside the region, just as Marion did. Outsiders can take a lifetime to be accepted into the fold by those born and bred in the far north, and Hamish was no exception. When he first moved to Lochdubh, he was treated as an outsider because he was from Ross and Cromarty, to the south of Sutherland. That's not too far to the south, but far enough for him to be regarded as an interloper. You shouldn't think, however, that those who live in the Highlands are inhospitable or unwelcoming—far from it. Many, after all, rely on the tourist trade for their livelihood, but newcomers who aim to stay longer, those who want to make a home in the Highlands, need to be patient to earn acceptance.

That's not something unique to the Highlands or something that creates a "typical" Highlander. Caution in the acceptance of strangers is simply human nature and an attitude that prevails to a greater or lesser extent in communities everywhere, whether rural or urban, especially if the strangers come with secrets to keep—and Hamish arrived in Lochdubh with a clutch of secrets. No one could quite understand how Constable Macbeth, as he was when he first arrived in the village, managed to have the police authority build him a brand-new police station and provide him with a new car. Nobody knew, and it wasn't something that Hamish felt inclined to explain.

Perhaps little mysteries like that provided enough intrigue to make the locals believe that their new police officer was something special, although at first he did nothing much to impress them. He seemed to want a quiet life and didn't go out of his way to find work, leading some to brand him as lazy—but he was always there when people needed him most. They discovered that he was perfectly capable of discreetly turning a blind eye to someone poaching the odd salmon or trout, even indulging in a little illicit angling himself, but anyone threatening the peace and tranquillity of Lochdubh, or running amok in the Sutherland countryside, had a very different Macbeth to deal with. His temper was as fiery as his flaming red hair and, at well over six feet tall, he was an imposing figure.

Surely that hair makes Hamish a typical Highlander? Marion described his hair as "true Highland red that looks like it has purple lights" but, despite his hair and his height, she shunned the stereotype of a burly Highland strongman. Hulking great Highlanders were famously prized as fighting men, recruited into armies throughout Europe at one time. In the early fifteenth century, Scotsmen formed the Garde Écossaise, elite personal bodyguards to the French monarchs for more than three centuries. Such was the reputation of the Highlander, yet Hamish isn't quite like that. He is tall and long-limbed but lanky rather than muscle-bound, a champion hill runner who won the top prize at the Strathbane Highland games five years in a row.

Unlike the residents of Lochdubh, who have had to spread their gossip nets far and wide to trawl for titbits about their policeman, I was fortunate enough to learn all about Hamish from Marion herself when I first began working with her. I was amazed that she didn't keep any notes about the cast of characters who appear alongside Hamish, but she didn't feel she needed any. She had created them all, from the salty old fisherman, Archie Maclean, to the sophisticated and beautiful Priscilla Halburton-Smythe, and knew all of their secrets and lies. She knew just what any of them would say or do in any given situation, allowing her to weave them into her stories whenever their presence was required to keep the plot moving forward.

Hamish, I learned, was the oldest of seven children, having three brothers and three sisters. Highland tradition has it that the oldest son works to help support the family until his siblings are able to lead their own lives, which is one of the reasons why Hamish has never married. Still a young man, although well beyond his twenties, he has now reached the age where, while continuing to contribute to the family coffers, he has been able to consider marriage, and he's been engaged three times. For many reasons best discovered by reading previous books, none of his engagements resulted in marriage.

It was a great pleasure to listen to Marion talk about Hamish and the other Lochdubh residents and, following her death, an immense privilege to be able to take them forward, using some of the many plot ideas we discussed. Whenever I'm wondering how best to deal with the latest predicament into which Hamish has been dropped, all I have to do is think of how Marion would handle it. She usually points me in the right direction.

So Hamish soldiers on in Lochdubh, dealing with friendly, familiar faces, as well as a few old adversaries. In *Death of a Traitor*, as you would expect from a plot involving treachery, he also has to contend with a whole host of secrets and lies, mainly perpetrated by a clutch of new characters. He is issued with a new uniform, has a new constable assigned to him temporarily and, perhaps, finds a new love. Needless to say, he has more than his fair share of trauma to deal with along the way, including the sad demise of a faithful old friend.

I hope you enjoy being back in Lochdubh as much as I do.

Rod Green, 2022

CHAPTER ONE

The wretch, concentred all in self,
Living, shall forfeit fair renown,
And, doubly dying, shall go down
To the vile dust, from whence he sprung,
Unwept, unhonored, and unsung.
Sir Walter Scott, *The Lay of the*
Last Minstrel

Gregor Mackenzie gazed out over the hillside above Lochdubh, leaning on his cromach walking staff and admiring his sheep grazing contentedly in the late morning sunshine. On a day like today, he mused, with a blue sky and a light breeze breathing the freshest of air across the mountains, gently ruffling the heather in soft purple waves, Sutherland was surely the most beautiful place on the planet. His mood was buoyed by the sound, healthy condition of his flock. He was immensely proud of his prize-winning animals and had a fine selection of lambs almost ready for the big auction at Lairg in September, sure to fetch a handsome price. As though they could read his thoughts, several of the North Country Cheviots turned their white faces towards him, their pensive expressions filled with false wisdom. When Gregor's border collie, Bonnie, pricked up her ears and raised her head, they immediately returned to their grazing.

"Ha!" Mackenzie let out a soft laugh and reached down to pat his dog. "It's like they don't want you to know what it is they're thinking, lass. Truth be told, I doubt they're ever thinking anything much."

It was then that he spotted a movement far below on the track leading to the main road. He immediately recognised the pink coat and hat of Kate Hibbert, the woman who had moved into the glen more than a year before. Her cottage was little more than a hundred yards from his. She was perfectly outlined against the distant view of Lochdubh and she appeared to be struggling with a large suitcase, dragging it down the rutted track.

"Where's that sly besom off to, eh, Bonnie?" Mackenzie reached into a battered knapsack, quickly laying a hand on his old binoculars without ever taking his eyes off the figure in pink further down the hill. No sooner had he fixed the woman in focus than she disappeared where the track dipped behind a heather-clad mound. He tutted, setting off down the hill to find a spot where he could catch sight of her again when she reappeared, Bonnie trotting at his heels. He'd heard nothing about Hibbert taking a holiday and his day was suddenly cheered by the thought that he might be rid of her for a couple of weeks. Wait, though—what if she were going for good? Man, he'd sink a dram or two of his best whisky to that thought as soon as he got home, no matter what his wife might say about him drinking in the afternoon.

Mackenzie stopped abruptly, his dog almost slamming straight into the backs of his legs. He looked down at the white, petal-like bracts and delicate purple flowers of the avern plants and took a detour off to his left. The avern, some called them cloudberries, marked the edge of boggy ground where he could easily sink up to his knee if he wasn't careful. Once he had a view of the track and the road running along the lochside, he raised his binoculars again. The glasses had been part of the trouble the Hibbert woman had created between him and his wife, Clara. He'd always kept the binoculars for spotting otters, or maybe an osprey, out on the water but Hibbert had told Clara she'd seen him spying on the women aboard the tourist yachts that came into the loch in the summer. Well, on warm days they were in bikinis—sometimes even topless. What was so wrong with taking a wee peek? That, of course, wasn't how Clara saw it.

He scanned the track and the road, waiting for Hibbert to reappear, musing over the problems she had caused. She'd interfered when it came to the peat. Clara had a fine, strong back on her and was well able to carry a sackload of peat down the brae to their cottage from where they cut it further up the hill. Hibbert had insisted on helping, always cheerful, always smiling but always bleating about what heavy work it was and how "poor

Clara shouldn't have to lug all that peat around." Clara never complained, but Hibbert kept on about it until, in the end, he'd been forced to agree that Clara shouldn't be carrying the peat and that he needed to do something about it. He bought Clara a peat barrow.

Even then, Hibbert gave him no peace. She was constantly round at their cottage, happily helping Clara to bring in the washing or clean the windows. She was forever drinking coffee, having lunch with Clara or happening to drop by just as they were about to sit down at teatime, making them feel obliged to invite her to share their evening meal. All the time, she was watching him, always looking for another chance to point out how he was failing his wife. When none came, she would conjure one up, saying things like, "That sofa's seen better days, has it not, Gregor? Surely Clara deserves a new one?" Gregor hated Hibbert but, while she never claimed they were the best of friends, Clara tolerated her at first. As time went on, however, Gregor could plainly see that Clara was starting to find Hibbert about as welcome as a midge in the bedroom on a warm night.

Things came to a head when Clara arrived home from doing some shopping at Patel's little supermarket down in Lochdubh to find the woman in their house, going through their mail and the old ledger where they kept their accounts.

"Aye, that was a grand day, Bonnie," Gregor said softly, the binoculars pressed tight against his eyes. "We were rebuilding the dyke all the way up in the top pasture, weren't we? We could hear Clara going mental even from there—such language as I've never before heard from her. She was right ashamed of the blasphemy afterwards. Attended the kirk every Sunday morning for a month. The bloody Hibbert woman steered well clear of us after that. But where has she got to now, eh?"

Mackenzie had a clear view of the track and the road but there was no sign of the woman in pink. Making his way down the slope, he took a look behind the mound that had obscured his view only to find the track deserted. He ran a hand over the greying stubble on his chin, shrugged and turned to head for home, itching to tell Clara he had seen that damned woman leaving their glen. With any luck, they'd heard the last of her.

Kate Hibbert was the furthest thing from Sergeant Hamish Macbeth's mind as he stood close to a small crowd gathered on the shore of The Corloch, enjoying the morning sunshine and listening to a story he hadn't heard since he was a child.

Auld Mary's Tale (part one)

"You'll neffer catch them now, John Mackay! They're free from your evil clutches at last!" The old woman stood on a small, rocky island ten yards from the shore of The Corloch. Silhouetted in the moonlight, her shadow cast long upon the water, the woman pointed a crooked finger towards the loch, the ragged folds of her black cloak hanging from her outstretched arm. *"They'll be in Sutherland territory afore an hour has passed. The Gordons will welcome them there, and you dare not follow."*

The three men on the shore stared out across the water to where a man and a woman were making their way steadily across the loch in a small boat. A ripple of water could be heard echoing over the surface each time the young man heaved on his paddle, yet they were still close enough for the three men to make out the pale, frightened face of the young woman staring back at them.

"Damn you, Mary! You gave them your boat!" raged the leader of the three. Each of them was barefoot, as they generally were come rain or shine, and dressed in a heavy plaid wrapped around the body, with a generous length draped over one shoulder, all held fast at the waist by a broad, leather belt. Each of them also carried a long, heavy sword, the steel blades glinting in the pale light.

"Just as you knew I would," the old woman cackled. "Don't try to pretend otherwise. It's all part of your plan."

"What's she talking about, John?" asked one of the other men, stepping forward. His beard and long hair were as dark as his leader's. "What plan?"

"She's raving, Jamie," scoffed the first man. "You hear that, Mary? You're raving mad. Don't you know who that is in yon boat? He's Malcolm Gordon, the son of a Sutherland laird, and the girl is Eilidh Mackay, daughter of our own laird. The laddie has been held hostage these past five years in order to keep the peace between us Mackays and the Gordons. Don't you realise what you've done? There will be no peace now!"

"Peace?" howled the woman, with a strength of voice that seemed alien to her frail, thin frame. "Don't you lecture

me about peace! The boy was neffer kept as a guarantee of peace. He was held hostage so that the Mackays could raid Sutherland, stealing cattle and causing havoc wi' no fear of reprisal! Now perhaps we'll see real peace at last!"

"You auld witch!" roared the third man. Even with the moonlight softening the foliage and the trunks of the ancient oak and birch trees to a misty grey, his hair and beard glowed a fearsome red. "You've given the Gordons a free hand to strike at us as they please!"

"Such is your fear," said the old woman, her voice now calm and steady. "You fear your enemies will take revenge, but your fear blinds you. Open your eyes as you should have done these past five years. Have you no' seen those two grow together—he as a prisoner in the laird's grand house and she as the laird's pride and joy? Have you no' seen the stolen glances and secret smiles? Have you no' seen the love that has blossomed? Young Malcolm's no' kidnapping Eilidh—they have chosen to elope together! They'll be wed afore the next new moon!"

"A Mackay woman wi' a Gordon man? Neffer!" growled John Mackay.

"Who are you to say such a thing?" the old woman laughed. "Married they will be and, in due course, blessed wi' strong, healthy bairns. And the bairns will have no hatred of the Mackays, their mother being a Mackay herself. And when Malcolm becomes laird, he'll no' send men to raid Mackay lands. He has friends here, and his wife's kin. He'll no' risk them being killed in battle, just as your laird will be loath to risk his daughter

*and grandchildren! There will be peace now, just as I
have ay predicted!"*

*"Predictions is it?" yelled John. "You're a witch, you
auld hag! A witch and a traitor!"*

*"There's a traitor among us, right enough," Mary
said softly, her voice carrying clearly across the water,
"but it's no' me, John Mackay."*

*"We'll neffer catch up wi' Miss Eilidh and the Gordon
laddie," Jamie groaned. "There's no other boat for miles
along this shore."*

*"Lamont could take him easy with his bow," said the
red-haired man, pointing his sword towards the boat.
"He could put an arrow through a sparrow's eye at this
distance."*

*"Aye, he's an easy target wi' this moon," agreed John,
"and the current would bring the lassie back to us.
Where is Lamont?"*

"You sent him to fetch the laird, John," said Jamie.

*"Then we've lost them," sighed John. "You hear that,
witch? We've lost the laird's daughter and you will pay
dear for this! We'll fetch a boat and come for you by sun-
rise. Traitor and witch—you will burn for your sins! You
will burn to cleanse our shore of your evil!"*

*"I'll no' roast on your devilish pyre!" yelled Mary.
"My ancestors settled here on The Corloch over a thousand years past. They built this crannog—my island. I've
lived here all my days and it is here my days will end."*

*From the dark folds of her cloak she drew a long dirk,
pointing the blade towards John Mackay and whispering*

the word, "Traitor." Then she spun the dirk in her bony hands, the tip touching her breast, and plunged the blade into her heart with a screech that stilled the waters of the loch.

"That's a grand story and well told," Hamish congratulated the narrator as the ripple of applause faded and the audience, a group of around a dozen tourists, trooped off along the makeshift bridge linking Auld Mary's Island to the shore.

"Thank you," the woman smiled. "They'll be back for a wee lecture about crannogs and part two of the story once they've had their afternoon tea at the picnic spot." She strode towards Hamish, holding out a hand to introduce herself. "I'm Sally Paterson."

Hamish pulled his hands out of his trouser pockets and reached forward to shake, but the woman suddenly withdrew her outstretched hand.

"Sorry, sorry," she said, wiping her hands on a cloth she produced from the waistband of her jeans and laughing. "Getting a bit muddy is an occupational hazard on a site like this."

"Aye, well, I'm fair used to getting my hands dirty in my job as well," he replied, taking her hand. "I'm Hamish Macbeth." Up close he could now see that she was taller than he had first thought, elegantly slim with a mane of ash-blonde hair and sparkling blue eyes.

"And what brings the police to Auld Mary's Island, Sergeant Macbeth?" she asked, glancing at the silver chevron badges on the epaulettes of his white uniform shirt.

"Just Hamish will do."

"So, 'Just Hamish,' I'm guessing you know The Corloch quite well."

"That I do, and I wanted to see for myself what's been going on up here," he said, shielding his eyes from the glaring sun with a flattened hand and squinting out over the loch. "Looks like the water's still disappearing."

"It is," she agreed, "and the engineers say we'll lose a bit more over the next couple of days before it begins to stabilise."

"I've never seen The Corloch so dry. It's a braw thing they're doing up in the hills with the new hydroelectric scheme but we don't want the loch here to vanish completely."

He looked out over parched, cracked areas of the exposed loch bed closest to the shore, scattered with ancient boulders and more recent driftwood deposited by the receding water. Auld Mary's Island stood on a shallow ridge that had been carved out of the landscape thousands of years before by a retreating glacier desperately trying to cling to the glen.

"Don't worry, Sergeant, it won't vanish. This warm weather has made it seem worse but the streams they have diverted will be flowing again soon and The Corloch will be back to its normal level by the time the winter rains set in."

"I hope you're right, but you're a historian, aren't you, not an engineer?"

"Actually, I studied geography at university, but that got me interested in geology, archaeology and anthropology."

"That's a lot of 'ologies.'" Hamish smiled, but the expression faded quickly and he looked away from her, casting his eyes over the rocky island. "Where we're standing is usually covered with water."

"It is," she agreed, "but with so much of the island now out of the water, it's given us a unique opportunity to study how it was built and to find out a bit more about how people lived here through the ages."

"There's a fair few of these crannogs scattered across the lochs."

"There certainly are. Some of them are thousands of years old. It's amazing to think that people back then had the ingenuity and skill to drive wooden stakes into the bed of the loch or pile boulders in the water to create these islands."

"I suppose living on an island was good protection from their enemies."

"And from wild animals—bears and wolves used to roam these parts. The original dwelling on Auld Mary's Island would have been a wooden roundhouse, but at some point it was replaced by a stone structure that was gradually enlarged." Sally pointed out the remains of the stone walls. "Auld Mary is thought to have been the last inhabitant. The old stories say that no one would live here after her death."

"She'd have had no bridge like that thing?" Hamish nodded towards a line of neatly laid wooden pallets that had turned a recently exposed loch-bed ridge into a walkway between the island and the shore.

"That's a temporary arrangement to let people visit the site here without sinking into the silt or slipping on rocks."

"So are you learning much about how they lived on—"

"Sergeant Macbeth! A word, if you please!" an unmistakable voice boomed out from the shore.

"Crivens!" Hamish lowered his voice. "Sounds like the big boss. What on earth is he doing up here?"

He turned to see Superintendent Peter Daviot beckoning him from the shore side of the palette bridge. Daviot was barely recognisable in stout walking boots, military shorts and a casual chequered shirt.

"Aye, it's the superintendent himself," Hamish sighed, turning back to Sally. "I have to go."

"Drop by again soon," Sally said, smiling and waving goodbye as Hamish loped towards the bridge. She raised her voice when he clattered across the palettes. "I'll be here for at least another two weeks!"

"Good afternoon, sir," Hamish said, a little out of breath by the time he joined Daviot on the shore. "I hardly recognised you out of uniform."

"I might say the same about you, Sergeant!" barked Daviot, plucking at Hamish's white shirt. "I saw you standing with your hands in your pockets, which you well know is not how we do things, and what is this?"

"My shirt, sir?"

"But it's not your uniform, is it, Macbeth? The correct uniform for a police officer on duty is the regulation black wicking shirt—and where is your equipment? You are wearing no body armour, you have no personal radio, no taser, no service belt, no baton, no handcuffs and you're not even wearing your cap! Where is your cap and your equipment?"

"Aye, well, I was chust...I mean I took a wee break and what with it being awful hot and...it's all in the Land Rover, sir."

"You know the force's insurance doesn't cover you if you are assaulted on duty and are not wearing protective equipment?"

"Aye, sir, I know that fine. I was..."

"Over here, Sergeant!" snapped Daviot, striding towards Hamish's parked police car and glancing back at a gaggle of middle-aged hillwalkers who were watching impatiently. He lowered his voice when they reached the Land Rover. "Listen, Macbeth, this isn't about your uniform, although you are most definitely incorrectly attired and...no, don't get me started on that again. I need you to rescue me from that lot." He nodded towards the hillwalkers.

"They seem harmless enough," Hamish said, with a shrug.

"You may have noticed my wife among them." Daviot's voice was now little more than a conspiratorial whisper. "It's one of her churchy charity things—a sponsored hillwalk. I need you to get me out of it. Those are, without doubt, the most appallingly dull, dreadful people I have ever had the misfortune to meet."

"Aye, they're a dry-looking bunch right enough,"

Hamish agreed. "Och, but … um … with the exception of Mrs. Daviot, of course. I mean …"

"Shut up and listen, man!" hissed Daviot, leaning a hand on the bonnet of the Land Rover. "I'm leaving my card on the car. When I go back to Susan and her friends, you give me ten minutes and then call me on the private mobile number. Talk for a bit as though you're reporting on an urgent situation at Strathbane. That way I can tell them I have to get back to the office urgently."

Hamish nodded. "Back to headquarters is it, or down to the Strathbane Golf Club?"

"Don't be insolent, Macbeth," warned Daviot. "Play along and I'll ignore the fact that you're loafing around out of uniform."

"Will do, sir, but," said Hamish, pausing to make it clear that their little negotiation was not quite concluded, "my white shirts still have years of wear left in them and, you know, people on my patch expect to see their local bobby dressed like a policeman, not like some special forces commando and—"

"I expect you to draw the appropriate uniform from the stores in Strathbane," Daviot interrupted, holding up a hand to silence Hamish. "Knowing you, I also expect you will wear exactly what you want on your own patch. Just make that call."

Hamish watched the senior officer striding back to the hillwalkers. He ran a hand through his shock of red hair and thought back over the number of times he had saved Daviot's bacon, not least when he was being blackmailed over some compromising photographs of his wife. Hamish had tracked down the photos and handed them over to Daviot, but he'd kept one. It was supposed to help him deter Daviot from closing down the police station at Lochdubh. That, he thought to himself with a sigh, was maybe a wee mistake. Daviot had sent the despicable Detective Chief Inspector Blair to steal the final photo but Blair had used it to blackmail Daviot himself. Blair was an evil scunner, but also a blundering drunk. Had Blair not been so inept, he might have succeeded in murdering Hamish when he'd become embroiled with Glasgow gangsters not so long ago.

Hamish felt a sudden chill, as though a cloud had passed across the sun. It was the Glasgow thugs who had murdered Dorothy, the woman he had been set to marry, on the morning of their wedding day. Hamish shook his head. All thoughts led back to Dorothy. Whenever he set foot somewhere they had been together—a beach, a hillside, even his own police station—snatches of conversation filled his head and he could hear her voice as clearly as if she was standing right beside him. He could see her smile, smell her hair, sometimes almost feel her walking arm-in-arm at his side. He thought about her all the time. But that was a good thing, wasn't it? He had heard that, when you lose someone you love, it can become difficult to picture them in your mind, as though they are fading away. That had never been a problem for him. He saw Dorothy's beautiful face every time he closed his eyes. That was his comfort. The fact that she was never far from his thoughts meant that, in a very real way, she was still with him. It meant that she would always be with him—

"Macbeth!" Daviot's voice echoed along the shore of The Corloch. "Stop daydreaming and get back to work!"

Hamish climbed into the Land Rover and waited ten minutes, by which time the hillwalkers were completely out of sight, before calling the number on Daviot's card.

"Daviot," came the voice after a few rings.

"Police headquarters here, sir," said Hamish.

"Well what is it, man? You know I've taken the day off."

"Aye, of course, sir. I...um..." Hamish knew he had simply to fill in time now while Daviot pretended to listen, as though receiving an urgent message, so he rolled out the first things that came into his head. "Well there's riots in the streets of Strathbane, there's been ten murders, the Strathbane Bank of Scotland's been robbed and Her Majesty the Queen is at the front desk because she's lost her crown jewels. That ought to do you, sir."

There was a click and a rustle of movement before Daviot's voice hissed, "You idiot, Macbeth! I had you on the loudspeaker. Everyone could hear that load of havers! Could you not have come up with something sensible?"

"Och, that's a right shame. I didn't realise..." Hamish was thinking fast. "You can ay tell them that police communications have been compromised by a hacker and you need to get back to headquarters to make sure it gets sorted out."

"Yes, yes, that will work," said Daviot, and hung up.

Hamish started the engine, then leant forward on the steering wheel and switched the car off again. He threw back his head and laughed. The thought of the looks Mrs. Daviot's kirk friends must have given her husband when they heard his report from "police headquarters" brought tears to his eyes. He hadn't laughed like that for months. Suddenly, he felt utterly exhausted. He started the car again and headed home to Lochdubh.

Hamish crossed the stone humpbacked bridge over the River Anstey and pulled the car over to the side of the road. He had one arm dangling casually out the open window and could feel the warm breeze snaking between his fingers. From here he could see all the way down the road into Lochdubh. The scattering of white-painted cottages, some larger than others, strung out along the road that skirted the edge of the loch, were bathed in sunshine. The air was tinged with the familiar dry smell of heather and the freshness of pine underpinning the faint, lemony scent of wild thyme. It was the smell of home. He drove on down the street, acknowledging a friendly wave from Mrs. Patel as he passed the village's small supermarket.

Then he spotted the formidable figures of the Currie twins, Nessie and Jessie, glowering at him from the pavement, two small clouds of misery on an otherwise glorious day. They were dressed identically, as always, their beige, lightweight summer raincoats buttoned up to the neck and their precisely permed grey hair making each a mirror image of the other. Nessie beckoned him.

"What is it, ladies?" he asked, stopping the car beside them. "I'm awful busy right now."

"What kind of woman is it that you've brought into the

village this time, Hamish Macbeth?" Nessie demanded. "By the looks of things—a painted harlot!"

"Painted harlot!" echoed Jessie, who had an enormously irritating tendency always to repeat the tail end of her sister's remarks.

"I really have no idea what you're talking about," Hamish admitted, shaking his head.

"Well, she's waiting for you outside your police station," Nessie said, indignantly. "As you would know if you were doing your job instead of traipsing off all over the Highlands. She's been pacing back and forth..."

"...back and forth..." repeated Jessie.

"...in her high heels and short skirt..."

"...short skirt..."

"...making your police station look like a..."

"Whorehouse!" squeaked Jessie, then cast her eyes to the ground to avoid her sister's withering stare.

"You two had best be on your way," said Hamish, enjoying the twins' discomfort at one of them having uttered such a shameful word. "I'll deal with my visitor, whoever she is."

Approaching the police station, Hamish could see a large red Range Rover parked outside and, sitting on the garden wall, a woman with long dark hair, smoking a cigarette. Her skirt was not as short, nor her heels as high, as the Currie twins had led him to believe but her clothes and her make-up were certainly more appropriate for a glitzy city cocktail bar than a sleepy Highland village like Lochdubh.

"Can I help you?" he asked, stepping out of his car.

"At last!" she threw her cigarette to the ground and crushed it beneath her shoe.

"Have you been waiting here long?" Hamish asked, eyeing the collection of cigarette butts on the pavement.

"Seems like forever," she snapped. "Where have you been?"

"Police business," he replied, staring straight at her. She was, he decided, really quite pretty, despite all the make-up and despite her current state of irritation bringing a waspish sharpness to her features. "Maybe you should have called."

"I did," she said, punching out the words in two short jabs. "Actually, we've spoken several times. I'm Diane Spears—Kate Hibbert's cousin."

"Aye, I recognise your voice now," he said. "You're the lady from Edinburgh. Why don't you come away inside and we can talk over a cup of coffee?"

"I don't have time for that. I just need to know what you're doing to find my cousin. It's been nearly three weeks since she went missing."

"There's nothing much I can tell you, really," Hamish explained. "Kate was last seen heading for the main road carrying a suitcase. I've spoken to everyone in the area that knew her and nobody has seen her since."

"And that doesn't seem odd to you? It doesn't seem strange that she should simply disappear?"

"Ordinarily it might," he admitted, "but this isn't the first time she's done something like this, is it? She's gone missing afore and had half the police in Scotland out looking for her. Last time it turned out that she'd spent the entire summer sunning herself by the Med at a swanky hotel in the south of France. That was afore she showed up here in Lochdubh."

"So you think she's gone abroad?"

"As far as we're aware, her passport hasn't been used."

"So she's still in the country? Look, I need to... damn!" Her phone rang with a shrill, urgent tone. She put it to her ear, exchanged a few brief words, then rang off and began tapping out a message on the screen before turning to Hamish. "I have calls to make and a business to run, but I'm not going anywhere until I get some answers. Is there anywhere decent to stay around here?"

"The Tommel Castle Hotel is on the edge of the village," Hamish advised, pointing out the right direction.

"Right. That's where I'll be. We will talk again, Sergeant—soon—and I'll want to hear about some progress on your part." She yanked open her car door, climbed inside and set off towards the hotel.

Hamish made his way down the side of the police station to let himself in through the kitchen door. There was no energetic and noisy welcome from his pets Lugs, a dog of various breeds and various colours, and Sonsie, his tame wildcat. He knew that on a fine day like this they would be dozing in the sunshine down on the beach or chasing the gulls. He hoped they weren't scrounging snacks from tourists. He checked the kitchen clock and realised that they would be home soon to be fed. Their stomachs kept better time than a Swiss watch. Rolling up his sleeves, he tackled the mountain of dirty dishes piled up in the sink. In the past he had generally had a constable working for him who would share domestic chores like this. Some had been more useful than others when it came to household duties but he didn't want to use the lack of a constable as an excuse to fall back into his old, lazy bachelor ways. Besides, mindless tasks like washing the dishes gave him a chance to think.

What was Diane Spears doing in Lochdubh? He could understand someone being concerned about a missing relative but she didn't seem the type to lose too much sleep over a cousin who had gone AWOL, especially one who had made it a bit of a habit. He recalled from his case notes that she was Hibbert's only real family, but Spears hadn't kicked up such a fuss when Hibbert had gone missing previously. And what about Hibbert? He had spoken to everyone in the area who knew her and they had all said the same thing—she was a very nice, helpful lass, yet nobody had been in the least bit upset that she had vanished. Nobody in the area had even reported her missing—it was Spears who had done that. No matter what people had said, he had the distinct impression that they were glad to see the back of her. Highlanders eked out the truth like a miser's pennies. Unless it was in their own best interest, they gave away only what they had to. In talking to the locals, Hamish knew full well that things had been left unsaid, and unless he had to dig deeper, he had no intention of stirring up trouble. The best thing was to sit back and wait for Hibbert to show up again.

Fortunately, that had been the official line from Strathbane as well. They didn't want him wasting his time chasing around after some woman who had shown herself to be perfectly capable of disappearing in the past only to show up when it suited her.

There was a sudden commotion and Lugs burst through the oversized pet-flap in the kitchen door, his claws scrabbling on the floor tiles as he tried to gallop towards Hamish.

"Steady, now, you daft dog," Hamish chided, stooping to tickle his pet's ears. "You've brought in half the beach wi' you. And where's...och, it's herself." He watched Sonsie make a more dignified entrance through the flap. It was an open secret around the village that Sonsie was more than just an overgrown moggie and everyone knew that the Scottish wildcat was an endangered species, yet no one would ever admit to an outsider that Sonsie was anything other than a domestic pet cat. They had seen how miserable Hamish had been without the cat when he had once tried to release her into the wild at the sanctuary on the Ardnamurchan peninsula and everyone had been hugely relieved when he eventually brought Sonsie home again.

"Let's get you two fed, then," he said, Sonsie winding herself around his legs. "I've a couple of venison sausages for you, Lugs, and a nice bit of rock salmon for you, Sonsie."

Having fed his pets, he strolled outside to check on his chickens and glanced up the hillside to where he grazed his small flock of sheep. The heather on the ridge line at the top of the slope was outlined against the blue sky and he knew that, beyond the ridge, the ground fell away into a small corrie where there was a tarn known as the Ruby Loch. Just above the loch was where he had laid Dorothy to rest. He kept the grave neat and tidy, visiting as often as he could. He knew full well that the locals called it his "shrine" but he couldn't care less what people thought. It was peaceful up there. It was somewhere he could go to think without any interruptions. They said he went there to talk to her, but that was nonsense. He wasn't the sort to waste words on a gravestone. The Ruby Loch had been a special place for him and Dorothy and it would always be special. If the gossips needed it to be more than that, that was their problem, not his.

The shrill bleeping of the police station phone drew him back indoors where he grabbed the receiver from his desk in the small front office.

"Macbeth."

"Oh, Sergeant Macbeth, thank goodness it's you. It's Sally, up at The Corloch. There's a body here—a dead body!"

"Not Auld Mary, is it?"

"No, this is a real body, floating in the water!" There was no mistaking the notes of panic and fear in her voice.

"Don't touch anything," warned Hamish. "I'll be there as quick as I can."

CHAPTER TWO

*Tricks and treachery are the practice of
fools that don't have brains enough to be
honest.*

Benjamin Franklin

Once he was out of Lochdubh, Hamish picked up speed
on the main Strathbane road, his Land Rover's siren and
flashing blue lights swiftly persuading the occasional
tourist to pull over and let him pass. Turning off to the
right to take the narrower road across the high moorland
up to The Corloch made progress frustratingly ponderous.
The road deteriorated to a single carriageway lined with
ditches, boulders or embankments as it wound its way
up into the hills, giving a succession of cars towing car-
avans or slow-moving motorhomes no opportunity to let
him pass save for at designated passing places. Approaching from the western end of the loch, the road looped all
the way round the shoreline. He took the shorter north-
shore route and, despite encountering another couple of

tourist vehicles, made it to the car park near Auld Mary's Island in record time. There was only one other vehicle there, a green Audi hatchback. Clearly the tourists who had stayed for part two of Sally Paterson's story had long since departed. He spotted her sitting at one of the picnic benches on the shore near the makeshift footbridge. She was being comforted by a woman Hamish did not recognise. They were the only two people in sight.

"Are you okay?" he asked, and both women looked up at him.

"I'll be fine." Sally's blue eyes were misty with tears and her face smudged with tear tracks. "It's all just been a bit of a shock. Horrible, really horrible."

"Where is the body?" Hamish asked.

"Round the back of the island . . . in the water. Her face is . . ."

"Aye, those in the water are the worst," Hamish said, making for the bridge. "Stay here and I'll go take a look."

Auld Mary's Island was roughly thirty yards long and twenty wide. Much of it was covered in yellow-flowered gorse bushes and on the highest ground in the centre of the island a tangle of hazel and beech limbs were battling to grow into trees, losing out each year to the devastation wrought when the winter winds scoured the loch. There was a large, clear space near the waterline where Sally and her team had been excavating and where the loch had receded, more of the rocks used to form the island had been exposed. Hamish clambered round to an area hidden from the shore and there, almost concealed in a cluster of boulders and driftwood, he could make out the shape of a woman's pink coat. He edged forward, pushing aside some overhanging gorse. Whin was what some of the locals called the plant, and it was said to bring dire bad luck. Giving the yellow flowers to someone, even inadvertently, meant that you would surely quarrel. Hamish reflected grimly on the bad luck that had befallen the woman in the water. She certainly wouldn't be quarrelling with anyone ever again.

A final couple of steps took him to where the corpse lay, the lower part in the water, the head and shoulders propped up on a rock. The face was turned towards him. This was what Sally had seen, he thought to himself. No wonder she had been upset. Flies were crawling all over the skin. He waved his hand across them and most of them rose in a buzzing cloud, revealing flesh that had turned a dark, waxy, greenish colour. The eyes were ragged, gaping cavities and the frayed lips were drawn back, exposing the teeth in a macabre grin. The fish had done their worst.

Hamish recoiled from the sight, stumbling backwards. He had seen bodies retrieved from the water before but this one was particularly grotesque. The warm weather would have played a part. Colder water might have preserved the body in better condition. The state of the corpse would prove a problem in establishing identity— they would doubtless resort to using dental records—but Hamish had no doubt who it was. The vivid pink of the coat shone through the grubby silt deposits that stained its surface, the man-made fibre showing no signs of deterioration despite its prolonged immersion. The elusive Kate Hibbert had turned up at last.

The flies quickly returned and he let them be, concentrating instead on what he could see of the rest of the body. There were ropes around the waist and the ankles, and through the clear water he could see that they were tied to rocks, obviously to weigh the body down. This had been no accident. The body had been dumped in the loch. Hibbert had been murdered.

Hamish removed his cap and stood with his hands on his hips, gazing out over The Corloch, squinting against the glare of the bright afternoon sun reflecting off the water. Hamish had been out on the water many times, fishing for brown trout. He knew that, even though this was not a sea loch, there was still a kind of tide that formed a reasonably strong current. The Corloch was almost four miles long but only a few hundred yards at its widest point. Lying west to east, the prevailing wind funnelled through the surrounding mountains, driving surface water towards the eastern end of the loch, where he was standing. This caused a build-up of pressure that was slowly released when deeper water flowed west. Would the falling water level have affected that? By his reckoning, if the body had been dumped from a boat when the loch was still full, the current would slowly have pushed it to Auld Mary's Island. The rocks he could see might have been enough to keep the body submerged, but wouldn't have withstood the relentless pressure of the shallow-water current.

Whoever had sent Hibbert to a watery grave couldn't

have known that the body would move, and certainly couldn't have known that the water level in the loch was about to drop. Had she been dumped in any of a dozen other mountain lochs in the area, she would still be missing.

Hamish sighed as he turned to go. He now had to call this in and report what had happened to headquarters in Strathbane. He'd let their people haul the body out of the water. He didn't envy them that job and, in any case, they'd want him to leave things just as he had found them. A murder squad team would descend on the area, pestering the locals with endless questions. The press would show up—newspaper and TV people causing chaos and pestering the locals all over again for any titbits of gossip about the victim. He thought about all of the people he had interviewed about Hibbert's disappearance and prayed that none of them was involved in her murder.

Then something else in the water caught his eye—a rectangular shape. Could it be a suitcase? He recalled that Gregor Mackenzie had mentioned seeing Hibbert heading for the main road with a suitcase when he'd interviewed him. Wading into the water a couple of steps, Hamish grasped the object and hauled what turned out to be a large suitcase to the surface, slinging it onto the rocks. Water gushed out of the case, cascading down the rocks back into the loch.

"Well," he said to no one in particular, "no harm in taking a wee peek, is there?"

He popped the locks, opened the suitcase and a sloosh of water drained out. Inside the case was everything you might expect to find when someone had packed for a long trip. There were clothes, shoes, and bags for toiletries and make-up. Everything was completely soaked through and there was nothing of any interest.

He was about to close the case when he noticed that the cardboard lining inside the lid had started to deteriorate, peeling away from the edges. He also noticed the corner of a black plastic bag behind the lining. Easing the soggy cardboard away from the lid, he retrieved a tightly wrapped black package about the size of a large book. He set the package aside, refitted the cardboard lining as best he could and closed the case. A shake and a quick wipe with his handkerchief dried off the package enough for him to tuck it inside his shirt. He would examine the contents at his leisure back in Lochdubh. If the package had no bearing on the murder, then he was doing no harm. If, on the other hand, it showed that someone in the area had been involved in Hibbert's murder, he wanted to know about it before any outsiders came storming in. He could then decide how to let the murder squad "discover" the relevant evidence for themselves. In the meantime, he had to call Strathbane.

Back on the shore, Sally was waiting patiently with her friend, who identified herself as Sharon Nolan.

"I'm a volunteer," Sharon explained. "I help out on the digs. It's kind of a hobby. Is the body really bad? Sally wouldn't let me see."

"No right-minded person would ever want to set eyes on something like that," said Hamish, then he crouched in front of Sally. "Are you going to be all right?"

"I'll be okay," she said, forcing a smile. "It's not the

first dead body I've seen at a dig, although the others have all been hundreds of years old!"

"That's the spirit," he said, straightening his long legs. "If you can hold on to your sense of humour, you'll be fine."

"Do you know who she was?" Sharon asked.

"I've a fair inkling," said Hamish, "but we can't be sure until the body's formally identified. Where are you both staying?"

"We're at The Corloch Lodge," said Sharon. "It's along the northern shore."

"Aye, I know it well. I'll have to ask you to bide here until the team arrives from Strathbane. They'll want to take statements from you and maybe have a wee look in your car."

"What for?" demanded Sharon. "Surely you don't think that we had anything to do with...?"

"No, no, of course not." Hamish held up his hands in a calming gesture. "But I'm sure you understand that we have to be thorough in circumstances like this."

"It's okay," Sally said, resting a hand on her friend's arm. "They have their job to do."

"You've been working on the crannog for a while now," said Hamish. "How come you didn't discover the body before now?"

"Up until this morning," Sally explained, "I should think it was still underwater. In any case, we've been working on this side of the island. You have to fight your way through a lot of thorny bushes to get to the back of the island. This afternoon, after I finished the crannog lecture, the water level had dropped enough for me to be able to make my way round on the rocks."

"I see." Hamish nodded. "Well, you must excuse me. There's things I have to do."

By the time the first cars arrived from Strathbane Hamish had closed the car park and secured the picnic area and a large section of the shore closest to the island with yards of blue-and-white tape. He was directing two constables to guard the approach road to the scene when his old friend Detective Chief Inspector Jimmy Anderson arrived.

"What have we got here then, laddie?" he asked.

"You mind of the missing person case I was dealing with, Jimmy?" Hamish said. "Well, she's not missing any more. This is a murder—no doubt about it."

He explained the situation, Jimmy listening intently, the concentration making his lean, foxy face seem even thinner.

"Right," Jimmy said, shrugging off his suit jacket and turning back towards his car, motioning for Hamish to follow. "If she went missing from Lochdubh, then we need someone down there manning the station and, since it's your station, that someone is you. We'll deal wi' things here. I'll be down to have a word wi' you later, once we've seen if these lads come up wi' anything."

Jimmy nodded towards the loch where divers in wet-suits were wading into the water and forensics officers in white suits were making their way round the rocks on Auld Mary's Island. He tossed his jacket onto the back seat of his car. The afternoon was sliding lazily into early evening but the temperature had yet to slip beyond shirt-sleeves level.

"Don't cut me out of this, Jimmy," Hamish said, lowering his voice and glancing towards where two detectives were talking to Sally Paterson at the picnic bench. "This is my patch and I need to be involved."

"Don't fret, laddie. You're busy enough running the station in Lochdubh without a constable to back you up but...I need you on this. Have a drop o' the good stuff ready for when I get down to Lochdubh. I'll be fit to murder a dram by then."

The usual exuberant welcome burst upon Hamish when he walked through the door of his police station in Lochdubh. Lugs, his eyes wide, his floppy ears standing as high as he could hitch them and his tail threshing the air, cracking against the kitchen table leg and the fridge door.

"Steady, lad," Hamish said, laughing as the dog reared up and planted his front paws in his stomach. "You'll break your tail doing that. Either that or you'll break the table."

Sonsie rubbed herself against his legs, the big wild-cat's purr vibrating like a small engine. She jumped onto a kitchen chair and stared up at him with pale yellow eyes, willing him to stroke her. He couldn't resist, petting both the cat and the dog at the same time, chatting to them as though they were children.

"Now, you two were fed earlier," he said, "and I'm that hungry I could eat the hoofs off a scabby donkey, so it's my turn now."

Setting the black plastic package from Kate Hibbert's suitcase down on the kitchen table, he soon had a frying pan of sausage, bacon and eggs sizzling on the stove. The package was a worry. It could hold the key to Hibbert's murder and it was all he could do to stop himself from tearing it open, but it would be a disaster if Jimmy walked in on him with its contents, whatever they were, spread out on the table. Leaving his food to cook itself, he took the package through to his office at the front of the building and slipped it into his desk drawer. Then he pulled the Hibbert missing person's file from his cabinet before he was drawn back into the kitchen by the irresistible aroma of frying bacon. He tended to his supper, then sat at the table with a steaming plate of food, a mug of coffee, a hunk of buttered bread and the open file.

His report listed all of the people he had spoken to about Hibbert's disappearance. She hadn't lived in the area for long and was still considered very much an outsider. Mind you, he thought to himself, you could live in the Highlands for decades and still be regarded as an interloper, and Sutherland was one of the most insular places in Scotland in that respect. Only those born in the area were considered by the locals to have a God-given right to live there. Anyone else had to prove themselves before they would ever be properly accepted. He had endured the same sort of experience when he first came to Lochdubh. Having been born in Cromarty and raised in Rogart, many Lochdubh residents still saw him as a newcomer, even though he had lived in the village for years.

It wasn't that the people of Lochdubh were an unfriendly bunch. They were far more gregarious than some and extended a warm Highland welcome to visitors, but generally preferred it if people didn't outstay that welcome.

Most newcomers who arrived from the south, looking for a quiet life surrounded by idyllic scenery, went scuttling back home once they had experienced the relentless ferocity of a Highland winter. Those who were made of sterner stuff and managed to avoid drinking themselves into oblivion on the long dark nights might eventually be accepted as part of the community although, when Hamish thought of it in terms of a family, they'd always be distant cousins rather than brothers or sisters—the kind of cousins most likely to drop off your Christmas card list. Kate Hibbert had never actually made it to cousin status and... he slapped a hand to his forehead and groaned, "Och, no..."

"Trouble, or was that just another midge? The wee devils are everywhere." Jimmy Anderson walked through the kitchen door, ruffling Lugs's ears when the dog bounced towards him. Sonsie glowered at him from the window ledge. She lost her cool for no one and only Hamish was ever permitted any display of affection.

"Kate Hibbert's cousin was here earlier, asking about her," Hamish explained. "She's at the Tommel Castle. I haven't told her we found the body."

"Well, you couldn't, could you, laddie? We need to be pretty sure that it's her afore we call in any family for formal identification. I doubt she'd recognise the poor lassie anyway, given the state the body's in. Anyhow, what about that dram? I'm fair parched. I've a mouth like the bottom o' a budgie's cage."

"Have you no' got Stevie driving you?" Hamish asked, glancing through the front office to where Jimmy's car was parked in front of the station. "I thought he was your bagman now."

"Aye, he is," Jimmy agreed, reaching for the glass of The Famous Grouse Hamish had poured him, "but he's on leave—sunning himself on a beach in Mallorca—and I'm short on manpower."

"You'd best take it easy on that stuff then, if you're driving yourself." He knew it was unlikely this was Jimmy's first of the day. He sat down at the table again with his unfinished coffee. "Better still, let me drive you back."

"How would that work?" Jimmy growled. "If you drive my car, you're then stuck in Strathbane. If we take your car, mine is stuck here."

"Well, spend the night here then," Hamish said. "You can't drive when you've been knocking back the whisky."

"You get a lot of freedom up here to do as you like," Jimmy said, giving Hamish a hard stare and pointing a bony finger at him, "but that doesn't include telling *me* what I can and can't do!"

"I chust think—"

"Well don't. That car just about kens its own way back to Strathbane by now." Jimmy relaxed back in his chair, helping himself to another generous measure. "Anyhow, it'll no' be dark and there'll no' be much in the way of traffic. So—what can you tell me about Kate Hibbert?"

"It was all in my missing person's report."

"Aye, well refresh my memory. I've more reports come across my desk than there are pebbles on your beach out there."

Hamish eyed the older man and Jimmy's watery blue eyes returned the stare. They had been through a great deal together over the years, working cases which, more often than not, were solved through Hamish's hard work and Highland intuition while Jimmy generally took all the credit. It was an arrangement that worked to the advantage of them both. Keeping Jimmy in favour with the hierarchy at headquarters put him in the best position to ensure that Hamish's precious police station remained operational, despite regular official plans for drastic cutbacks that would close it down, putting an end to the quiet life he so loved in Lochdubh.

"She'd no' lived here long—just over a year. She moved into a cottage up Hurdy's Glen on the other side of the loch. I went to see her when she first arrived, just to say hello, and she seemed very pleasant. Lots of smiles and lots of chat. I never set eyes on her much after that. It's the people living in the glen who knew her best but you know what it's like around here—everybody knew who she was and everybody had an opinion about her. Ask them now that it's a murder enquiry, of course, and nobody will know a thing."

"Was she well liked?" Jimmy took another gulp of whisky.

"Most people seemed to like her just fine. They said she was ay cheerful and happy."

"That would get right up my nose afore too long."

"Aye, but it's no' really a motive for murder, is it?"

"What did she get up to when she was here?"

"She kept herself busy. She had a couple of wee cleaning jobs, one for Morgan Mackay, who lives in a big house up Hurdy's Glen, and one for Hannah Thomson, who lives on the outskirts of the village. She's getting on a bit and struggles with the housework. Apart from that, she seems to have put in a lot of time helping people out wherever she could."

"A right do-gooder, eh? This lassie sounds too good to be true, does she no'?"

"Maybe, but she certainly got somebody's back up. Somebody ended up hating her enough to murder her. What did the pathologist have to say?"

"He reckons she was probably strangled. Difficult to tell with the state of the body but we'll know more after the post mortem."

"Do they have any idea how long she'd been in the water? We need to establish her movements after she was last seen leaving the glen."

"Hold on a wee minute there, laddie. I've a team of detectives who will be working on this case and I'm running the show here, not you. I'll let you know what I need from you. What I don't need is for you to overstep the mark and cause me problems back at headquarters by sticking your nose in where it's no' wanted. So far, the press haven't caught wind o' this, but by tomorrow, word will be out and they'll be clogging the road to The

Corloch and swarming all over Lochdubh. We'll handle things up at The Corloch but you'll have to keep a lid on things down here. Have a word wi' the people who knew Hibbert best and tell them to keep their traps shut. We can't run the risk of letting the killer read everything we know in the morning paper. We have to try to control what appears in the papers, on the TV and online. No one is to talk to the press except me."

"How am I supposed to keep everyone quiet? The press have ways of loosening tongues," Hamish said, rubbing the fingertips of his right hand against his thumb in the universal sign for money.

"Bully them, frighten them, threaten them," Jimmy said simply, refilling his glass.

"Aye, right." Hamish sighed. "That's no' the way to deal with folk around here, and you know that fine yourself."

"But you know your own folk better than anyone," Jimmy pointed out. "So get out to see them first thing tomorrow, afore the press turn up, and see if you can get anything else out o' them about Hibbert. My team will deal with the archaeologist and her sidekick and anyone else around The Corloch who might have seen the body being dumped."

"So how long was she in the loch?"

"You know very well that would usually be hard to say." Jimmy rubbed the back of his hand over tired eyes. "But we had a lucky break there. She was wearing a fancy gold watch wi' a date window. It was smashed either when she was dumped or just afore, and it stopped—two days after she went missing."

"That means she never left the area. If she had done, she'd have been dumped somewhere else. Why would anyone go to all the trouble and run the risk of getting caught bringing a body back here to dispose of it in The Corloch? She was held somewhere around here for those two days."

"And that means it's more than likely we're looking for someone who lives here," Jimmy grunted.

"Could be someone renting a place for the summer," Hamish suggested, reluctant to admit that the killer might be local. "There's plenty o' holiday lets in the area."

"Aye, I'll get the team to start checking those out." Jimmy nodded, then took a short breath. "How are you coping yourself?"

"Well, it can get a bit hectic without a constable," Hamish replied, "but I've been keeping on top o' things."

"I didn't mean 'How are you coping without a constable?'" said Jimmy with a sigh. "I meant, how are you coping... without Dorothy?"

"I'm doing just grand." Hamish shifted uncomfortably in his chair. "You don't have to worry about me. I don't want anyone making a fuss. Folk in the village sometimes look at me like they expect me to collapse and start bawling like a bairn or something, but I just need to be left to get on with things."

"I heard you gave the counsellor from Edinburgh short shrift when she tried to talk through it all wi' you."

"I never asked for any kind o' trauma counselling. I only agreed to see her because Daviot wouldn't let me back to work unless I did."

"You can understand why, though, eh, laddie? It's no' everyone that could cope wi' his fiancée being murdered and then being shot in the head."

Hamish fingered the scar, now hidden beneath regrown hair, where a gangster's bullet had creased his skull.

"You wouldn't want some stranger messing wi' your head, Jimmy, and neither did I."

"Right you are, then," said Jimmy, getting to his feet and patting Hamish on the shoulder. "Good lad. Let me ken straight away if you come up wi' anything about Hibbert. We can talk tomorrow."

With that, he was gone and Hamish was left staring at the kitchen chair where Jimmy had sat—the kitchen chair where Dorothy had often sat. He wanted to see her there, smiling, laughing, beautiful, sitting with him, the two of them together again. In his mind's eye, he could picture her there, but more tangible was the feeling that she was still with him. Sometimes he thought he could smell her perfume, or pick up the scent of her hair when he walked through the house, as if she had been there just ahead of him. He knew the experts said that the sense of smell was the most powerful memory trigger but, when he was being honest with himself, he also knew those moments were only his imagination telling him lies that he wanted to be true. Dorothy had been in the station many times in her role as a police constable, but never in her intended role as his wife. She had never lived with him in the station. She never even spent the night there. He had banished everything of hers from the station because he couldn't bear to be reminded of what might have been, couldn't bear to endure the dark descent into the brooding, sullen moods that had dominated the days and weeks following her death.

The only keepsake he had was a photograph on his phone and that, he told himself, was hardly likely to leave any scent about the place, was it? His head sank in a penitent nod before he heaved his lanky frame upright and walked outside. On the hillside up to his left, the soft sunshine was starting to turn the heather a misty pink as the gloaming, the dusky twilight that would endure until almost midnight, was beginning to set in. Up there, beyond the ridge, lay the Ruby Loch. Maybe he'd pay the grave a visit tomorrow. He turned to his right and took four strides to reach his small back garden. From here he could see out across the water towards Hurdy's Glen, lying between the two highest peaks that looked down over Lochdubh—the Two Sisters.

Legend had it that the Two Sisters were once one huge mountain, higher than any other in the whole of Scotland—Ben Cral. The mountain had been created by God at the dawn of time to trap a demon named Cral in the bowels of the earth. Then, one hot day a giant named Hurdy came lumbering across the countryside, planning to take a swim in the sea as no loch was deep enough for him. A witch, in league with Cral, tricked him into believing that there was a huge treasure hoard hidden inside Ben Cral, so Hurdy took his giant axe and, with a single blow, lopped off the top half of the mountain. Cral immediately leapt out and, realising he had been fooled, Hurdy tried to force him back in again. The two fought and, although he wasn't quite as big and powerful as Hurdy, Cral could scoop great handfuls of molten rock from inside the mountain to hurl them at the giant. Hurdy took a swipe at Cral with his axe and missed, cleaving what remained of the mountain in two, whereupon the molten rock drained into Lochdubh, bubbling and hissing as it cooled, creating a huge cloud of steam. Hidden from Cral's sight by the cloud, Hurdy picked up the top half of the mountain and, as soon as the steam cleared, hurled it at Cral. The force of the blow propelled the demon through the air until he fell into the sea two miles off the coast. The mountain top trapped him under the seabed, the very summit of what had been Ben Cral standing above the surface as a rocky mound now known as Cral's Island. The demon remains buried to this day, struggling to escape from time to time and making the ground shake. Where Hurdy had sliced the remains of the mountain down the middle, the two peaks came to be called the Two Sisters and the molten rock thrown by Cral cooled to become the huge boulders that litter Hurdy's Glen.

Hamish had always loved the story and found himself wondering what Sally Paterson would make of it. Volcanic activity, glacial erosion and earth tremors, no doubt. Then again, she had made a grand job of telling Auld Mary's tale, so she was clearly more than an analytical, rational scientist—there was a touch of artistry about her, too. He shuddered at the thought of her finding Hibbert's body and decided to pay her a visit the following day to make sure she was holding up. Right now, however, he wanted to investigate Hibbert's hidden package.

Sitting at his desk in the front office, he closed the blinds and switched on his desk light. Pulling on a pair of latex gloves, he placed the black package on the desk in front of him. The plastic was already covered in his fingerprints, but he could clean it up if he needed to. He had to be a good deal more careful with the contents if they were ever to be used as evidence. The parcel was well sealed with tape. He fished a pair of scissors out of his desk drawer and carefully cut it open at one end. Inside he could see a number of large brown envelopes. He slid one of the envelopes onto the desk. It was not sealed and he tipped out the contents. Half a dozen identical blue envelopes cascaded onto the pool of light cast by his lamp. Each of them had been sealed but then slit open along the top edge with a knife or letter opener. None was stamped nor addressed.

Hamish chose one of the envelopes. It contained a single sheet of writing paper. Unfolding it, he read a hand-written note.

My darling Kelpie,
I'm writing this now with thoughts of you still
flooding my senses and the tender feeling of your
embrace still warming my heart. How I hated
it when you had to leave! One day things will be
different. We will have more than a mere evening
together. There will be no more goodbyes. It will
be just you and me, together forever.

    **I can scarcely bear to wait until we can see
each other again. Please let that be soon! I long to
stroke your beautiful hair and feel your lips touch
mine. It is madness that you are not here with me
now! Talk to me as soon as you can. Tell me again
that you love me and all will be well.**

    With all my heart
    J. P.

He refolded the letter and put it back in its envelope. It
was clearly intended to be an intimate, passionate note
and had been written by a man—he was certain that
it was a man's handwriting—to his lover, but it was
embarrassingly awful. It read as though it were written by someone desperately attempting to be romantic in the crass style of a cheap, old-fashioned romance
novel. Whatever Hibbert had seen in "J. P." it certainly
had nothing to do with his skill as a writer of love letters.
Hamish felt suddenly guilty at having read the letter, and
worse for having judged the writer. Then he shrugged.
He was a policeman. It was his job, as Jimmy had put it,
to go sticking his nose in where it wasn't wanted. Had
Kate Hibbert been involved with someone? If she had
been, she had done a very good job of keeping it quiet.
Secrets turned to tittle-tattle in less time than it took to
boil a kettle once folk around Lochdubh had their minds
set on tea and gossip. In any case, why would she want to
keep it a secret? Was her lover a married man? Who was
this "J. P." and, for that matter, why was his sweetheart

name for her "Kelpie"? Kelpies were mythical monsters that dragged people to their deaths in lochs and rivers— not exactly a tender or endearing term for your lover.

He read through a second letter—another sparse few lines of gushing drivel dedicated to "Kelpie" and signed "J. P." He examined the envelopes. With no address, the letters had clearly been delivered by hand. That meant there was also no date-stamped postmark and, as the notes themselves weren't dated, it was impossible to tell when they'd been written. He looked at the plastic parcel again. He could understand Hibbert wanting to take letters like these with her, wherever she was going, but why wrap them in plastic and hide them inside her suitcase? He'd been on flights abroad before and once, sitting by an emergency exit that allowed more room for his long legs, he'd looked out the window while the jet was still on the ground and spotted his suitcase on a baggage train, waiting to be loaded. It was raining hard outside and all of the baggage was drenched. Was that why Hibbert had wrapped her most precious possessions so well—to protect them while she was in transit? Perhaps, but that didn't explain why she had then hidden the waterproofed package inside the lining of the case. If the lid hadn't started to rot, he'd surely never have found the package.

The big question, of course, was where was she going? Was she heading off to meet her lover for a romantic tryst in some far-flung, sun-kissed paradise where they could stroll hand-in-hand without fear of being recognised? That theory seemed all wrong to him. When he had talked to people about Hibbert's disappearance, he had been fairly sure that some of them were holding something back, but there was no way that everyone would have been able to keep quiet about her having an affair. There was always someone, usually someone with their own axe to grind, who would blurt out a tasty morsel of gossip like that.

Setting the letters aside, he slid the remaining envelopes out of the package. One was more bulky than the others, and inside he found two black velvet pouches. He was unfastening the drawstring to open the first pouch when his mobile phone rang. The screen announced that the caller was Jimmy.

"Macbeth."

"Hamish...it's Jimmy." The voice sounded weak and strained.

"Aye, Jimmy, what is it?"

"Crashed...car's crashed. I'm on the Strathbane road. I need you, Hamish...need you to come...I'm hurt bad..."

"Stay on the phone, Jimmy!" Hamish called. "I'm on my way, but you stay with me—keep talking."

Hamish swept the contents of the plastic package into his desk drawer, grabbed his service belt and, all the while supporting Jimmy by phone with a steady stream of encouragement and reassurance, he dashed to his Land Rover.

CHAPTER THREE

I don't want to go to Heaven. None of my friends are there.

Oscar Wilde

For the second time that day, Hamish roared along the road to Strathbane with the Land Rover's blue lights flashing. More than once he heard the engine race as he crested a rise and all four wheels left the ground. He used his phone handsfree to keep talking to Jimmy and his radio to call for an ambulance. He slowed as he approached a bend in the road where it cut through two rocky outcrops—the spot Jimmy had described to him on the phone. Beyond the cutting he screeched to a halt. Jimmy's car was on its roof, wedged in a roadside ditch at a crazy angle, the driver's door wide open, the surface of the road closest to it littered with broken glass.

Just beyond the car, Jimmy lay flat on his back, his mobile phone in his right hand. His face was deathly pale, with even the blue of his half-open eyes looking like the colour had drained out of them.

"Man, am I glad to see you..." he breathed as Hamish dashed to his side. "Reckon my leg's broke...back and neck hurt like hell...left arm doesn't want to move."

"But you made it out the car on your own," Hamish said, looking at the scuff marks in the road dust where Jimmy had obviously dragged himself clear of the car. He checked Jimmy over as best he could without moving him. "You don't look like you're bleeding. There's a few wee cuts on your hands from the broken glass and that leg's sitting at a funny angle. Can you move your other leg? Don't try—just move your foot a wee bit."

Jimmy did as instructed.

"That's braw. You're going to be all right, Jimmy," Hamish said, slipping three fingers into Jimmy's right hand. "Now squeeze those fingers—good. How about the left hand? Good, that's working, too. Bide where you are. I'll be right back."

Hamish dashed to the Land Rover, then paused for a moment. What he was about to do was wrong but, even as he hesitated, he knew he had to go through with it. He was loyal to Jimmy as a true friend but Jimmy was also his only real ally at headquarters. Having Jimmy looking out for him in the past had helped to make sure that his station in Lochdubh hadn't been shut down. He walked back towards his injured friend, carrying an electronic breathalyser machine.

"You're surely no' going to..." Jimmy sighed.

"An ambulance is on its way and other police will be here afore it," Hamish explained. "If you've no' had a breath test, they'll surely do one. You'll test positive, you'll lose your licence and, since you've banjaxed one o' their bonny motors, Police Scotland will sack you."

Hamish breathed into the machine and held up the reading for Jimmy to see.

"I've no' had a drink, so we have a negative reading stored on the machine. Now take this, but do NOT drink any." He thrust a silver hipflask into Jimmy's right hand. "They'll smell whisky on your breath, but I'll tell them I gave you this to ease the pain AFTER I'd breathalysed you."

"Hamish, you don't have to . . ."

"Wheesht now, Jimmy. I'll do this just this once. You get in a car wi' a drink on you ever again and I'll arrest you myself. No second chances. Stick to the story for the medics as well as the other cops."

Right on cue, they heard the sound of sirens and a police car appeared from the direction of Strathbane. Two uniformed constables leapt out, and Hamish stopped them before they approached Jimmy. He had no need to explain who Jimmy was, both officers recognising him straight away, but he informed them that he had performed a breath test and showed them the breathalyser reading. They looked at it, looked at each other, and smiled. Hamish sent them off, one in either direction, to close the road.

"They didn't believe a single word you said," Jimmy croaked as Hamish knelt beside him again.

"Aye, but they're good lads and they'll play along," said Hamish. "Now, how did you manage to end up in the ditch?"

"It was them." Jimmy didn't attempt to move his head, but focused his eyes some distance beyond Hamish's right shoulder. "I came round the bend and they were all over the road."

Hamish turned to see a small flock of around a dozen Blackface sheep staring back at him, watching the proceedings with concerned faces and innocent dark eyes. He stood to look at the tyre marks on the road.

"So you swerved to avoid them, rode up the embankment and clipped that boulder. That flipped the car and sent it sliding across the road on its roof till it ended up in the ditch. You're lucky to be alive, Jimmy."

"Well, let's try to keep him that way, shall we?" came a female voice. The ambulance had arrived and two green-uniformed paramedics were rushing to Jimmy's side. They knelt to examine him, the male medic snapping open a medical bag before the woman, her blonde hair tied back in a knot, stood to face Hamish. She scarcely came up to his shoulder, yet the frown etched on her face made him feel like a wee boy in class about to feel the wrath of the teacher.

"You gave him this, did you?" She waved the hipflask at Hamish.

"Aye, well, it iss chust that... well, hisself was..." The sibilant tones of his Highland accent always became more pronounced when Hamish was feeling angry or uncomfortable.

"You great dunderhead!" She held the hipflask up near his face. "You can't give a badly injured man alcohol and you should know that, Sergeant! I can't believe you did that! If you had twice the brains you've got, you'd still be an eejit!"

He went to take the hipflask but she snatched it away from him, unscrewed the cap and made to empty the contents onto the road. Then she paused, sniffed at the open neck of the flask and replaced the cap again. She glanced from Hamish to Jimmy and back again, then slapped the flask into his hand.

"Take it," she said. "A friend of yours, is he?"

"Aye, a friend—and a colleague. He's a DCI."

"Has he a wife you can call?"

"He's a couple of ex-wives," said Hamish, "but I doubt they'll care too much about him being in hospital. I'll go with him."

"Stay out of our way in the meantime," was all she said before crouching back down beside Jimmy.

Late that night, Hamish sat on a plastic-cushioned, plastic chair in one of Braikie Hospital's many corridors, staring out of a window at the stark whiteness of the new LED lights illuminating the car park and the street outside. He couldn't help thinking that the old, orangey-yellow streetlights created a more mellow atmosphere but they had been scrapped when it was shown that they were releasing vast amounts of carbon dioxide into the atmosphere while using double the electricity of the new

LEDs. That, he supposed, was scientific progress moving Sutherland in the right direction, and the new lights did a fine job in fighting off the gloomy grey that passed for darkness at this time of year, but they weren't as cheery as the friendly old orange lights.

Those were the sorts of things that filled your head when you'd been sitting for hours in a hospital corridor with nothing but the smell of disinfectant and a copy of last week's *People's Friend* magazine for company. The Hibbert case, of course, broke into his thoughts again and again, screeching and spinning around in his head like gulls in a gale, a jumble of envelopes, love letters and velvet pouches. Where had Kate been going? Had she been having an affair? Where was she for the two days before her body was dumped in The Corloch? He heard the squeak of a rubber sole on polished vinyl flooring and looked round to see the female paramedic approaching.

"I'm just about to go off shift," she said, offering a gentle smile far removed from the fearsome expression he'd experienced earlier, "so I thought I'd check in with you to see how your friend was doing."

"Broken leg, broken ribs, dislocated shoulder and bruising to his back and neck," Hamish reported, standing to talk to her, "but it could have been a lot worse, I guess."

"He must mean a lot to you for you to put your job on the line for him."

"For me to…what? I don't know what you mean," Hamish lied.

"I know what you did," she said softly. "He'd been drinking, you took the breath test for him and then gave him that flask."

"Nope." Hamish shook his head. "Still no' wi' you."

"He hadn't been drinking from that flask. He was reeking of whisky. The flask had brandy in it."

Hamish sighed and cast his eyes to the floor.

"It wasn't your flask, was it?" she said. "Otherwise, you'd have known."

"A hillwalker gave me it last winter," Hamish admitted, "after I found him lost in the snow. I stuck it in the car and never thought about it again until today."

"You can't let him carry on drinking and driving," she warned, a trace of her earlier frown beginning to put in an appearance. "He'll end up killing himself or, worse, someone else."

"It won't happen again," Hamish promised. "By the time Jimmy's back at work, he'll have his driver again and, well, I think he's had enough o' a fright this time to stop him driving wi' a drink on him ever again."

"You need to make sure he doesn't," she said, turning to go, then looking back at him over one shoulder. "I suppose I'll . . . see you around."

"Aye, of course . . . I suppose so," Hamish said. For the first time, he noticed that she was actually very pretty, with big brown eyes and the kind of smile that left you helpless to do anything but smile in return. "Another time, another accident . . ."

As the paramedic disappeared round a corner, a male

doctor with short dark hair and wearing blue scrubs emerged from the door beside which Hamish had been sitting.

"She's a right cracker, eh, Hamish?" The two knew each other of old, Hamish having paid numerous visits to Braikie Hospital over the years.

"Aye, well... aye, she seems very nice, Mike..."

"Her name's Claire and she's single, would you believe? But you keep your mitts off her." He grinned, waving a warning finger. "I'm about to ask her out and I saw the way you were looking at her."

"Me? No, no, you've got that all wrong. Now, how is he doing?"

"DCI Anderson is currently sleeping like a baby," said the doctor, "and that's what you should be doing, too. Go home and get some rest. You'll be able to talk to him in the morning."

Hamish headed home and went straight to bed, resisting the temptation to take another peek at the contents of the black plastic package. He knew that he was too tired to make any sense of it and decided to leave it well alone, but *it* would not leave *him* alone. Thoughts of envelopes, love letters and velvet pouches spun through his mind, and then there was the paramedic, Claire. She was a smart lass, and very attractive too, with a cheeky little sexy smile. He immediately felt guilty that he had thought about her in that way, as though he were betraying Dorothy. Yet he hadn't thought about Dorothy today since... but he was asleep before he could think of how long it had been.

* * *

The instant he woke, while his eyes were still closed, Hamish had a strange feeling that he was secretly being watched. It was something he'd heard others talk about. Something beyond the normal senses of sight, sound, smell and touch. It made his shoulders tense and the back of his neck feel like it was caught in a cool breeze. He lay very still, daring only to squint through eyelids open barely a crack. There were eyes on him. Two sets—Lugs and Sonsie were sitting on the bed staring straight at him.

"What are you two up to?" he said, propping himself up on his elbows. Daylight was streaming in through the open curtains and he reached for the clock on the bedside table. "It's only five o'clock. Just because it's light doesn't mean it's breakfast time."

Sonsie glared at him, looking horrified, as though convinced he was lying to them, but Lugs, delighted merely to see him awake, bounced towards him, tail wagging, and licked his face.

"All right, all right!" Hamish laughed, fighting off the dog. "I'll feed you afore I have my shower." Lugs thundered downstairs ahead of Hamish, a blur of paws, wagging tail and flapping ears, while Sonsie sashayed casually along behind, tail held high, purring contentedly to herself as if this had been her plan all along.

Once he had showered and dressed, Hamish stood at the door to his office, a steaming mug of coffee in one hand and a bacon sandwich in the other. He stared at the drawer into which he had shoved the contents of the package the night before. That, he decided, would have to wait until he could go through it all without any distractions. This morning, he planned to visit Jimmy in Braikie, then Sally Paterson at The Corloch Lodge, then Gregor Mackenzie over in Hurdy's Glen on the way back. In the afternoon, he'd sit down with the package and study it properly.

He rounded up his pets, loaded them into the back of his Land Rover, and set off for Braikie. Lugs and Sonsie were used to travelling the length and breadth of Sutherland with him and knew they'd always be given time to explore a beach, a hillside or a riverbank somewhere along the way.

"You'll have to bide in the back there while we're at the hospital," Hamish called to them while driving along Lochdubh's main road by the seawall. Curtains were opening and the village was starting to wake. "But I'll leave the window open and you can have a good gallop around when we're up at The Corloch." By the time they reached Braikie Hospital, the dog and the wildcat were curled up together on their blanket, snoozing gently.

Jimmy had a small room to himself in the hospital and Hamish was pleased to see him sitting up in bed when he arrived, albeit because the top half of the bed had been raised.

"Good to see you looking bright and awake, Jimmy," he said.

"Aye, and I've had a braw cooked breakfast," Jimmy replied. "Man, I was famished."

"So what's happening wi' you?"

"Well, the leg's been set and it's got some kind o' splint on it for now, but they're putting it in plaster in a few minutes. The shoulder's going to need a wee operation, but the rest will mend itself in time."

"You're a lucky lad, Jimmy. You're sticking to the story about the breath test, right?"

"Aye, that's no' a problem. What is a problem is the Hibbert case. I'm going to be stuck in here but I want to know what's going on. I need you to keep me in the loop."

"Jimmy, you need to rest and—"

"To hell wi' rest. Strathbane's that short o' cops that they'll have to bring in someone else to head up the Hibbert case, and you know what that means, eh? When I get back, some other bugger will have his feet under my desk and I'll be sidelined. I need to stay involved, Hamish. I need you to help me keep my finger on the pulse."

"Aye, all right, Jimmy, I'll do what I can, but I'm no' in there at headquarters."

"I've friends in Strathbane who'll let me know what's going on there. Some o' my lads might be taken off the team, but there'll ay be someone there I can talk to. You're on the ground, though, laddie. You can root about and get to the bottom of this murder afore anyone else."

"They'll likely no' want me investigating anything."

"Aye, right," Jimmy snorted, "and when has that ever stopped you in the past?"

"Fair enough," said Hamish. "Now, about our wee ruse wi' the breathalyser. Only the sheep saw what happened.

They'll no' tell a soul and neither will I, but I'll no' do that for you again, Jimmy. In future, if you're drinking, you're no' driving."

"You've made your point." Jimmy looked angry at having been lectured, but quickly relaxed. "And you're right. When I thought I might take my last breath in a ditch at the side o' a road in the middle o' nowhere... You'll no' see me behind the wheel wi' a drink on me ever again. You have my word."

"Good," Hamish said, bluntly, that one word making it clear that they need never talk about the matter again. "I'll let you know what I find out and you let me know what the investigating team turns up. That way we might be able to crack the case afore they do."

He wondered for a second whether he should tell Jimmy about what he'd found in the suitcase, but decided to wait until he had worked out if Hibbert's mysterious hidden package had any bearing on her murder.

"Get your skates on, then, laddie," Jimmy said, urging Hamish to make a move. "Life's wearing on and you're a long time dead."

Hamish arrived at The Corloch Lodge an hour later, releasing Lugs and Sonsie by the waterfront. With the loch having receded so far, there was substantially more shoreline for them to explore and Sonsie leapt onto a boulder in the sunshine where she began a fastidious fur-cleaning regime. Lugs bounded towards the water and leapt in, swimming round in circles. Far off to the east, beneath the trees at the head of the loch, Hamish could just make out the white shapes of two police vehicles with their blue-and-yellow Battenberg reflective markings. His own Land Rover was plain white, never having been updated with the new livery. He wondered who was on duty there at Auld Mary's Island and if they had found anything else of interest, making a mental note to try to have a chat with them as soon as he had the chance.

Turning towards the lodge he could see that, despite the early hour, there was plenty of activity. Windows and curtains were open and the sound of a number of different conversations drifted from the building in the still morning air. The lodge was not a large hotel like the Tommel Castle down in Lochdubh and neither did it have the castle's pretensions to historic medieval origins. Both had been built by wealthy Victorians, Tommel Castle as a romanticised vision of what the architect believed a historic French chateau should look like, with towers, turrets and battlements. It was a huge country house, its interior swathed in Victorian opulence, while its walls wore a cloak of appropriated Gallic grandeur.

The Corloch Lodge, on the other hand, was an unashamedly Victorian building, its solid stone walls extending to a modest two storeys and set with large windows beneath a many-gabled slate roof. The pleasing outlines created by the roof's multitude of angles served to accommodate bay-window structures on the east and south flanks of the building, providing views over the loch from the reception rooms and the main upstairs bedrooms. The lodge looked, as had always been intended, like a comfortable, welcoming country house where the original owner, a prominent Edinburgh barrister, could entertain friends for weekends of hunting, shooting and fishing. Hamish was about to head inside to seek out Sally Paterson when he heard someone calling his name.

"Hamish! Over here!" Sally was standing near a set of French doors that opened onto a sunny patio area.

"Good morning," he said, striding over to a table where they both took a seat. The remains of a hearty breakfast were in evidence.

"There's coffee here, if you'd like some. It should still be hot, and do help yourself to a croissant. Sharon hasn't come down yet. She stayed up late last night in the bar with a crowd of anglers telling tales about the one that got away."

"Aye, this place is a favourite for the fishing," Hamish said, accepting the coffee and reaching for a croissant, "but they're banned from The Corloch at the moment because of the water levels."

"They were all up early, heading further afield," she agreed. "What brings you here?"

"Well, you do, actually. I wanted to see how you were after that business yesterday."

"That was awful"—she shuddered—"and we're not allowed back to the dig." She smiled, shifting a foot clad in a walking boot from under the table. "Still, it means I can do a bit of hillwalking instead. Not sure if Sharon's going to be up to it."

"How long have you been staying here?"

"Six days," she replied with a slight frown. "More questions? I already answered so many from those other policemen yesterday."

"Aye, I know and I'm sorry you have to go through all this," he said with genuine sympathy that he followed with a blatant lie, "but it looks like the body is linked to my missing person's case and I have to fill out my own report."

"Okay," she said with a sigh, sipping her coffee, "fire away."

"Where do you live?"

"Bearsden, just outside Glasgow."

"Aye, I know where that is," he said, flipping open his notebook, "but that's no' a Glasgow accent you have on you."

"Originally I'm from Tunbridge Wells."

"Turn-bridge...where?"

"It's in Kent, not far from London."

"I see. Do you know many people in this area?"

"Not really. I've never been to this particular part of Scotland before."

"And Sharon? How do you know her?"

"We first met at university in Edinburgh. We've been friends ever since."

"I see..." said Hamish again, then winced inside, realising that he may have made that sound like he was inferring something from her answer that really wasn't there. Folk in Lochdubh might tut and gossip about what

Police Scotland officially referred to as "sexual orientation" in their "diversity" missives, but Hamish couldn't care less about how people were wired as long as they treated others with respect and obeyed the law.

"Just what do you mean by that? We're good friends, Sergeant—that's all."

"Och, of course," Hamish blurted. "I didn't mean anything else by that, I..."

Sally watched him squirm for an instant, then burst out laughing.

"You really shouldn't let your interviewees wind you up like that, Hamish." She smiled, then stood to greet Sharon, who appeared from the lodge looking pale and tired.

"Sharon, you look like a walking hangover." Sally pulled up a chair for her friend. "Walking will cure it, though. Have a cup of coffee before we get going."

They chatted while they finished their coffee, Hamish taking notes from time to time, then he bade them farewell and headed down to the loch to round up his pets and drive back to Lochdubh. On reaching the bridge over the Anstey, rather than crossing it to reach the village, he kept going, taking the road leading along the north shore of the loch towards Hurdy's Glen. The bright morning sunlight had turned the surface of the loch to liquid silver and on a sandbank exposed by the ebb tide lazed a handful of seals basking blissfully before the sun grew too severe.

Turning off into Hurdy's Glen, the road quickly

deteriorated to a track, the Land Rover bumping and swaying as it climbed towards Gregor and Clara Mackenzie's cottage. Hamish knocked on the front door, then stepped back, marvelling at the freshly painted, glossy blue woodwork. Each year the summer sun followed the blasting of the winter storms, to leave the paint flaking and peeling. Each autumn, Clara scraped, sanded and repainted the door. This year, she had clearly tackled the job early. She opened the door and gave him a warm greeting.

"Gregor's up on the hill wi' his sheep," she said, craning her neck to see past Hamish. She was a slim, energetic woman with a ready smile. She was always busy, always eager to forge ahead with whatever was next on her list of "things to do," but Hamish knew exactly why she was now distracted. She was looking over his shoulder because Clara loved animals.

"They're in the car," he said, smiling.

"Och, lovely," she said, swelling with excitement. "I'll fetch them. I'm making a batch o' mutton pies and I've a wee bit o' something for them ben in the kitchen. I'll have a coffee waiting for you on your way back down."

"Thank you, Clara," said Hamish. Lugs loved to be everyone's friend but Clara was the only person, apart from himself, in whom Sonsie had ever shown the slightest interest. "They'll be pleased to see you. I'll have a wander up to find Gregor."

From his vantage point up on the hillside, Gregor had seen the white Land Rover arrive and waved as Hamish made his way up the hill. After greeting his visitor, Gregor sat on the pile of rocks he was using to repair a collapsed dry-stone wall, while Hamish sat in the shade of the wall itself.

"You made good time up the brae, Hamish," Gregor congratulated him, "and you're barely out o' puff. Will you be defending your title at the Strathbiggie Games this year?"

Hamish was known far and wide as the man to beat when it came to the hill run at Strathbiggie, and he knew exactly why Gregor was asking.

"It'll be a wee wager that you're thinking of, is it no', Gregor?"

"Aye, it makes the sport that bit more exciting, is what I think."

"And you know that if I run, as a competitor I'm no' allowed to bet."

"Is that right?"

"You well know that it is, Gregor Mackenzie," Hamish said, laughing, "but if I gave you money to bet, you'd doubtless be willing to split the winnings with me."

"The thought might have crossed my mind..."

"Well, let's talk about that nearer the time. Right now, I need to talk about Kate Hibbert."

"I've already told you all I know about that woman."

"Maybe, but I need to go through it again."

"Is this to do with the body in The Corloch? Is it her?"

"Bad news travels fast, eh?" Hamish shook his head. "I can't say anything about that. Walk down with me to where you spotted her."

The two men made their way down the slope, Gregor's dog trotting by his side.

"So she disappeared behind those boulders," Hamish said, pointing to the outcrop, "and you went off in this direction, sticking to the dry ground."

"Aye, that's right. I went this way and lost sight o' her completely."

"And making your way down here," Hamish said, following in Gregor's footsteps, "you can't see the track down to the main road at all. In fact," he added, "because o' the way the ridge runs, you can't see where it carries on up the glen to the Mackay house."

"True," said Gregor, "and that's the smoothest stretch o' the track. There's only Morgan's place up there, so it doesn't get rutted wi' traffic the same way that it does down here."

"I don't really know Morgan," Hamish admitted. "I've only ever met him a couple o' times. What's he like?"

"Keeps himself to himself in the main. We talk from time to time when I see him hiking down to the loch wi' his fishing rod. He'll drop something off if he's had a good day on the water. We've had some nice pollock from him and I mind him sharing a salmon wi' us no' so long ago. He ay says that auld house up there is too much for him. That's why he was glad to have Hibbert help him out. He's got some sort o' servant there since she disappeared. Somebody who keeps the house and garden and does a bit o' cooking."

They carried on down to where Gregor had last seen Hibbert.

"In the time it's taken us to walk down here," Hamish pointed out, "a car could have come from the road, picked her up and driven off again without you seeing it. Did you no' hear a car on the track?"

"My hearing's no' really that good," Gregor admitted, wrinkling his nose, "but motors ay struggle coming up the track off the road. Even wi' the four-wheel drive you have to rev your engine. I would have heard a car, even if I couldn't see it, so where she went is a mystery to me."

"Do you know anyone who might have wanted to harm Kate—anyone who might have fallen out wi' her or have a grudge against her?"

"I've no idea about that," Gregor said, slowly shifting his gaze to the right as though he were taking in a view of the loch he had seen many thousands of times before.

"Aye, right." Hamish nodded, studying Gregor's features. "Come on, then. Clara's got some coffee on the go."

Sitting on a bench by the front door of the cottage, each with a mug of strong coffee and their faces tilted towards the sun, the only thing spoiling the moment for Hamish was the fact that he knew Gregor Mackenzie was lying to him. Why had it been so easy for him to tell when Gregor was hiding the truth, yet so difficult to see when Sally Paterson was pulling his leg earlier? Was it because he was a weather-beaten Highland crofter, while she was a sophisticated, attractive woman from the south? Maybe he was losing his touch. On the other hand, maybe he'd always been a wee bit too easily distracted by a pretty face. He leant forward to take a sip of his coffee.

"It's a grand view you have here, Clara," he said, surveying the grassy slope that gave way to heather and gorse beyond the garden wall where the glen slipped away towards the shimmering waters of Lochdubh. "You've the peace and quiet here, but you're only a few minutes' walk from your neighbours' cottages down there. The nearest one is where Kate lived, isn't it?"

"It is," Clara agreed, looking towards him. "Empty now, though. Mind you, it stood empty a fair bit when she was living there, too. She was ay rushing around, ay had somewhere she needed to be."

"When did you last see her?"

"Afore she disappeared, I had scarce laid eyes on her these past three months."

"I thought she helped out around here a bit."

"That she did," Clara said, turning her face back to the sun, "and an extra pair of hands was right welcome, but I'm guessing she found other places she needed to be."

Clara, Hamish decided, was an even worse liar than her husband. Her relaxed tone was not that of someone who enjoyed having a friend helping out, then lost that friend in strange circumstances. She clearly did not miss Hibbert in the slightest.

"Well," he said, standing and placing his empty coffee mug on the bench, "thanks for the coffee but I'd better away down to the station."

Clara fussed over Lugs and Sonsie one last time before she and Gregor waved Hamish off, watching the Land Rover trundle down the track towards the road.

"He thinks we're up to something," Clara said.

"Och, away wi' you," Gregor replied. "Hamish knows us. He'd never suspect us o' having anything to do with Hibbert going missing."

"I hope you're right," Clara muttered, collecting Hamish's mug and heading back to the kitchen.

Hamish made it back to the police station in time to hear the office phone clamouring for his attention. He snatched up the receiver.

"Lochdubh police station."

"Is that Sergeant Macbeth?" came the voice of a woman in some distress. "Can you come quickly, please? You have to help me! They're in my kitchen! They're going to get me!"

"Calm down now, madam. Who's in your kitchen?"

"There's two of them! Both of them huge."

"Give me your name and address," said Hamish, making a note. Her name was Moira Stephenson and she was in Cromish. "Stay calm. I'm on my way."

"Oh, thank you! Thank you!" said the woman. "Please hurry. I can't abide spiders."

"Spiders . . . ?" Hamish let out a deep breath. "You had me thinking there were intruders in your house! I'm a police officer, no' Spider-Man! I'm no' coming all the way up the coast to Cromish to deal wi' a couple o' creepy crawlies. If you can't just give them a battering wi' a rolled-up *Sunday Post*, then walk outside your front door and find someone to do it for you."

He made to slam the phone down, then thought better of it and placed it gently back in its base. Breaking the phone would make things worse, not better. He retreated to the kitchen where he made himself a cup of tea and a cheese and ham sandwich for lunch before returning to his desk. Brushing breadcrumbs from his shirt, he pulled on a fresh pair of latex gloves and retrieved one of the velvet pouches from the drawer. He untied the drawstring and tipped the contents out onto a sheet of white printer paper.

A pair of gold earrings tumbled out of the pouch. Each had a gold horseshoe shape at the top from which dangled three strands of gold links, each link set with a small diamond. The longest strands had a dozen links and a large diamond suspended at the end. The shorter ones had proportionately smaller suspended stones. Even in the flat yellow light of the desk lamp the diamonds sparkled with such brilliance that Hamish could tell the earrings were high-quality jewellery. They looked far from new, but not old-fashioned enough to be antique.

"*Vintage* is what Tommy would say," he muttered to himself, thinking of an old jeweller and occasional fence he knew in Strathbane. "Vintage, but where have I seen these afore?"

Concentration furrowed his brow as he tried to place the jewels, or something like them, on women he knew. Dorothy had liked new things and he had never seen her with earrings like these. Elspeth, the TV reporter to whom he had also been engaged at one time, would not have worn anything quite so flamboyant. Then there was Priscilla, the third of his ex-fiancées, whom he knew sometimes borrowed expensive jewellery from her mother. Had he seen Priscilla with something similar to these? He shook his head, admitting temporary defeat, carefully slipped the earrings back into their pouch and replaced it in the drawer, swapping it for the second pouch.

Turning its contents out onto the paper, he found himself studying another piece of jewellery, although this one he considered to be more "arts and crafts" than the earrings. It was a silver chain with a silver pendant in which was mounted a dark brown nut. The nut was almost heart-shaped with a cross, which appeared to be naturally part of the nut, like a crucifix at its centre. He held it up to take a closer look, letting the pendant sway on its chain.

"Where did you get that?"

The voice came from the office doorway where stood Elspeth Grant, her auburn hair sleek and shining, a far cry from the wild locks she had when working as a reporter in the Highlands. As a television presenter based in Glasgow, she had adopted a far more glamorous image, yet her beguiling silver-grey eyes could still fix you with an inescapable gaze.

"Elspeth! What are you doing here?" he said, realising that he had left the back door wide open, and sliding his desk drawer closed.

"What do you think?" She sighed, flopping down into an office chair. "The word is out that a body was fished out of The Corloch and when anything like that happens, I'm the one the news editor sends. Local knowledge, local connections, still a local girl despite everything I've done over the years in Glasgow."

"You can't deny where you come from." Hamish shrugged, "And it's good to see you, even if you are here under protest."

"Och, I'm not protesting really." Elspeth smiled. "It's good to be out of the city for a while and I've been looking forward to seeing you. How are things?"

"Things are just fine," he replied, holding up a hand to fend off further questions.

"Well, that's good," she said softly. She knew Hamish better than anyone, and knew not to press him further about the turbulent times in his recent past. "So does that pendant have something to do with the dead body? Was it a murder like people are saying?"

"I don't know where you get your information from," he responded, "but you know fine I can't talk to you about anything to do wi' The Corloch. And this thing," he said, turning back to the pendant, "is just a strange piece of lost property."

Elspeth stared at him. Generations of women in her family had been gifted with a kind of second sight, an intuition that allowed them to see and feel things that others could not. Right now, all of her senses were telling her that Hamish was lying.

"Well, if you're looking for the owner, you're looking for a midwife," she said.

"What makes you say that?"

"That's a birthing amulet. It's a kind of tropical plant seed that sometimes washes ashore here, carried on the Gulf Stream all the way from the Caribbean. The most highly prized examples have that little cross on them. They used to get them blessed by a priest and midwives would give them to women to hold, to help with the pain of childbirth and to help ensure the baby was born healthy."

"Well, well . . . a midwife's charm, eh?" The telephone interrupted his thoughts. "Lochdubh police station."

"Hamish, it's Alex," came the voice of an officer in Strathbane Hamish had been friends with for many years.

"Aye, hang on a wee minute, Alex," he replied, then covered the mouthpiece with his hand, turning to Elspeth. "Sorry, but I need to take this."

"No problem," she said, standing to leave. "I'm staying at the Tommel Castle. Drop by later for a drink."

"That sounds good," he agreed, then returned to his call. "What is it, Alex?"

"You need to get your arse down to Strathbane sharpish, Hamish. Daviot wants you here and it looks like all hell's about to break loose!"

CHAPTER FOUR

*The best way to find out if you can trust
somebody is to trust them.*
Ernest Hemingway

Hamish hit the road to Strathbane again, this time travelling at a more leisurely pace. If Alex was right and "all
hell" was inflicting itself upon police headquarters, he
was in no hurry to get there. It was a beautiful day for
a drive up onto the high moors and into the mountains.
He let the warm air flood into the car through open windows, cruising in a small, well-spaced convoy of tourist
traffic along the shore of Loch Assynt. Any other drivers
tempted to try a spurt of acceleration to overtake on the
narrow road thought better of it when they realised that
the white Land Rover in their midst was a police vehicle.

He scanned the motorhomes, family cars and motorcy-
cles jockeying for space at the car parks by the Loch Assynt
Islands and Ardvreck Castle, making sure they were all
behaving themselves, although he expected no trouble. He

knew that the glorious weather, along with the breathtaking views of the mountains, the lochs and the moors would have lulled the majority of visitors into a relaxed bliss that would last at least until they hit roadwork and heavy traffic way beyond Sutherland on their journey back down south. By then, they would be someone else's problem.

Passing through Inchnadamph, the white walls of Inchnadamph Lodge dazzled in the sunshine to his left. The house had been built as a manse for the old kirk down near the loch around two hundred years ago but was now a popular bed-and-breakfast place, the decline in religious dedication among the populace having more-or-less coincided with the rise of the tourist trade. Up the glen beyond the lodge, the massive presence of Ben More Assynt dominated the skyline, luxuriating in the sunshine without the customary cloak of cloud shrouding its summit. His route followed the River Loanan to Loch Awe—not to be confused with the far larger Loch Awe further south in Argyll, although he had lost count of the number of tourists who had—and beyond to where the road meandered between the Cromalt Hills to his left and the peaks of Cùl Mòr and Cùl Beag to his right.

Sutherland, he told himself, not for the first time, was the finest place in the whole world. There were few things that could mar the loveliness of such majestic scenery but, as the road looped down towards the coast and he rounded a bend that brought him out of an area of forest, one such disfigurement lurched into view—Strathbane. Once a thriving port, the demise of the fishing industry had decimated the town's trawler fleet and with the fishing boats went the shipbuilding, maintenance and repair industry. A variety of regeneration schemes had been launched, resulting in shabby industrial estates on the outskirts of town housing a succession of ultimately ailing and failing electronics, textiles and toy manufacturing businesses. Decrepit tower blocks, a dismal city centre blighted by vacant shop units and dingy back alleys populated by drug dealers and their junkie clients rounded off the town's sleazy image. Hamish shook his head. He knew he only ever saw the worst of the place and that he would never be able to shake his impression of the town as a concrete scab on the otherwise beautiful face of his beloved Sutherland.

He parked outside the grey, functional structure that was Strathbane police headquarters and made his way up to the fourth floor. Nodding greetings to colleagues he recognised, he strode into the small outer office of Superintendent Peter Daviot. By the door to Daviot's private office sat his secretary, Helen, who guarded her boss's inner sanctum like a Rottweiler with a cardigan and a perm. Looking up from her computer keyboard to see Hamish enter, her face set in a scowl. Whenever the big Highlander put in an appearance it generally meant trouble, and she despised him for his casual manner and lack of reverence.

"Hello, Helen," Hamish greeted her with a smile, making for the door to Daviot's office. "Is he in?"

She rose from her chair with commendable speed to insert herself between Hamish and the door.

"The Superintendent is busy," she said. "Take a seat and I will let him know you have arrived."

"That won't be necessary, Helen," said Daviot, opening the door. "Would you bring us some tea, please, and maybe a plate of biscuits?"

"I've your favourite Tunnock's Tea Cakes," she offered eagerly.

"That would be splendid," he replied, turning back towards his desk. "Come in, Sergeant."

"Bung a few garibaldis on the biscuit plate, Helen," Hamish said with a wink.

"Sit down, Hamish," Daviot said, as Hamish closed the door behind him. A slight chill of apprehension made the hairs on the back of his neck bristle. If Daviot was using his first name, even though they were alone, something was up.

"Is there a problem?" he asked, taking his seat.

"I do hope not," Daviot said, "but I wanted to have a chat with you about the Hibbert murder case."

"It's officially a murder now, is it?" Hamish asked. "And we've a positive identification on the body? Any personal effects about her person? We need to know where she was going and work out where she'd been for two days. Also, she has a cousin staying at—"

"Yes, yes, all in good time," said Daviot, waving his arms to stem the flow of questions. "At the moment my main concern is DCI Anderson."

"I understand Mr. Anderson will be in hospital for some time yet."

"That is correct," Daviot agreed, "and his accident has

left me in something of a quandary. We are very short on manpower at the moment and I have no one of equivalent rank to take over DCI Anderson's team."

"Can't one of his lads step up to take the lead?"

"That idea has been vetoed by the powers-that-be. They're sending us someone on temporary assignment."

Both men fell silent when Helen appeared bearing a tray laden with a teapot, milk jug, cups, saucers, sugar bowl and a fully stocked biscuit plate. She placed it on the desk between them.

"Thank you, Helen," said Daviot.

"You're most welcome, sir," she said, giving Hamish a sideways glance as she left.

"So who is it?" Hamish asked, once they were alone again, although he suspected he already knew the answer.

"Blair."

"No! Why him?"

"I don't want him here any more than you do, believe me, but on paper he looks like the right man for the job."

"DCI Anderson will be livid. Blair is a bungling eejit. We both know he can't be trusted. He's ay looking for a short cut or a way to line his own pocket."

"Be careful what you say about senior officers, Sergeant," Daviot warned, his voice taking on a formal tone once more. "I know that you have had issues with DCI Blair in the past. You know that I have, too, but he clearly now has friends in high places and has been given carte blanche to run the investigation as he sees fit. He will be bringing a few of his own team with him."

"Aye and that's what all the fuss is about around here, isn't it? He's kicking Jimmy's boys off the squad. I'm betting you have some very unhappy senior detectives on your hands."

"I will deal with that," Daviot said, letting out a sigh and pouring them both tea, "but I need you to deal with Blair."

Hamish's hazel eyes narrowed as he thought about the last time he had been forced to "deal with Blair." He had cornered Hamish in the shrubbery at the Tommel Castle, where he thought there were no witnesses. Blair had a gun and was prepared to shoot Hamish to stop him from revealing his links to the Glasgow underworld. He might have done it had it not been for the mysterious American, James Bland, who helped Hamish disarm Blair. Such was Hamish's fury over Blair's involvement with the gangsters who had killed Dorothy, he had then turned the gun on him. Only the arrival in the increasingly crowded shrubbery of Mary, Blair's long-suffering wife, had prevented him blowing Blair's brains out.

"I can never work wi' that man."

"You won't really be working with him," Daviot explained. "You'll be working for me. I need you to report to me on every aspect of the investigation. I'm under a great deal of pressure from higher up on all sorts of fronts and if Blair makes a mess of this, the top brass will start taking an unhealthy interest in our division."

"He won't let me anywhere near his core team. He hates me."

"You'll find a way. I can't afford this case to fall apart, and neither can you. There are those far higher up the food chain who are itching to reorganise policing throughout this whole area. If you can keep tabs on Blair and help to make sure the case is brought to a swift resolution so that he is returned to Glasgow as soon as possible, I can make *this* go away."

He handed an official Police Scotland report across the desk. It was headed "Regional Office Closures and Rationalisation." Lochdubh police station was at the top of the "closures" list. Hamish felt a surge of anger rising but resisted his first instinct, which was to hurl the whole report back across the desk at Daviot, and forced himself to remain calm. His station was under perpetual threat of being shut down and he'd had to face up to that challenge many times in the past, but it was intensely galling to see it there, in black and white. He took a sip of tea followed by a mouthful of garibaldi and eyed Daviot across the desk. Maybe there was a way to make this work to his advantage.

"So you're threatening me?" he said, allowing a harsh note of anger in his voice. "You're going to take away my station—my home—unless I spy on Blair for you. I'd say that was blackmail."

"No, no, no," Daviot spluttered. "Nothing of the sort. All I'm saying is that I'm prepared to stick my neck out for you, if you'll do a favour for me in return."

"I get to keep my station," Hamish said, his tone hard and steady as he laid out his terms, "and you'll get me off any closure list for at least five years. I'll also be needing a new Land Rover, the old one will no' make it through another winter."

Daviot's mouth dropped open, but for a moment no sound came out. He had been expecting this to be an awkward meeting, perhaps even with Macbeth's notorious temper playing a part, but he had not expected such a hard-nosed negotiation.

"You drive a hard bargain," he said at last, "but I guarantee you I will do my utmost on the five years. As far as the car is concerned, I will juggle budgets somehow to make that happen."

"Then we're done here." Standing to leave, Hamish picked up another garibaldi. "I'll keep in touch but, for now, I'll bid you good day."

"Sergeant Macbeth," Daviot said as Hamish reached the door, "it is accepted practice to use the term 'sir' when addressing senior officers. You have not. Not once. I expect you to do so in future, most certainly in public."

"Aye, I'll remember that," said Hamish. "Good day to you, *sir*."

"And Macbeth," Daviot added, reaching for the phone on his desk, "I'm calling down to the stores department now. Make sure you pick up your black uniform shirts on the way out."

Hamish crossed the outer office, stalked by the predictably dour expression of Daviot's secretary.

"Keep smiling, Helen!" he called, waving without turning round.

Out in the corridor, he leant against the wall, letting out a melancholy sigh of disbelief. Blair—back in his life again. He could feel his blood beginning to boil at the mere thought of that scunner strutting around Lochdubh again. Mind you, Blair had no great love for the village. He wouldn't set foot there unless he felt he absolutely needed to. He was every bit as predictable as one of Helen's sour looks. No, he would leave Lochdubh to Hamish and concentrate his efforts elsewhere, doubtless on some wild goose chase. If Blair played true to his usual form, Hamish would be able to anticipate his every move and stay one step ahead of him.

"You—Macbeth!" His thoughts were interrupted by the guttural, gravelly voice of DCI Blair himself, as though he'd been summoned by Hamish's ruminations. "Get your lazy arse in here now!"

Blair was standing by an open office door, retreating inside when Hamish began to move towards him. In the office was gathered a group of four male and two female detectives. Hamish recognised one of the men and one of the women as Jimmy's officers, the rest were Blair's people. Three of the men wore suits, one without a tie, and the fourth, a younger man, was more casually dressed in a polo shirt and jeans. Hamish judged the dark grey suit that the portly Blair was wearing to be expensive and guessed Mary had bought it for him. It was sorely in need of dry cleaning, the tell-tale stains betraying too many beer-and-pie pub lunches. He looked at Blair's face, reddened and bloated with booze, and noted the small scar on his cheek.

"I am now in charge of the Hibbert murder enquiry," Blair announced pompously, glaring at Hamish from beneath heavy, dark brows, "and I'll be running operations from here."

"So they've confirmed she was strangled?" Hamish asked. "And you've confirmed that it's Hibbert?"

"It's her, right enough," Blair barked. "We've got dental records. The pathologist says she was strangled. There was no sign of a handbag, phone, purse or passport, even though it looked like she was going on holiday, so I'm treating this as a robbery that went wrong. She hitched a lift and the driver turned nasty. He throttled her when she tried to fight him off and he then panicked, drove to The Corloch and slung her into the water."

"That's rubbish," Hamish objected. "A thief would simply have shoved her body in a ditch, not driven all the way up to The Corloch. And she couldn't have been pushed into the loch—she had to have been dumped from a boat."

"You listen to me, laddie!" Blair marched towards Hamish to stand in front of him, his forehead level with the big Highlander's chin, and jabbed his chest with a podgy finger. "You'll do as I say and keep your opinions to yourself."

"Poke me one more time wi' that finger," Hamish quietly promised him, "and I'll snap it like a twig."

"Did you hear that?" Blair whined, backing away from Hamish and turning to the others. "Who heard him threaten me?"

The officers in the room avoided eye contact with Blair, studying the paperwork on the desks in front of them or staring at the floor. The young detective in the polo shirt gave a short laugh, which he quickly turned into a diplomatic cough before popping a stick of gum in his mouth.

"Get away to that backwater ye call home, ye useless teuchter!" Blair snarled at Hamish, the unmistakable aroma of stale whisky engulfing every word. "If you'd done a better job when this was a simple 'missing persons,' then we wouldn't all be wasting our time here now! You're to re-interview all the inbreds up there in the back of beyond and put the fear of God into them. This is now a murder investigation and if any of them is holding anything back, I'll do them for obstruction and have them behind bars before they can say 'haggis'!"

Hamish could feel his neck flush red with fury and his stomach tightening. He moved towards Blair and suddenly the young man in the polo shirt was at his side, also facing Blair. He was tall, though not quite as tall as Hamish, and powerfully built. His shoulder subtly touching Hamish was enough to prevent him from reaching Blair unless Hamish knocked the younger man out of the way.

"You said something about me going with Sergeant Macbeth, sir?" he said, the words bracketed by a barrage of chewing.

"Aye...aye," Blair said, his bluster collapsing under Hamish's withering stare. "Forbes is assigned to you in Lochdubh. Now get out, the pair of you."

"You looked about ready to kill him in there," said Forbes as they walked along the corridor. "He's not worth it. He's a joke."

"The man iss no choke," Hamish muttered, his accent cutting through his hushed tone.

"Seemed to me he was more than a wee bit feared of you."

"He hass effery right to be."

DCI Blair was the last of his small team to check into the Strathbane Spa Hotel. There were cheaper places to stay in the area but he didn't see why he and his lads should slum it, even if the police hierarchy was imposing rampant budget restraints and spending cuts. Spoiling his team helped to keep them loyal. He had booked himself into a suite and now, hauling his small suitcase from his car in the hotel's underground car park, he justified the expense to himself by having offloaded Forbes onto Macbeth. Forbes would now stay at the police station in Lochdubh free of charge, an obvious cost saving should anyone ever ask about it. As he thumbed the button on his key fob, he began wondering what he would find in the minibar in his room. It had been a couple of hours since he'd had a drink at the pub near headquarters.

"Drinking and driving, Chief Inspector?" Hamish stepped from the shadows. "I smelled whisky on your breath earlier. By rights I should now breathalyse you."

"What are you doing here?"

"Forbes is checking out," Hamish explained, walking slowly towards Blair. "He's collecting his things afore I take him up to Lochdubh."

"Aye, well, just you get on wi' it, then," Blair blustered, puffing out his chest. "I have important things to do."

"You mind your step while you're back here," Hamish

said quietly. "Start throwing your weight around on my patch and you might no' live to regret it."

"You keep away from me!" Blair whined, but Hamish already had hold of him, grabbing two fistfuls of jacket and slamming him against his car.

"How did you manage to avoid getting your throat slit by the Glasgow gangsters you were mixed up with?" he snarled.

"Do you think my head buttons up the back?" Blair said. "I'm no' stupid. I took out insurance. I know enough about that lot to send them all to the jail and cost them millions into the bargain. I've put it all down in black and white. Anything happens to me and those papers will land on the desks of some real hard-hitters, from the Chief Constable to the Lord Advocate. So you see, I'm worth more to the Glasgow lot alive than dead."

"Well, you're worth nothing to me! See that wee scar on your face? That's where I shoved the barrel o' the gun you threatened me with, is it no'?"

"Don't be daft now," Blair whimpered. "I was only... you know... trying to give you a bit o' a fright."

"Well, I'm no feared o' a wee shite like you!" Hamish replied. "You'd better stay out o' my way, Blair, or the Glasgow mob will be the least of your problems!"

"Ready to go, Sergeant?" Forbes's voice echoed across the car park.

"Aye, I'm ready, all right," Hamish grunted, releasing Blair and stepping away from the car. He strode towards the spot where he had left his Land Rover. "Let's get out of here. There's an awful bad smell about the place."

With the Land Rover rumbling out of Strathbane, Forbes did his best to make conversation. Hamish was driving, and remained stubbornly monosyllabic. He didn't know what he could say to this young man. He seemed perfectly upright and honest but he'd been assigned by Blair, and Blair had sent officers to spy on Hamish in the past. Was young Forbes another of his snoopers? Was everything he said and did now going to be reported straight back to Blair? How could he have Forbes living in the station and still keep the package from the suitcase a secret? How could he find out what it was that Gregor, Clara and the others might be keeping from him when Forbes was hanging around, desperate to tell all to Blair? And how could he stick to his deal with Daviot when Blair knew his every move?

"It's a lovely part of the country once you're out of Strathbane," Forbes said.

"Aye."

"Will it take us long to reach Lochdubh?"

"No."

"You must love being out here, away from the city noise and crowds."

"Aye."

"Och, come on, Sergeant," Forbes said with a little laugh. "If I'm going to be working for you, it would be good for us to be able to have a bit of a chat. You might think that I'm just one of Blair's cast-offs but I'm really looking forward to working for you. I see it as a real feather in my cap."

"Why? You know nothing about me."

"I know more than you might think. I know what it said in the papers when the headlines were all about the 'Hero Cop Shot in Head.'"

"Then you still know nothing," Hamish snorted. "You can't believe what you read in the papers."

"Aye, you're right there," Forbes agreed, "so I've been asking around and looking back at some of your old cases. I've been doing my homework. It pays to know who you're working for."

"And yet you've been working for Blair."

"Not out of choice. From what I've found out about him, I think he's lucky not to be behind bars or, from what you were saying in the car park, rotting away at the bottom of the Clyde."

"You heard...?"

"Enough. I know you hate him. I can't stand him either. He's sent me off to work with you because I don't fit in with his motley crew and he doesn't trust me."

"Aye, right," said Hamish. "Well, seeing as how we're being all open and chatty, you might as well know that I don't trust you either."

They drove the rest of the way in silence.

Instead of taking the most direct route to Lochdubh, Hamish branched off towards Braikie. He saw Forbes looking at the Lochdubh signpost and merely said, "I need to pay someone a visit. Won't take long."

At Braikie Hospital, Jimmy was sitting up in bed, a wall-mounted television tuned to a news channel and an iPad in his hand. He was swiping through images on the screen when Hamish walked in.

"Ah, the very man," Jimmy greeted him. "I heard you'd been summoned to Strathbane."

"You heard right," said Hamish. "Blair is back."

Jimmy nodded and listened intently as Hamish explained everything that had happened, leaving out only the incident in the hotel car park.

"So," Hamish said through a sigh, "I've got my station under threat *again*, Daviot wants me spying on Blair, Blair's already heading in the wrong direction and he's sent one of his people to spy on me, and we've still got a murderer out there on my patch somewhere."

"All right, laddie, calm down," Jimmy said with a slow, steady tone. "You can easy deal wi' Daviot—all he needs is a regular update. Blair will blunder around wi' his robbery theory until that runs out o' steam, so we've a good chance to stay ahead o' him."

"No' if his pet detective constable is breathing down my neck."

"David Forbes is no' the problem you think he is," said Jimmy. "In fact, the laddie's a real asset."

"You know him?"

"His father, Ian, is a superintendent down south, over on the east coast. I've known him since we were at the police training college in Tulliallan together. Wee Davey is my godson, Hamish, although he's no' so wee these days is he?" Jimmy laughed. "More muscles than Rambo last time I saw him. He loves his rugby and he's a smart lad. You can rely on him."

"Well, that's a relief." Hamish nodded. "I've got the feeling I'm going to need all the help I can get. Now, I need to ask you about the watch you mentioned Hibbert was wearing. Can you mind anything about it? What make was it?"

"I know exactly what make it was. It was an eighteen-carat gold ladies' Rolex Oyster, probably from around 1978. It's no' every woman's choice o' a watch—maybe a wee bit too big and flash for some—but it's a fine timepiece nonetheless."

"Jimmy, when did you become an expert on ladies' watches?"

"Ever since I had nothing else to do but play wi' this thing," said Jimmy, holding up the iPad. "So it's got me thinking, what is a woman who takes on cleaning jobs to make ends meet doing wi' a gold watch worth five grand?"

"And if this was a robbery," Hamish added, "why didn't the mugger take the Rolex?"

"Maybe it was broken in the struggle and he thought it wasn't worth the bother?"

"Maybe, but the Rolex is ringing a bell, Jimmy. I need to check this out. I also need to talk to Hibbert's cousin now that the body's been identified. She's at the Tommel Castle."

"Do that first, laddie," Jimmy advised. "Far better she hears it from you than from Blair."

Hamish made his way down to the hospital car park where he had left Forbes sitting in the Land Rover. He found him perched on the bonnet, tapping a message into his smartphone.

"So how is Uncle Jimmy?" Forbes grinned.

" 'Uncle' is it? Why did you no' tell me you're practically related to DCI Anderson?"

"Because I wanted to win your respect myself, but Jimmy tells me," he added, holding up his phone to show how Jimmy had told him, "that, in his words, 'there's no' time for that crap.' I'm here to help, Sergeant, if you'll let me."

There followed a quiet moment during which Hamish appraised the young detective with a critical eye. He judged Forbes to be around fifteen years his junior with dark hair, dark eyes and an honest, open face. The honesty was what resonated most with Hamish. He had heard no lies from Forbes, and he was certain he would have known if Forbes had tried to hoodwink him. The younger man returned his gaze with a solemn expression that he wore like an unwanted necktie.

"If Jimmy vouches for you," Hamish said eventually, "that's good enough for me."

"I'd rather have got there on my own," the younger man admitted, "but I'm not too proud to take a helping hand from Uncle Jimmy."

"So what should I call you?" Hamish offered his hand.

"Davey's what my friends call me," said Forbes, taking the handshake.

"Davey it is then." Hamish smiled.

"Thank you, Sergeant."

"It's just Hamish, unless we're out on a job," Hamish said, looking at his watch, "and that's what we need to be doing now. Kate Hibbert—we need to inform the next of kin."

Afternoon was drifting into evening by the time they arrived at the Tommel Castle. In the wood-panelled reception hall, Mr. Johnson, the hotel manager, was talking to a tall, slim woman who was standing with her back to them. There was, however, no mistaking the smooth bell of blonde hair. Prompted by a nod from Mr. Johnson, who then disappeared into his office, Priscilla Halburton-Smythe, daughter of the hotel's owner, turned to welcome them.

"Hamish, how lovely to see you," she said with a cool smile. It was, as always, a perfectly polite, amicable greeting but it lacked any of the warmth one might have expected from someone with whom Hamish had once considered himself to be deeply in love. As things had transpired, it was her very lack of ardour, and lovemaking devoid of passion, that had made Hamish decide to call off the engagement. Priscilla was stunningly beautiful, but her coldness had made him realise that he did not relish the thought of spending the rest of his life with her. He knew now that he had never really been in love with Priscilla, not the way that he had loved Dorothy. No one could ever come close to Dorothy.

"I...um...didn't expect to see you here," Hamish said. "Are you up from London for long?"

"I'm helping to get things organised for the Grand

Gourmet Night," Priscilla explained, indicating a poster mounted on a board near the reception desk. "Gourmet Night is Saturday. Freddy is going to excel himself, I'm sure."

"Freddy was once my constable here in Lochdubh," Hamish explained to Davey.

"Hello, I'm Priscilla," she said, holding her hand out to Davey and cocking an eye at Hamish. "I thought I'd better introduce myself in case Hamish never got round to it."

"Constable Davey . . ." Davey said clumsily, then shook his head. "I mean, Constable Forbes."

Hamish looked to the ceiling and sighed. Davey wasn't the first man he'd seen mesmerised by Priscilla's stunning good looks.

"Don't they give constables uniforms nowadays?" Priscilla teased him.

"Actually, I'm a detective constable—sort of on loan to Sergeant Macbeth," he said.

"We've had detectives staying at the hotel in the past," Priscilla replied. "They all seemed to wear suits."

"That's not mandatory," he explained. "We're supposed to dress appropriately for whatever it is we're doing."

"I see." Priscilla nodded. "Pointless you wearing a suit to go undercover in a nudist camp, eh?"

"No, that's . . . ha!" Davey laughed a little too loudly at Priscilla's joke and Hamish grabbed his arm, guiding him towards the main bar.

"We're here to talk to Diane Spears," he said to Priscilla. "I can see her in the main bar. This way, Constable."

"She's quite something, isn't she?" Davey said quietly, once they were well out of earshot.

"Aye, she's certainly something," Hamish muttered. "Now get a grip, man—we have work to do."

Diane Spears was sitting at a table and looked up as the two men approached. She no longer bore the look of an angry, frustrated woman but wore a forlorn expression, her dark eyes moist with tears although, Hamish noted, none had spilled out to tarnish her perfect make-up.

"It's her, isn't it?" she asked, her voice so soft that it could scarcely be heard above the background noise from the TV on the wall in the corner of the room. "The body in the loch."

"Aye, well," said Hamish, "I'm sorry to have to tell you that a body has been recovered from The Corloch. It has now been positively identified as that of your cousin, Kate Hibbert."

"We already know, Hamish." Elspeth Grant arrived from the bar carrying two gin-and-tonics, setting one on the table in front of Spears. "Footage from the press conference is about to be screened on the TV news."

"What press conference?" Hamish asked.

"That one." Elspeth nodded at the screen now filled by the jowly face of DCI Blair. His voice sounded even more gravelly when broadcast electronically.

"The body of a woman in her early forties was found at a place called Auld Mary's Island on The Corloch yesterday," Blair announced. "Evidence gathered so far has led me to instigate a murder enquiry."

"How was she killed, Chief Inspector?" called one reporter.

"That's no' something I can discuss at this point," Blair responded.

"Have you any idea who the murderer is?" called another journalist.

"My enquiries are still at a very early stage," said Blair.

"Who was the victim, Chief Inspector?" Elspeth's face flashed on screen as she put her question to Blair.

"The victim has been identified as Kate Hibbert and her family has been informed," Blair snapped, pushing his way through the scrum of reporters to avoid any further questions.

"Except I wasn't, was I, Sergeant Macbeth?" Spears said flatly, staring at Hamish.

"That's no' the way this is meant to happen," Hamish said, scarcely able to believe that Blair had talked to the press without checking that he had spoken to Spears. "I'm awful sorry, Miss Spears. You should have heard about your cousin from me, not from the press."

"Blair was desperate to be able to say something positive," Elspeth said. "He blurted that out without thinking."

"We are truly sorry, Miss Spears," said Davey. "You have our heartfelt condolences for your loss."

"Elspeth explained that Blair is a loose cannon," Spears said, taking a sip of her drink. "I'm not blaming you two." Then, looking at Davey, she added, "Whoever you are."

Hamish introduced Davey before warning Spears that the press pack would be hounding her before long.

"I talked to Diane earlier today," said Elspeth, "so I

knew she was staying here. She's promised me an exclusive on her cousin and her background. None of the rest of the press has any clue where she is."

"I'll have a word wi' Silas," Hamish said, turning to Davey. "He's another one o' my former constables who works here. He's in charge o' the hotel security. He'll make sure nobody tells the press you're here, Miss Spears."

"Thank you, Sergeant," said Spears, holding up her mobile phone. "My neighbours in Edinburgh tell me they're already being plagued by the vultures, so I'm in no rush to go back there. And please call me Diane. Miss Spears makes me sound like a primary-school teacher."

"Are you staying for a drink?" Elspeth asked.

"I'll maybe pop back later," said Hamish. "There's still things I need to do right now."

"Bring your friend, too," said Diane, looking up at Davey. "It would be nice to have some company this evening."

Once they were back in the car, Davey let out a low whistle.

"Man, she was a real looker, eh?" he said as Hamish started the engine.

"Elspeth?" Hamish snapped. "Look, Davey, there's a few things you need to know…"

"Take it easy, Hamish," Davey said, slipping another stick of gum in his mouth. "I know about you being engaged to Priscilla and to Elspeth. I know about Dorothy—and I can't even begin to tell you how sorry I was to hear about that—and I'm not here to cause you any grief. What I meant was that Diane Spears is seriously hot. Did you see the way she looked at me? I think I'm in there, pal."

"I wouldn't do that."

"Ah, yes, there's a wee problem, isn't there? We have to look at her as a potential suspect. That doesn't stop me getting friendly with her though, does it? I mean, I could find out more about Hibbert if we had a few wee quiet chats."

"I meant the chewing gum," Hamish said. "You shouldn't be seen by the public chewing gum on duty and if anybody around here spotted you, you'd be blamed for every blemish on the pavement from here to Braikie."

"Of course, sorry," Davey apologised, removing the gum, wrapping it in a tissue and pocketing it for later disposal. "Force of habit."

"Sounds like you could say that about Diane, too."

"What do you mean?"

"You got all tongue-tied over Priscilla and then you went all mushy over Diane—'heartfelt condolences' is a bit over the top, is it no'?" Hamish smiled. He didn't want it to seem as if he was being too harsh. He was beginning to like the lad. "Don't let lust for the ladies get in the way o' the job we have to do, Davey."

"Point taken," Davey agreed. "I'll do my best...but she was gorgeous."

"Aye, right," said Hamish, "but no' terribly upset about her cousin. As soon as Elspeth told her Hibbert was dead, she did a deal for her 'exclusive.' She's all about the money, that one. If you're ever strolling hand-in-hand wi' her, make sure you keep your other hand on your wallet, lover boy."

CHAPTER FIVE

O wad some Pow'r the giftie gie us
To see oursels as ithers see us!
It wad frae mony a blunder free us,
An' foolish notion:
What airs in dress an' gait wad lea'e us,
An' ev'n devotion!
Robert Burns, "To a Louse"

"So it was her that they fished out of The Corloch." Ian Duncan took a sip of tea and carried on eating his supper. The TV news report moved on to a story about climate-change protesters gluing themselves to petrol pumps.

"Aye, and there are now whole teams of detectives out there looking for whoever killed her," said his wife, Fiona, her voice trembling. "Hamish Macbeth was at the Mackenzies' place asking about her. What am I going to say if he comes here? It'll no' take him long to get the truth out of me—ye ken what I'm like."

"Don't speak to him," said her husband, shovelling a

forkful of mince and tatties into his mouth, then wolf-
ing it down. "Tell him to come and see me. I'll deal with
him."

"He won't think we had anything to do with it, will
he, Ian?"

"He's no' got any evidence that points to us."

"But you ken fine there *is* evidence. How do you ken
he's no' already seen it?"

"Because if he had, he'd already have been knocking
on our door. Say nothing and send him to me. I'll take
care of it, Fiona, I promise."

"You'd better. If he finds out, we're done for."

At Lochdubh police station, Hamish sent Davey upstairs
to settle into the spare room while he fed Lugs and Sonsie.
The pets had given the newcomer their usual welcome—
Lugs had treated him like his long-lost best friend and
Sonsie had ignored him completely. When Davey reappeared, Hamish set him to work in the kitchen, frying
pork chops and boiling potatoes for their supper, while he
headed for his office.

He had a couple of large filing cabinets where he kept
local crime reports. The paperwork was also all on his
computer but Hamish always felt that having the physical
report in his hand helped him to recall more about a case
than simply scrolling through it on a computer screen.
He plucked a five-year-old burglary report out of the cabinet, sat at his desk and began reading through it. The
woman whose house had been broken into was Hannah

Thomson, then aged seventy-six, a widow and retired midwife—that was what had first set alarm bells ringing in Hamish's head. According to the report, someone had forced an entry through the back door of her cottage, although "forced" was perhaps an overstatement. Hamish knew that, like most people around Lochdubh, Hannah's back door, as well as her front door for that matter, was probably never locked. Two items had been stolen and photographs of the items, previously taken for insurance purposes, were in the file—a pair of diamond earrings and a ladies' gold Rolex Oyster.

He resisted the urge to retrieve the earrings from his drawer to compare them with the photograph. He didn't want Davey to know anything about the package he had taken from the suitcase, and the lad might walk in on him at any moment. Jimmy may have vouched for him and he seemed an honest soul, but he couldn't risk the possibility that Blair was holding something against Davey, something he could use to force Davey to do his bidding. He may have been doing the young detective an injustice, but Hamish couldn't afford to slip up if he turned out to be a traitor. In any case, it would be hard to explain to an outsider why he wanted to check out the contents of the package before he let anyone know it existed. It might turn out that the package had nothing to do with the murder, but he had removed it from the scene and if Blair found out, he would use that breach of protocol to make sure Hamish was sacked. He couldn't risk that, so he had to keep Davey in the dark.

As far as the earrings and the watch were concerned, however, he had no doubt that they were the ones reported stolen five years ago. The birthing charm he had also found in one of the pouches sealed the deal—Hannah Thomson was a retired midwife. So how did Kate Hibbert get hold of these things? She had only arrived in Lochdubh around a year ago and was a stranger to the place. It was highly unlikely that she burgled Hannah's cottage five years ago, but she may have got her hands on the jewellery and the watch while she was working as Hannah's cleaner. That, of course, would mean that the earrings and the watch had never been stolen—the burglary never happened. He looked at the insurance photographs. Hannah would have received a handsome payout from her insurers. Maybe the old lady had staged the burglary because she needed the cash. He would have to pay her a visit.

"Food's ready!" Davey popped his head round the office door. "What's that you've got there?"

"Och, it's nothing," said Hamish, slipping the folder back into the filing cabinet. "An old burglary report—let's eat."

They made short work of the food and, Hamish was pleased to note, Davey had managed the simple meal without burning anything. He might only be there temporarily but it was good to know that he'd be able to do his share of the cooking. Once they'd finished, they freshened up before heading off to the Tommel Castle Hotel again. The heat of the day had surrendered to a cool evening breeze wafting in off the loch, but it was still warm enough for them to walk along the waterfront in shirtsleeves. Davey's shirt was a green-and-gold paisley pattern cut in such a way that, while the buttons were not straining, it was close-fitting across his arms and torso. He caught Hamish scrutinising it.

"Cool shirt, eh?" He grinned. "I bought it in Glasgow in one of those designer shops in Buchanan Street."

"Did they no' have a bigger size?" Hamish asked. "Those muscles of yours look like they're about to burst out."

"This is the fashion nowadays, Hamish." Davey laughed. "Close-fitted shirts are trendy."

"Aye, well, if you say so," Hamish said, looking down at his own, far looser blue shirt, which he still regarded as his best new shirt even though he couldn't actually remember exactly how many years ago he'd bought it. "The latest fashions can take a wee while to reach Lochdubh—some never make it at all."

They chatted as they walked, Hamish proudly presenting Lochdubh to its newest resident, pointing out the Two Sisters, the local pub, Archie Maclean's fishing boat and some of the oldest of the ancient white cottages along the shore road. The further they walked, the more they relaxed into each other's company and, by the time they reached the Tommel Castle's main bar, Hamish felt he was beginning to get to know the young detective, and finding him hard not to like.

Diane and Elspeth were sitting on barstools, each

enjoying a glass of red wine, although, judging by the way Diane's skirt had ridden up and by the way her waves of long dark hair were now looking dishevelled rather than elegant, she had enjoyed a few more glasses than Elspeth.

"Look at this, Elspeth!" said Diane, too loudly. "It's our two favourite cops—Starsky and Hutch!"

Elspeth caught Hamish's eye, grimaced and gave a slight tilt of her head towards Diane, clearly indicating that she had had too much to drink. She hopped down from her barstool and made as if to give him a warm welcome.

"Keep an eye on her, Hamish," she whispered in his ear. "She's more upset than she'd like us to think. I wouldn't let her have any more wine. She's had enough."

"Aye, I can see that," he replied.

"My, my!" Diane said, appraising Davey and placing her glass on the bar. "This one fills a shirt well, doesn't he?" She reached out a hand, squeezed Davey's bicep and toppled sideways off the stool. In the blink of an eye, Davey dipped, caught her before she hit the floor and returned her gently to the stool.

"Good catch," said Hamish, clearly impressed.

Diane looked slightly confused at finding herself with her arms around Davey's shoulders. "What just happened?" She giggled. "Never mind. I feel very safe in the long, and ever so strong, arms of the law."

"Diane," Elspeth said with a reproving tone, almost as though she were talking to a child, "I have to make some phone calls. I'm going to leave you with Hamish and Davey. I won't be long."

"Take as long as you like." Diane laughed, sipping her wine. "I'll have both of them all to myself!"

Hamish ordered beers for himself and Davey while they chatted with Diane about Elspeth's job, the hotel and Lochdubh. Then there was a lull in the conversation and she suddenly looked at Hamish with tears in her eyes. Unlike earlier, a couple spilled out, coursing down her cheek.

"She didn't suffer, did she?" she asked. "I can't bear the thought, you know, that she was terrified, all alone, suffering..."

"She wouldn't have known what happened," Hamish lied. "It would all have been over in an instant."

"You must have been very close to Kate," Davey said.

"Not really." Diane sighed. "She was the only real family that I had left, and I suppose I was the same to her, but we were quite independent people. We didn't see each other much but we spoke fairly regularly. We were business partners, as well as cousins."

"What sort of business?" Hamish asked.

"The rag trade," Diane explained. "I import fashion items and sell them on to retailers all over Scotland."

"Kate doesn't seem to have been the type to get involved in the fashion business," said Hamish.

"She was a kind of sleeping partner. Kate was ten years older than me and always a bit of a mystery. I can't remember her ever having had a permanent job, yet she was able to come up with money from time to time and she invested in the business with me."

"How much did she invest?" Davey asked.

"Not always a huge amount. A few thousand here and there. She told me that I was her 'pension fund.' The last time she made a really significant investment was when she got back from France and came to stay with me in Edinburgh."

"You weren't the one who reported her missing when she disappeared off to France, were you?" asked Hamish.

"No, I had no idea she'd gone at first. It was somebody she knew in Aberdeen who decided to tell the police that Kate had vanished."

"And she had money when she came back from France?" Hamish was beginning to see things more clearly. Hibbert having money was making the way forward seem a whole lot simpler. "Where did she get it?"

"Not a clue." Diane shrugged. "She said she could earn a lot now and again but not regularly, which is why she wanted the business as a pension. She told me she would invest a huge amount very soon—around half a million. That, along with the money that I've saved myself, was going to fund our own shops."

"Half a million!" Davey whistled. "That's serious money."

"Aye," Hamish agreed. "Serious enough to kill for."

Diane began to cry, her shoulders heaving with great, breathless sobs. Davey put his arm around her, telling her that it was perfectly natural for her to cry, that she should let it all out, that none of this was her fault and that it was a truly awful ordeal for anyone to have to go through.

Hamish could see that the tears were real. Diane was a tough cookie but it had all finally become too much for her. His mind, however, was focused less on the tragic circumstances than on the money. Where had Hibbert been getting the money she invested with Diane? She certainly couldn't raise half a million by stealing and selling bits and pieces like Hannah Thomson's jewellery. No, there was a simpler answer. If the jewellery in the black package didn't belong to Kate Hibbert, then neither did the letters nor any of the other contents. Yet they were still valuable enough for Hibbert to hide and there could be only one reason for that. Hamish was furious with himself for not having worked it out earlier. Now he knew without a doubt that the murderer's identity lay somewhere in that package and he was desperate to get back to the station to find out what else was waiting to be discovered in his desk drawer.

"What's been going on here?" Elspeth demanded, hurrying over to Diane. "I only left you alone for a few minutes..."

"I think that the harm was done long afore that," said Hamish. "It's all finally got to Diane, I'm afraid."

"Come on, Diane," Elspeth said, helping her down off the barstool and leading her towards the hotel reception area. "Let's get you to your room. You'll feel better after a good night's rest."

No sooner had they reached the main staircase than Hamish was striding towards the front door, heading back to the station at a brisk pace Davey struggled to match. Ignoring the welcome from Lugs and Sonsie, he made for his office, leaving Davey to raid the fridge for a snack. He hid the package inside his shirt, something that he noted Davey would not have been able to do, then announced that he was exhausted and heading upstairs for an early night. Sitting on his bedroom floor with his back against the door to keep out any unwanted visitors of either the two-legged or four-legged variety, he retrieved the package and tipped the entire contents onto the floor in front of him. He set aside the two velvet pouches and scanned through the love letters. Each was addressed to "My darling Kelpie," and each was signed "J. P." They all appeared to contain the same sort of cloying declarations of undying love, but he paused when he came to a passage in the fifth letter.

> **You must leave him. Then we can be together.**
> **Leave him and come to me. I will look after you.**
> **We can get away from this place and have the**
> **rest of our lives together, if only you can find the**
> **courage to leave him.**

"Leave him?" Kate Hibbert had neither boyfriend nor husband. Clearly, like the jewellery, the letter did not belong to her. Hamish opened another brown envelope and a selection of polaroid photographs spilled out. They appeared to show a rather overweight Batman and a distinctly chunky Catwoman in various stages of undress, indulging in adventurous sex in a variety of positions.

Hamish had no idea who the man posing as Batman was, but he was positive that the woman in the Catwoman costume was not Hibbert.

He opened another envelope and a piece of paper fluttered out—a receipt from a company in Galashiels called Lothian Livestock Services. There was nothing on it to say what it was for or who had paid the bill, just a date, an amount and the words "Paid in Full." Hamish tucked it away again and opened the final envelope. It was a printout of a computer spreadsheet showing columns of numbers and, at the bottom of the first column, three names—Vadoit, Serdonna and Ralbi—each followed by a string of numbers shorter than those above. Hamish shook his head. The spreadsheet was a mystery, as was the receipt from the company in Galashiels, although that could be checked out. He was in no doubt, however, that those items had been used by Hibbert for the same purpose as the jewellery that Hannah Thomson falsely claimed had been stolen, the compromising photographs of the superhero couple and the love letters—blackmail.

Hibbert might have made a good detective. She had pried into people's private lives to find a weakness, a failing or a closely guarded secret in the same way that a cop investigates a suspect, delving into the subject's affairs, probing and generally ferreting around to see what turns up. Hibbert's motivation, however, was not to bring a criminal to justice, but to extort money from her victims. How much had she forced Hannah Thomson to stump up? That was where he would start. Poor old

Hannah was an unlikely blackmail victim but she was living on her own and she was vulnerable. Once Hibbert knew her secret, it wouldn't have taken much to persuade her that she would be treated as a despicable pariah in Lochdubh if word ever got out that she had defrauded an insurance company. She would never be able to hold her head up in the community again and she would certainly be expelled from the kirk—at least that's the picture Hibbert would have painted.

Hamish sighed, replacing everything in the plastic package. The truth was that most folk in Lochdubh wouldn't have cared a bit about Hannah's misdemeanour. Most of them had probably done something similar, or worse, when it came to overstating or falsifying insurance claims. "Victimless crime" was what it was often called, except now the crime had two victims— Hannah and Kate Hibbert. He got himself ready for bed and rested his head on the pillow, thoughts of Hibbert's blackmail victims whirling through his mind. Who were they all? Hannah was here in the village, but were the others her neighbours over in Hurdy's Glen? He would start with Hannah first thing in the morning, then pay another visit to Hurdy's Glen. Of course, if Hibbert had fleeced another victim—or victims—before she fled to France, then maybe the person in Aberdeen who had reported her missing might have caught up with her. The murderer didn't *have* to be someone from Lochdubh, did it? Kelpie and J. P., or the owner of the mysterious spreadsheet, might live in Aberdeen. There was an awful lot to think about... He had almost drifted off to sleep when Lugs headbutted the bedroom door open and he and Sonsie flopped on the bed at his feet.

Following a hearty breakfast that required two frying pans to contain the mountain of sausages, bacon and eggs that would fuel Hamish and Davey for the rest of the morning, the two policemen set off to walk to Hannah Thomson's house, Hamish having explained to Davey that she was the first of Kate Hibbert's known associates they should re-interview. As they walked, he wondered how he would manage to broach the subject of the jewellery without giving away the whole blackmail affair to Davey.

Hamish was in uniform, although not the version of which Superintendent Daviot would have approved, and Davey was more casually dressed in a dark blue polo shirt. The morning sunshine was not quite as intense as it had been of late and, scanning the mountains surrounding the loch, Hamish could sense a change in the light, giving him the impression that the glorious summer weather they had been enjoying might not last much longer.

If it was possible to walk through Lochdubh in the daytime without bumping into Nessie and Jessie Currie, Hamish had yet to discover how it was done.

"Go easy wi' these two, Davey," he said, indicating the twins marching towards them on the pavement by the seawall. "They've ay got a bee in their bonnet about something, but their hearts are in the right place."

"So this is what our bold policeman gets up to while there's a vicious woman-killer on the loose," Nessie said as they drew near. "He's out in the sunshine having a wee dander..."

"...a wee dander..." Jessie repeated.

"...while we are all living in fear of being murdered in our beds!"

"...murdered in our beds!"

"Well, you'll be safe enough for the time being, ladies," Hamish said, smiling, "since you're no' actually in your beds right now."

"I suppose that's the best we can expect from you, Hamish Macbeth," said Nessie, indignantly. "Flippant flimflammery!"

"...flimflammery!"

"We'll be pursuing enquiries later this morning," Hamish explained, keeping his tone official in an effort to placate the twins. "At the moment we are doing a quick tour of Lochdubh to acquaint my new colleague, Detective Constable Forbes, with the area."

"A pleasure to meet you both," Davey said, and found himself bowing slightly, as if meeting royalty. In fact, it was difficult not to bow, or at least stoop a bit, since the two little old ladies craning their necks to talk to them made Hamish and Davey seem like giants. Davey could have been fooled into thinking he was in Lilliput rather than Lochdubh. He was perplexed by their beige raincoats. "Are you expecting rain today?"

"This is Lochdubh," Nessie said, looking at Davey as

though he were an imbecile. "If it's not already raining, it will be soon. We're always prepared."

"...always prepared," came Jessie's echo before they both marched off, the heels of their sensible shoes clicking on the bone-dry, rain-free pavement, Jessie's clicks just a moment behind Nessie's.

Hamish spotted Angela Brodie, the local doctor's wife, leaning against the seawall, staring out over the loch. She waved when she saw them approaching.

"Looking for inspiration?" Hamish asked. "Angela is a writer," he explained to Davey, introducing the two. Angela shook Davey's hand and welcomed him to Lochdubh.

"Of course, I already knew who you were." She smiled. Hamish had always marvelled at the way Angela's smile transformed her whole appearance. She had wispy brown hair and an unremarkable appearance until her smile released a flood of warmth and geniality that lit up her face, revealing a rare and fascinating beauty. "News travels fast in the village."

"Have you seen Hannah Thomson recently?" Hamish asked. "I was wondering how she was doing."

"I saw her yesterday evening," Angela said. "She's a lovely lady but she wasn't really herself. She seemed preoccupied with something. I put it down to that awful news about Kate Hibbert. They were quite close at one time."

"Aye, I believe they were," agreed Hamish. "Maybe we'll pop in and check on her while we're out and about—just to make sure she's all right."

"I'm sure she would appreciate that, Hamish," said Angela, and the two men strolled on in the direction of Hannah Thomson's house.

"Angela's no' the biggest gossip in the village by a long chalk," Hamish explained to Davey once they were out of earshot, "but we'll have been seen chatting to her and..."

"...someone will ask what it was all about," Davey said, finishing Hamish's sentence. "Then it will be all over the village that we paid Mrs. Thomson a courtesy call rather than visiting her for any other reason, such as her being part of a murder enquiry. That saves her any awkwardness or embarrassment."

"You catch on quick," said Hamish, casting him a sideways glance.

"People are people," Davey said, with a shrug, "and gossip is gossip, whether you're in Lochdubh, Lochgelly, Linlithgow or anywhere else."

Hannah Thomson's cottage, set back from the pavement opposite the seawall, had thick stone walls resplendent in a heavy coat of white paint to protect the masonry from the elements. Wide ledges on the windows either side of the front door betrayed the thickness of the walls, with a window-box display of begonias and geraniums creating a cascade of yellow and pink blooms. Hamish rapped the brass knocker on the front door.

A small, round woman leaning heavily on a stick opened the door to them.

"Sergeant Macbeth," she said, looking more than a

little surprised to see Hamish. "How lovely to see you. Come ben and I'll get the kettle on."

"That would be grand, Hannah," Hamish replied, removing his cap and introducing Davey before both men ducked under the lintel to enter the cottage.

Coming out of the sunshine, the cottage seemed dark inside at first but it was far from gloomy. They stepped straight into the small living room where the flagstone floor was brightened by colourfully hooked rugs and the walls were painted a delicate primrose yellow. Oak beams straddled the ceiling and two solid, high-backed Orkney chairs stood either side of the fireplace with an overstuffed, floral sofa facing them from the opposite wall. Hannah shuffled across the rug that lay between the chairs and the sofa, inviting them to take a seat as she headed to the kitchen. Hamish parked himself in one of the Orkneys while Davey sank into the sofa and Hannah conducted a conversation from the kitchen, mainly focused on how long the warm weather would last. She spoke with the soft, slow precision of a Scot whose first language was Gaelic rather than English.

Davey heaved himself out of the sofa to take a tea tray from Hannah, who was struggling into the living room, having abandoned her stick to carry the tray. He set it on a small table and Hannah served tea.

"So what brings you to see me today, Sergeant Macbeth?" she asked, lowering herself into the vacant Orkney.

"You'll have heard about this terrible business with Kate Hibbert," said Hamish. "Can you think of anyone who might have wanted to harm her?"

"No, no, not at all," Hannah said, shaking her head and staring down at her tea cup. "She was ay cheerful, and ay a great help to me."

"Did she tell you she was planning to go away?" asked Davey.

"No...I...I hadn't spoken much wi' her in the weeks afore she disappeared," Hannah replied.

"I know it's difficult, losing such a good friend," Hamish said, "but I've something here might cheer you up—some lost property." He reached into his shirt pocket and produced the silver pendant.

"Oh...my birthing charm!" The old lady's voice was trembling and her eyes were filled with delight. "Where did you find it?"

"I think you know where I found it," Hamish said, handing it to her.

"Aye...I suppose..." Hannah hesitated, glancing briefly at Davey.

"Constable Forbes," Hamish said quietly, nodding towards the front door, "could you give us a wee minute, please?"

Davey looked from Hamish to Hannah, said, "Of course, Sergeant," and headed out into the sunshine.

"Was she...wearing it?" Hannah asked.

"No," Hamish replied. "She took it, didn't she—along with the earrings and the watch?"

"Aye." Hannah sighed. "Stole them from me, she did, and more besides."

"But you shouldn't have had them anyway, should you? You reported them stolen in the burglary."

"You'll no' send me to the jail, will you, Sergeant Macbeth? I didn't mean to do anything wrong."

"Tell me the truth, Hannah, and I'll see what I can do."

"The earrings were left to me by my aunt and the watch was a gift from a rich lady in Helmsdale after I delivered her bairn. I kept them safe in wee velvet baggies in my dressing table upstairs, but one day I must have decided to hide them on top o' my wardrobe. Well, my memory's no' what it used to be, Sergeant, and I forgot I'd moved them. I searched everywhere and started thinking someone must have come in the house and taken them."

"So you called me to tell me you'd been burgled, and after I'd come to see you, I recommended that you talk to your insurance company."

"Then they sent me all that money..." Hannah's chin wrinkled, her bottom lip trembled and a tear fell from the corner of her eye. "It was months later that I found the earrings and the watch, and by that time I'd spent all the money on a new stove, the new central heating and..."

"It's all right, Hannah," Hamish said, leaning forward. "You made a mistake, that's all. I'm guessing you hid the things away again."

"Aye, I did that. What else could I do? I couldn't bear the shame of everyone knowing what a fool I'd been. I put them back on the wardrobe along wi' the letters from the insurance folk."

"So Kate Hibbert found them and figured out what you'd done."

"She said she was my friend. How could I have believed such a woman? She was supposed to be doing a bit o' cleaning for me, but she was in at everything, nosying around my whole house. She knew I shouldn't have the earrings and the watch, so she took them, and she took my bonny wee birthing charm at the same time. She was never my friend, was she, Sergeant? She was a wicked, wicked woman and I'm...I'm glad she's dead!"

"Did she ask you for money as well?"

"Aye...just the cleaning money at first, even though she stopped doing the cleaning. Then a bit more...and a bit more. If she hadn't gone when she did, I think she'd have had my whole savings."

"You must have hated her—someone you thought was a friend turning on you like that, like a traitor."

"I hated the sight of her...but in a strange way I felt sorry for her, too—sad that the best thing she could do in life was to prey on an auld woman like me. What will happen now, Sergeant? Will you have to arrest me?" She held out the pendant, returning it to Hamish.

"Keep it," Hamish said, taking Hannah's frail old hand in both of his and gently folding her fingers closed around her birthing charm. "This is yours. I promise I'll get your earrings back to you as well. The watch, I'm no' going to be able to do anything about. You keep the birthing charm, Hannah, and I'll keep your wee secret. Don't talk to any other policemen about this, and everything will work out just fine."

Hamish stepped out into the sunshine to see Davey standing opposite the cottage, leaning against the seawall and playing with his phone. He joined him on the other side of the street and they made their way back towards the station.

"What was all that about, then?" Davey asked.

"Just setting a poor auld woman's mind at rest," Hamish replied, placing his cap on his head.

"Och, come on, Hamish," said Davey, a note of frustration in his voice. "I wasn't born yesterday. We're in the middle of a murder enquiry and you're messing about with old burglary reports and lost property? What's going on?"

"Nothing you need worry about," said Hamish, firmly. "Now let's get going. We need to pay a visit to Jimmy afore we do anything else."

"What have you two got for me?" Jimmy asked, sitting up in bed surrounded by his iPad, his phone, the TV remote and copies of the local newspapers. He made no attempt at pleasantries and Hamish was struck by the keenness of his stare and the alert, expectant look on his foxy features. Hamish suspected that the hospital food, although not what you would call a gourmet experience, was better by far than Jimmy's normal diet and all this time without a glass of whisky in his hand was clearly doing him a power of good.

"Well, I'm now pretty sure Hibbert was up to something," Hamish said.

"How do we know that?" Jimmy asked quickly, turning to Davey. "What was she up to?"

"Actually, it's not that easy to say right now," Davey said, slowly. "There's nothing concrete and...we're... we're still pursuing..."

"Enough!" snapped Jimmy, holding up a hand to cut Davey short and fixing Hamish with a furious stare. "He hasn't a clue what you were talking about. Why not?"

"Aye, well, certain information has come into my possession—" Hamish began, only for Jimmy to shake a fist at him.

"'Certain information'?" he growled. "Information that you haven't shared wi' Davey. Why? Why would you no' want Davey to know about it? How did you come by this 'certain information'? No...don't answer that. You've been up to your auld tricks again, haven't you? Whatever you've done, I don't want to know about it. If it all goes arse up, I'll deny all knowledge wi' a clear conscience, but I can't have you flying solo on this, Hamish. Make sure you bring Davey up to speed wi' whatever it is. You can trust him. He can help."

"Aye, okay, Jimmy," Hamish said, sheepishly. It was years since he had seen Jimmy so sharp, so clearly focused. "What's Blair up to?"

"He's sent two o' his team to Aberdeen to follow up on whoever it was that reported Hibbert missing last time she did a bunk," Jimmy said, "and he's pressing Diane Spears for everything she knows."

"She'll tell him about the money Hibbert promised

her." Hamish nodded gravely. "Blair will want to follow the money trail. If he even suspects that Hibbert had
a pile o' cash, he'll be after it. Recovering big sums o'
money ay makes good headlines."

"Did she have money?" asked Jimmy.

"I don't know, but I suppose she might have done."
Hamish pondered a moment. "Did forensics pick up
anything?"

"They didn't come up wi' much," said Jimmy. "There
were a few tiny flecks o' what appears to be blue paint on
her coat, but they couldn't say where that came from."

"That might not even have anything to do with the
murder," commented Davey. "You could get that from
leaning on a bus stop, or whatever."

"Aye, you're right," said Jimmy, "but it's worth bearing
in mind. Now listen," he continued, lowering his voice.
"According to the autopsy, death was by strangulation but
Hibbert had three broken fingers on her left hand and two
on her right. There were marks on her wrists and ankles
where she had been tied up. She had a couple o' cracked
ribs and it looks like she was beaten about the face."

"Jeez…" Davey let out a long breath. "She was tortured."

"Aye, and that means that she had something somebody
else wanted," Jimmy reasoned, turning to Hamish once
again. "Does that fit in wi' your 'certain information'?"

"It might," Hamish confirmed, "and if she didn't give
them what they wanted, whoever tortured her might now
think they should be going after the people who knew
Hibbert."

"Why would they do that?" asked Davey.

"Because..." Hamish hesitated, then decided to come clean, "Hibbert was a blackmailer. If she was murdered by one of her victims without her killer getting his or her hands on whatever it was that Hibbert was using to blackmail them, they might just turn their attention to the people they think were her friends in order to find the blackmail material."

"In the name o' the wee man..." Jimmy breathed. "Who on earth lives around Lochdubh who would be capable of torture and murder?"

"People can be capable of all sorts of things when the chips are down," said Davey.

"Aye," Hamish agreed, "and sometimes people are no' quite as harmless as you might think. Come on, Davey, we need to get to work afore someone else ends up at the bottom o' a loch."

CHAPTER SIX

*Truth will ultimately prevail where there
is pains to bring it to light.*
George Washington

"Leave me alone! I don't want to have anything to do
with you, do you understand?" Her voice was trembling
with emotion but there was no mistaking the determined
insistence or flat notes of hard anger. She swapped the
phone from one hand to the other, pressing it against her
ear again as he spoke.

"I know you don't mean that. Please don't say that, my
darling Kelpie." His voice was soft, filled with pain and
an almost childlike distress that someone could inflict
such cruelty upon him.

"I mean it, all right!" she yelled. "And don't call me
that stupid name!"

"But, Kelpie, I—"

"Shut up and listen! I've just seen Hamish Macbeth

and his new sidekick walking into Hibbert's old cottage. If they find out..."

"They won't find out anything, Kelpie, honestly. You're worrying too much."

"It's you that should be worried! If they come up with anything, I'm not going to be the only one to suffer— I'll make sure you do, too! Now stay away from me, or I might just decide to have a wee word with Macbeth anyway!"

She hung up, viciously jabbing the button to end the call and then dropping the phone, as though hoping that any lingering echoes of his voice clinging to it would be eradicated by the clatter when it hit the floor. What was she going to do? It was all such a mess! Macbeth was going to find out, she was sure of it, and that would mean the end of everything.

"I checked the place out when she first went missing," Hamish said to Davey, stepping across the threshold of Kate Hibbert's small cottage. They had come straight from seeing Jimmy, Hamish having decided that this was a good place to start bringing him up to date. "She bought the cottage outright—no mortgage or anything. It's no' worth a fortune but if she'd been going away for a bit, you'd think she'd have asked somebody to keep an eye on it."

The front door opened onto a narrow hallway with a living room off to the right, a bedroom to the left and a kitchen and bathroom at the back of the house. The walls in the hall and living room were painted in a bland beige and hung with a few cheap prints. Davey smiled when he saw Van Gogh's *Sunflowers* hanging in a thin wooden frame on the living-room wall.

"My granny had one like that," he said, "only hers had a darker background. Apparently, Van Gogh did loads of different versions."

"Is that right?" Hamish said, making no attempt to conceal his disinterest. "We've no' much time here. Blair is bound to have his lads stomping around the place afore the day's out. Now take a look around. What do you see?"

"It all looks very neat and tidy," said Davey, scanning the living room. "The furniture's a bit old-fashioned. That sideboard looks like it weighs a ton and so does the sofa. The carpet's a bit plain, but it's very clean, and the fireplace has been cleaned out as well. In fact... it's all so tidy, it's almost like nobody lived here."

"Aye, I thought that, too," Hamish agreed. "I can imagine that somebody might want to leave things in good order if they were going away for a while, but this feels a wee bit too perfect, and it's the same in the other rooms. Everything's had a major spring clean, which is a bit odd given that Hibbert left in a hurry, without telling anyone. Now look at this..."

Hamish crouched at the base of the sideboard and Davey knelt beside him, running his hand over indentations on the carpet.

"The sideboard's been moved," Davey said, "but it hasn't been put back in exactly the same place."

"It's the same wi' that sofa," said Hamish, nodding at the marks made by the sofa's feet. "I never thought much about it when I first took a look around, but it's no' right, is it?"

"Hibbert would have needed a friend to help her move these things," Davey noted.

"She would that," Hamish agreed, "but I think she'd run out of friends around here. She didn't move this furniture. I think the whole house has been searched very thoroughly, and then a nice job has been done tidying up afterwards."

"But rooms that have been searched usually end up looking like a tornado has ripped through them," Davey argued.

"Maybe they do," said Hamish, "but I'm thinking that whoever went through this place didn't want anyone to know they'd been here."

"Why? What do you think they were looking for?" asked Davey.

"Let's get back to the station," Hamish said with a heavy sigh. "I'll show you what I've been puzzling over."

At the station, Hamish left Davey fussing over Lugs and making a pot of coffee while he went upstairs to retrieve the black plastic package from where he had hidden it under his bed. He then explained about finding it in the suitcase before spreading the contents out on the kitchen table.

"The earrings belonged to Hannah Thomson, as did the watch Hibbert was wearing when she was fished out of The

Corloch," Hamish explained. "Hannah lost them, thought they'd been stolen and put in an insurance claim. When she found them again, the insurance money had long been spent. Hibbert found out and was blackmailing her."

"Really?" Davey was genuinely surprised. "The insurance thing isn't exactly the crime of the century, is it? Coming clean would be better than leaving yourself at the mercy of a blackmailer."

"Davey, you have to understand what it's like in Lochdubh for a respectable woman like Hannah. She would have imagined that every eye in the kirk was on her when she attended the service, and that every whisper she heard was her name being dragged through the mud. The truth is, it would have been nowhere near as bad as that, but Hibbert would have made it sound like a scandal fit for the front pages of all the Sunday papers."

"The poor old woman must have been worried sick," said Davey, shaking his head and taking a sip from his mug of coffee. "So you think that all these other things were also being used by Hibbert to blackmail people? That's why you took the package in the first place, isn't it? It was hidden, so it was important, and if it involved any of your folk from Lochdubh, you wanted to be able to protect them."

"That's about the size of it." Hamish nodded.

"Taking care of your own is one thing, Hamish, but you've risked your job and your home by hanging on to this evidence."

"It's evidence," Hamish said, scanning the table, "but

maybe nothing to do wi' the murder—not all of it, anyway. If we can find out who Hibbert was using these things against, then we can eliminate suspects without their private lives hitting the pages o' the gutter press, and find the murderer in the process."

"That assumes that what the murderer was looking for is actually here on this table. It could be something else—something that they've already found when they searched the house."

"Aye, that's true," Hamish said, ruffling Lugs's ears when the dog stuck his head in his lap, "but if they found what they wanted in Hibbert's cottage, why bother putting everything back so neatly? I think they tidied up so that nobody would know they were still looking for something."

"So it's right here ... the thing they searched for ... the thing they murdered for ..."

"Aye, and tortured her for it as well."

"Why did she not just give them what they wanted?"

"Maybe she thought that this package of blackmail material was all that was keeping her alive. Once they had it, they were bound to kill her."

"Or maybe they went a bit too far and she died before they got her to talk."

"I'm afraid that's also possible," Hamish agreed, nodding grimly, "but they slipped up. They didn't find the package when they grabbed her and, had the suitcase not started to fall apart in the water, I would never have found it either. They probably thought that she'd left it somewhere safe. If you were in their place, where would you look next?"

"I think... well... I might assume that she'd given it to someone for safekeeping. A friend, or..."

"... a relative." Hamish finished off Davey's thought for him.

"Diane!" Davey gasped, jumping to his feet. "We need to warn her that she might be in danger!"

"We do," said Hamish, quickly repacking the black parcel, "and we need to have a word wi' everyone who knew Hibbert—tell them to keep their wits about them and their doors locked. I'll drop you at the Tommel Castle. You talk to Diane, Elspeth and Silas. I'll call in on Hannah Thomson. She's the nearest person anyone might think was one o' Hibbert's 'friends' and she's the most vulnerable."

They dashed to the Land Rover and set off down Lochdubh's main street at pace. With Hamish driving, Davey phoned ahead to let Silas know they were on their way.

"Say nothing to anyone about the blackmail, Davey," Hamish warned. "We have to keep that to ourselves for now. No one must know that we have Hibbert's blackmail package."

"Right," said Davey above the sound of the car skidding to a halt in the Tommel Castle's driveway. Silas walked down the front steps of the hotel to greet them. "I'll tell them we have reason to believe that the killer thinks someone close to Hibbert saw her being abducted, so they have to be on their guard."

"Good idea," said Hamish, racing off as Davey slammed the door. The Land Rover's tyres kicked up a fountain of gravel from the drive.

"I wish folk wouldn't do that," Silas tutted, using his foot to sweep gravel back into the wheel ruts Hamish had left. "It takes ages to rake all this lot flat."

"Never mind that now," said Davey. "We need to have a word with Diane Spears and Elspeth."

"They're in the lounge," said Silas with a look of concern about Davey's urgent tone. "They were having a bite to eat and then ... a visitor arrived."

Before Silas could say another word, Davey dashed into the hotel and was in the hall when he heard the bellow of a familiar voice.

"So where did you think she was going to get that kind o' money?" Blair yelled. "Do you think the fairies were going to magic it up for her?"

Davey walked in to find Diane and Elspeth seated at a table laid with tea and sandwiches, Blair looming over them and one of his female detective sergeants hovering in the background. Diane looked shocked, her features frozen, hardly able to believe what she was hearing. Elspeth's silver-grey eyes flashed with fury from beneath a furrowed brow.

"There's really no need for that sort of tone, Chief Inspector," she snapped.

"Och, is there no'?" Blair softened his voice as best he could, raising his eyebrows in an expression of mock sympathy. "I'm right sorry, but there was me thinking this was an investigation into a serious crime—a murder, no less."

"We know what you're investigating," Elspeth said, scowling at him, "but Miss Spears is distressed enough about her cousin. You should *not* be treating her like a suspect."

"Don't you dare try telling me how to do my job, Miss High-and-Mighty TV News Floozy!" Blair roared, reverting to his default setting of blustering bully. "I'm now of the opinion that this woman's business, including her flashy red car, have been funded in part by the proceeds of crime. Why did you no' establish where Kate Hibbert got the money she invested wi' you?" he added, glowering at Diane. "Where did she say she got it?"

"I, well…" Diane began, flustered and confused. "She … she always had some sort of explanation for it."

"And what sort of explanation did she have for the half million you just said you were expecting?"

"We…we hadn't got round to discussing that yet," Diane admitted, her voice cracking and her eyes brimming with tears.

"Had you no' now?" Blair took a step closer, towering above the seated woman. "I think maybe you had. I think maybe she changed her mind and was making off for a bit o' sunshine in the Med like she did afore. I think you were mighty pissed off to be missing out on that money and maybe decided to take it anyway. Money is ay the best motive for murder. So you see, Miss Grant," he went on, sneering at Elspeth, "I have every right to treat your client as a suspect—and if it turns out that you've done a deal wi' a murderer for her exclusive story, it's really going to put the brakes on your career. We might no' have to put up wi' you looking down your nose at us from the TV screen much longer!"

There was a short moment of silence, broken by the ringing of the female detective's phone. Elspeth then spotted Davey standing in the doorway and, following her eyes, Blair turned to face him.

"What are you doing here?" he demanded.

"Hamish...I mean, Sergeant Macbeth asked me to call in to make sure that Miss Spears was all right."

"Oh, did he?" Blair snarled. "Get him here right now. I want a word wi' that ginger-headed—"

"Sir," said the female detective, interrupting him, "I have a police inspector in Edinburgh on the phone looking for Miss Spears. It seems her flat has been burgled—ransacked by the sound of it."

"No..." Diane gasped, tears spilling from horrified eyes. She leapt to her feet. "I can't believe this is happening! I have to get back there. I need to see what's going on. I need to pack a bag."

"I'll come with you," said Elspeth, throwing a comforting arm around Diane's shoulder.

"Maybe you should send your sergeant with them, sir," Davey suggested to Blair. "You know, to keep an eye on them."

"Aye," Blair agreed, then grunted at the female officer, "don't let them out of your sight."

When Diane objected to having a police escort, an argument ensued, Blair bickering with Diane all the way out of the room. Davey discreetly drew Elspeth to one side.

"Stay close to the sergeant," he said quietly. "We think the murderer believes Diane saw him. If that's the case, he might come after her next."

"You think she's in danger?" said Elspeth, sounding alarmed.

"Well, yes, it's a possibility," Davey admitted, "but she'll be fine if she's with you and the sergeant."

"How do you know that Hibbert's murderer thinks Diane saw him?" Elspeth asked.

"Him...or her. We don't know that it's a man..."

"You said 'him' and 'he.' "

"That's just a turn of phrase. All I meant was..."

"What's going on, Davey?" Elspeth fixed him with a stare. She was a Highlander, and she had the Highlanders' unerring ability to recognise when they are not hearing the truth. She didn't need her second sight to tell her that Davey was lying. "What's Hamish up to?"

"Nothing...It's just...Look, I can't tell you the whole story, but Hamish thinks someone should be keeping an eye on Diane for her protection."

"I'll want the truth from you eventually," Elspeth warned him, walking off just as Blair came barrelling back into the room.

"Are you still here?" he snarled at Davey. "I thought I told you to fetch Macbeth."

"Yes, sir, I'm on my way now and..." He cut himself

short to answer his phone. "Just a sec, sir. It's Sergeant Macbeth on the line now."

"Give me that!" Blair spat, snatching the phone from Davey.

"Listen, Davey," Hamish said quickly, unaware that he was talking to Blair. "I need you here right now. Hannah Thomson is dead."

"Is that right?" crowed Blair. "And why would you be phoning your pal here instead of calling it in straight away to Strathbane? You bide right where you are, Macbeth. I'm on my way."

Hamish ended the call. Blair! That was all he needed! He'd wanted Davey to secure the scene and call Strathbane. He needed to be over in Hurdy's Glen talking to those who knew Hibbert, warning them to be on their guard. Blair would have him on sentry duty outside old Hannah's cottage for the rest of the day.

He looked across the living room to where Hannah sat in one of the Orkneys. She had no obvious injuries but her hands clutched the arms of the chair and her skin was disturbingly pale. Her head rested against the chair's tall back, her features slack and devoid of expression, but her eyes were open, staring straight at him with a look of absolute terror. Hamish had seen quite a few dead bodies, many with the eyes still open. When the eyes were open, it was always crystal clear that the person was dead. You could check for a pulse or any other signs of life, but the eyes never lied. He'd often heard people say that "the eyes are the windows to the soul." He was pretty sure that it was some kind of Shakespeare quote, but he had never bothered trying to look it up. He knew it was true because when you looked into a dead person's eyes, there was nothing there—no sign of interaction, no inkling of thought, no flicker of communication. Looking through those windows, you could tell that the soul had departed. The eyes were the coldest part of a corpse.

He'd also heard some say that if you looked into the eyes of a corpse you might see a reflection in those windows—a reflection showing the last thing the dead person ever saw. How often would that reflection be the image of a murderer? How much easier would that make his job? The notion was nothing more than a silly super-stition and looking into Hannah Thomson's eyes he could see no such image. He was, however, overcome with a feel-ing of dread. There was an unmistakable look of horror in Hannah's dead eyes. She had been terrified when she died, he was in no doubt about that. What had frightened the old lady so badly? She was looking towards him, towards the door. Was she scared and desperate to get out, or was she frightened by someone coming in? Suddenly he shivered, a chill feeling creeping across his upper arms and down his back. He was about to walk outside to feel the warmth of the sun when Blair barged in with Davey in tow.

"Have you touched anything?" Blair barked.

"Of course not!" Hamish responded. "I checked for signs of life and then left her alone. I'm no' exactly a beginner at this."

"Aye, right," said Blair, "but it wouldn't be the first time you'd buggered up a crime scene. What were you doing here?"

"You told me to re-interview the people who knew Kate Hibbert. Hannah was a known associate."

"Heart attack," Blair sniffed, wiping the back of his hand across his nose. "I've dealt wi' enough 'sudden deaths' to know a straightforward heart attack when I see one. I called Strathbane on the way here and I'll have uniforms here soon. Outside, both o' you," he added, pointing towards the door. "I need a word wi' you and I'm no' doing it in here—she's giving me the creeps."

They stepped out into the sunshine, standing among the green foliage of azalea and hydrangea bushes that bordered the short garden path, the large blue flower heads of the hydrangeas having taken over when the azaleas had dropped their red blooms earlier that summer. Hannah, Hamish thought, scanning the array of geraniums in the window boxes, had clearly loved her flowers.

"What have you been up to?" Blair demanded.

"What do you mean?" Hamish asked.

"I told you to get those interviews done, yet your car was seen on the road to Braikie!" Blair's face flushed with colour as his temper escalated. "That's no' where you were supposed to be, is it?"

"Maybe it wasn't our Land Rover," Davey offered, with a shrug. "I saw one this morning that looked just like ours, only it was silver. From a distance, in the sunshine, the silver looked just like—"

"Bollocks!" Blair silenced him. "You were off to see Jimmy Anderson, weren't you? Keeping him up to date, I bet. Well, he's no' working this case—I am! If I hear you've been taking time out to visit him, I'll have you both suspended. Understand?"

"Clear as a fog horn." Hamish nodded, gritting his teeth to control his own temper. He knew people would be watching, and he knew Blair was counting on that. There would be witnesses if he so much as laid a finger on the man.

"Good," said Blair, with a sly sneer. "I will take charge here. When the lads from Strathbane get here, the press are also bound to show up and they'll expect a statement from a senior officer. Now, what is it that you've been hiding from me, Macbeth?"

"What do you mean?"

"About Hibbert. I know you're holding something back."

"There iss nothing…" Hamish began, the sibilant tone of his Highland accent becoming more pronounced as his irritation with Blair grew.

"I've got two o' my team on the road back from Aberdeen." A mean smile strained against Blair's heavy jowls. "They've followed up wi' the people that reported Hibbert missing last time. It turns out that they only wanted us to find her because she had their money. They were a husband and wife. The husband had been having an affair and Hibbert was blackmailing him. As it happens, the wife was also having an affair and Hibbert was blackmailing her, as well.

"After Hibbert disappeared, the couple got divorced

and everything was out in the open. They had nothing to hide any more and when they each found out the other was being turned over by Hibbert, they decided to prosecute her to get their money back."

"Then they're now murder suspects," said Davey.

"Aye, well, they would be," Blair agreed, his smile widening to a devilish grin, "except that all o' this brought the pair back together again and they've just flown in after spending the last month on their second honeymoon in Cyprus. They have a perfect alibi."

"So where do you think that leaves us?" Hamish asked, dreading the answer.

"That leaves us wi' a murdered blackmailer," Blair said, staring Hamish straight in the eye, "and if she made money wi' the blackmail afore, I'm betting she tried it again. I'm betting she tried it on somebody around here—somebody wi' a secret that was worth half a million. Who do you know that has that kind o' cash?"

"There's no' many in Lochdubh could easily lay their hands on that much," Hamish admitted, "but some might find a way."

"No' her inside, anyway," said Blair, jerking his thumb at the cottage door. "I want to know who Hibbert was milking. Now you get out there and get those interviews done. If there's the slightest thing that doesn't tally wi' their original statements, my team will take over and give them a grilling. I'm having everybody wind up their other lines o' enquiry, so I want your report by tomorrow morning. Jump to it . . . *Sergeant.*"

Hamish bristled at the way his rank was slapped down at the end of the sentence like an insult. Blair was taunting him, daring him to step out of line. He refused to be baited, instead turning on his heel and walking away.

"Well done," Davey congratulated Hamish as they climbed into the Land Rover.

"Well done for what?"

"For not losing your temper," Davey said, "for not giving him a poke in the eye, and for not saying anything to make him suspect you have any kind of evidence."

"He's going to work that out for himself eventually. Hibbert's package is under your seat. Phone the number on that receipt from the Galashiels company—Lothian Livestock. Find out what that's about. I'll call Daviot and give him an update to keep him happy."

By the time they reached Hurdy's Glen, Hamish had spoken to Daviot, giving him a carefully truncated version of the true situation and Davey had finished a long conversation with the woman who ran Lothian Livestock.

"They sell all sorts of farm equipment," he explained as Hamish turned left after crossing the bridge over the Anstey, taking the road around the loch towards Hurdy's Glen. "They also supply animals for breeding. She's checking their records to find out what the receipt was for. She'll call back. She sounded really nice. Wonder what she looks like."

"Keep your mind on the job, Davey," Hamish said with a sigh, then spotted a woman in a meadow that stretched from the track to a stream known as the Hurdy

Burn. She was surrounded by four ponies, stroking their noses and ears while they crunched the carrots she was offering them. "There's Jean Simpson. She knew Hibbert really well."

"She works part time for a bank in Strathbane, doesn't she?" said Davey, showing that he had done his homework and read through Hamish's initial report.

"Aye, so we're lucky to catch her here today."

He stopped the car and called "Hello" to Jean before he and Davey let themselves through a gate into the meadow. Despite the presence of the stream, which filled a sizeable pond before cascading through a culvert under the main road and into Lochdubh, the grass was dry, parched by the recent spell of sunshine. Hamish introduced Davey, who immediately asked Jean's permission to pet the ponies. He stroked the neck of one and a second nuzzled his hand for attention.

"What can I do for you, Hamish?" Jean asked. She was slim and fit, in her early forties with long black hair pulled back, held by a sparkling silver "scrunchy" that seemed out of place with her muddy waxed jacket, jodhpurs and wellies.

"Well, we were wondering if you had seen anyone suspicious hanging around lately," Hamish explained. "We're worried that whoever murdered poor Kate Hibbert might think that one of her friends saw her being abducted. She used to help you wi' your ponies, didn't she?"

"Aye, although she wasn't really that interested in them. A bit frightened of them, I'd say."

"Aw, how could anyone be frightened of these guys?" Davey said, grinning. "They're adorable."

"You're like my girls." Jean laughed. "They love the ponies. Ride them whenever they can."

"They're at the high school in Braikie, are they no'?" Hamish asked. "How did Kate get on wi' them?"

"She was never really around when they were home," Jean answered. "She'd join me here on my days at home, but she was always glad to get up to the house for a tea or coffee."

"When was the last time you had a coffee wi' her, Jean?" Hamish asked.

"A week or so before she disappeared," Jean said, a note of concern creeping into her voice, "but I've told you all this already. Why are you asking again?"

"Och, I've just been asked to go over a few things with people again," Hamish said. "How did she seem when you last saw her?"

"She was...fine," said Jean, ruffling the mane of a chestnut pony and staring off towards the pond. "Same old Kate."

Some might have taken Jean's slight hesitation as a tinge of sadness at the loss of her friend. Hamish, on the other hand, smelt a lie.

"Did you part on good terms?" he asked. "Still friends?"

"Aye...still the same," she answered, continuing to gaze down towards the pond and the loch beyond, avoiding eye contact. Hamish followed her stare, taking in the water, then admiring the ponies and slowly coming to a realisation that he was astounded had not occurred to him before.

"Strange that Kate should be so keen to spend time here when she was actually feared o' the ponies," he said, slowly, "isn't it, Kelpie?"

"What did you just call me?" Jean turned towards Hamish, a horrified look on her face.

"Kelpie—it's a mythical spirit creature that they say lives in rivers and streams. Out of the water it takes the form of a beautiful woman or a sleek black horse. Either way its aim is to lure people to their death in the water."

"Aye...I know what a kelpie is..." She looked straight into Hamish's hazel eyes and he knew immediately that his guess had been spot on. "Why did you call me that?"

"Because that's what he calls you, isn't it? That's J. P.'s pet name for you."

"How did you find out?" She let out a long breath and turned to stroke a pony that was nuzzling her back. "Was it those bloody letters?"

Hamish nodded. "Hibbert was using them to blackmail you, wasn't she?"

"How could she do that?" Jean turned back to Hamish, angry tears coursing down her face. "I treated her as a friend...and she took me for every penny I had. If Tom ever finds out..."

"Tom—your husband," said Davey. "Works as an accountant with a timber merchant in Strathbane? Used to be with Highland Rugby Club? I saw him play a couple of times."

"Tom will kill him—and then what about my girls?"

"When did the affair start?" Hamish asked.

"Affair? There was no affair! He won a kiss under the mistletoe in a charity raffle at a Christmas gala dinner in the Strathbane Spa Hotel. There were hundreds of people there. It was just meant to be for a laugh. I was there with the folk from work. It was one kiss—a bit of fun for charity—only afterwards, he wouldn't leave me alone. He kept pestering me to meet him for coffee or to go out for dinner. I told him I was married. I made it clear I was definitely not interested in him. Then the letters started appearing."

"They were delivered by hand."

"Aye, and always when Tom was at work. I never saw him stick them through the letterbox. I swear I never wanted anything to do with him. You have to believe me."

"I believe you, Jean." Hamish nodded. "I know you'd never do anything that would upset Tom or the girls, but why did you keep the letters? Why no' just burn them?"

"Because I thought I might have to use them at some point to get some sort of restraining order put on him."

"How did Hibbert get hold of them?" Davey asked.

"I never saw one of the things being delivered, but she did. She missed nothing, that one. Once she had one of the letters, she went looking for the rest and found them among my pony files while I was making her a cup of tea. I told her the letters were nonsense but she said that Tom and the girls wouldn't see it that way. She would have ruined my whole life!"

"That's a pretty powerful motive for murder," said Hamish.

"I know…" Jean sobbed, fishing a tissue out of her pocket and blowing her nose, "but I didn't kill her, Hamish, honestly. I couldn't ever do such a thing."

"I don't believe you could," Hamish agreed, "but what about J. P.? Did he know about the blackmail?"

"I told him—I told him what a mess he'd got me into. He said he would give me money to pay her off, but I didn't want his money. That would have put me in his debt. I just wanted the whole thing to go away."

"We have to regard him as a suspect," Hamish said, gravely. "Who is J. P., Jean?"

"I'm not saying … I can't …"

"It's Morgan Mackay, isn't it?" said Davey.

"What? How did you…?" Jean's misery was now complete.

"Kelpie was his wee pet name for you." Davey explained his reasoning: "The beautiful woman, the horses by the water—he clearly thought it fitted. The kiss under the mistletoe was at an event you attended with other bank workers. Morgan Mackay also used to work for a bank, so it's safe to assume he might have been invited to a charity dinner involving bank staff. J. P. Morgan was a famous banker and his company is now a massive international investment organisation. Signing himself off 'J. P.' was a secret joke he must have wanted to share only with you."

"Mackay thinks he's so clever," Jean sniffed, "but he's just a … wee shite!"

"I have six letters," Hamish said. "Are there any more?"

"No, that's them all."

"All right." Hamish grasped Jean's shoulders tight in his hands and bent down to look her straight in the eyes. "You will never see those letters again. You will never hear from Mackay again. I'll deal wi' all o' this, but you must tell no one. If you tell any other police officers about this, I won't be able to stop it all coming out. You have to keep it to yourself, understand?"

Jean nodded.

"Good." Hamish smiled. "But mind you lock your doors and keep your wits about you. Until we catch Hibbert's murderer, you need to keep yourself and your family safe."

Jean whispered, "Thank you," throwing her arms around Hamish's chest to give him a huge hug before he and Davey made their way back to the Land Rover. They set off along the main road, heading for the track that led up Hurdy's Glen. Once Hamish turned off the road, they quickly left behind the flatter ground where the meadow lay to begin climbing the steep, deeply rutted section of track that snaked up the hillside. Hamish raised his voice above the revving of the engine when he dropped down a gear to keep the car bumping and swaying up the track. "They're ay talking about laying a proper road surface here. The going gets easier further up, beyond most of the houses. We carry on to the end of the track—the last house in the glen."

"Morgan Mackay's house," said Davey, consulting a

notebook he produced from his trouser pocket. "Retired, with some sort of live-in home help."

"He had Hibbert doing chores for him afore he moved the home help in," Hamish said. "A Polish bloke by the name of Bogdan."

"From your interview notes, I thought at first they might be together. You know—a couple?"

"There's been talk," Hamish said, "but the way he pestered Jean Simpson surely means they're no' in any kind o' relationship like that."

"Maybe he's a man of varied tastes," Davey suggested.

"And as long as he wasn't causing trouble for anyone else that's no' a problem either." Hamish shrugged. "Our problem is that Morgan Mackay is now both a victim and a suspect. He was tangled up in Hibbert blackmailing Jean and could well have decided to get rid of Hibbert."

"Sounds more like he wanted to pay her off than bump her off."

"Well, we'll soon get the chance to find out."

They passed a succession of white-painted stone cottages, some clustered together in small groups as if to share their warmth during the harsh winter months, some slightly larger farmhouses standing proudly alone on the hillside. He saw Gregor Mackenzie sitting outside his cottage with Bonnie, watching their progress.

"Just by that big mossy boulder," Hamish said, pointing out the mound, "is where Gregor last saw Hibbert."

As they passed the spot, the track became smoother

and they were suddenly able to talk more quietly again, the lurching of the vehicle easing, the engine calming, the springs and bodywork ceasing their creaking complaints. Eventually they reached a point where the track petered out and Hamish drove through an open five-bar gate onto a short gravel driveway before parking outside a two-storey Victorian house. Most of the building was of grey stone beneath a roof of grey slate, bleak enough, in Hamish's view, especially as the outlook from the main windows was up the valley rather than down towards the loch. To the side, an ugly extension had been added—a double garage with windows above that suggested at least one more room. A large grey car was parked in front of the garage. In the main part of the building, two men stood at the largest window, watching the arrival of the police car.

"It's that policeman again—Macbeth."

"What should I tell him?"

"Tell him nothing. Just stick to the story."

"What if he's been talking to Simpson?"

"She knows better than to say anything."

"But he's good at getting people to open up. She might have talked."

"That could end very badly—especially for her."

CHAPTER SEVEN

*What each would give to know how much
the other knows—all this is hidden, for
the time, in their own hearts.*
Charles Dickens, *Bleak House*

"Can I offer you tea, gentlemen?" Morgan Mackay smiled politely, his narrow lips chasing wrinkles across his cheeks. He was the sort of man who always looked like he had just shaved and his thinning brown hair sat neatly in place, combed back from his face. He was wearing a freshly ironed cotton shirt and crisply pressed flannels.

"That would be grand." Hamish nodded, removing his cap. He and Davey had been shown in to the front room where two burgundy leather armchairs and a matching sofa were arranged around a large fireplace with a dark wooden mantelpiece. A fire screen showing a panorama of hills and lochs blocked drafts from the chimney and paintings of similar Scottish scenery decorated the walls. The décor made the room look the way that Hamish imagined a gentlemen's club would. The largest of the paintings was above the mantelpiece—a powerful stag standing proudly against a background of misty mountains.

"*The Monarch of the Glen*," said Davey, examining the painting. "It's not a print, is it?"

"Not a print," Mackay agreed, admiring the painting, "but a copy. Rather a nice copy, but there's no way I could stretch to four million, so it's not the original."

"It's no' a monarch, either," Hamish pointed out. "He's a royal stag wi' twelve points to the antlers. A monarch has sixteen."

"If only someone had told Sir Edwin Landseer that," Mackay chuckled, "he could have added a few more points. Bogdan, would you be so kind as to fetch us some tea?"

"Just afore you do," Hamish said quickly, "and while I have you both here, have either of you noticed any strangers in the glen over the past couple of days—anyone suspicious?"

"Not that I can think of," Mackay said, turning to the fourth man. "What about you, Bogdan?"

Bogdan was in his mid-thirties, perhaps twenty-five years younger than Mackay. He was powerfully built with short dark hair and black eyes that stared out from beneath a heavy brow.

"I have seen nothing," he said slowly, his deep voice resting on an even deeper accent, "but last night we heard something outside the back door. It was very late. I looked out but there was nothing. I thought maybe a fox or a deer."

"Constable Forbes, why don't you go with Bogdan?" Hamish suggested. "Take a look out the back."

"What's this all about, Sergeant?" Mackay asked as the others left the room. "Please, take a seat."

Mackay relaxed into one of the large armchairs. To its left was a small side table on which Hamish noted a copy of the *Scotsman*, with the crossword almost finished.

"Do you lock your doors at night, Mr. Mackay?" he asked.

"I do." Mackay gave another little chuckle. "I know that many around here don't, but ever since I moved up here from Glasgow nearly forty years ago, I've kept the habit of locking up at night. Why do you ask?"

"We are concerned that Kate Hibbert's killer may suspect that one of her friends saw her being abducted." Hamish let the lie flow so easily that he almost believed it himself. "I'm sure there's nothing really to worry about, but best be on your guard."

"We will, Sergeant. Are you saying that the killer might come after any potential witnesses?"

"I doubt it. I think whoever murdered her is probably long gone," Hamish assured him, seamlessly backing up one lie with another. "You lived in Strathbane when you first came north, is that right?"

"You know it is, Sergeant." Mackay was starting to sound slightly cagey, and he gave Hamish a suspicious glance. "I worked at the Strathbane Savings Bank."

"Aye—you worked your way up to 'Regional Manager' as I recall, but you retired early."

"I did. They were cutting back on branches—everyone uses internet banking now—and looking to make staff cuts. I was offered a retirement pension package too tempting to resist."

"Do you keep in touch wi' any o' your old colleagues?"

"I try to stay in touch with old friends. Some even visit me here from time to time. I take them walking and fishing."

"And do you visit your old friends in Strathbane? Maybe attend the occasional charity function, for example?"

Mackay sat back in his chair, folding his arms, a resigned look settling his features.

"Okay, I see where this is going," he said. "It's about me and Jean, isn't it?"

"It's about you harassing Mrs. Simpson, yes."

" 'Harassing'? Since when is wooing a lady such a crime?"

"Since the lady chooses not to be wooed. She's a married woman with a family, so you just leave her alone, 'J. P.' "

Mackay's hands went to the arms of the chair. He eyed Hamish with a wounded glare.

"Aye, I have the letters," Hamish said, nodding, "and I know what Hibbert was up to."

"Jean told you everything?"

"She didn't have to. I worked it out from the letters. She didn't come to me—I confronted her. She did, however, tell me that you offered to pay off Hibbert."

"Jean wouldn't let me. I don't know why. It's only money. I'd do anything for her."

"Including murder?"

"I didn't kill Kate Hibbert." Mackay sighed. "In fact, I quite liked the woman. Mind you, if she hadn't given up her cleaning job here, I would never have got Bogdan, and he's made all the difference around here. He's transformed the garden and he's quite a handyman. He's also my alibi, Sergeant. When she went missing, I was here—I never left the house that day. Bogdan will confirm that."

"I'm sure he will," Hamish said slowly. "So now Hibbert is gone, your pestering of Jean Simpson has to stop. It ends here, or you'll have me to deal with."

"Are you threatening me, Sergeant?"

"Call it what you like, but I have those letters and if you ruin Mrs. Simpson's life, you can bet your 'pension package' I will ruin yours. I know folk in Strathbane as well. I can use those letters and your pathetic attempts at 'wooing' to make you a laughing stock. It will get very lonely up here in the glen when the dinner invitations dry up and your walking and fishing friends find other places to walk and fish."

At that moment Davey reappeared, a concerned look on his face.

"There's a muddle of fresh footprints in one of the flowerbeds out the back," he reported, "and it looks like someone tried to force open the scullery window. There are marks where some sort of tool was used as a lever."

"I think maybe I scared them off when I switched on

the lights in the kitchen," said Bogdan, following Davey into the room with a laden tea tray.

"I'm sure you're right," Hamish agreed, giving Mackay a sharp look. "Mind what I said, Mr. Mackay, and you'll be fine. I'm afraid we've no' got time for tea, Bogdan. We need to be on our way—police business."

Hamish fitted his cap firmly on his head, signalling the end of their meeting.

As he and Davey climbed back into the Land Rover, Davey looked across at him with a raised eyebrow.

"That was a bit of an abrupt exit, wasn't it?" he said. "I take it you spoke to Mackay about Jean Simpson?"

"Aye, I did that. I doubt he'll be bothering her again."

"What about the attempted break-in? Mackay and Bogdan might not be safe tucked away up here."

"That's a worry, all right, but abducting a lone woman is one thing, breaking in and taking on two men is a different story, and Bogdan looks like he can handle himself."

"You're right—he wouldn't look out of place in a rugby scrum," Davey agreed, then added, "I got a call from the woman at Lothian Livestock while I was outside. The receipt was for a ram—a real handsome beastie, apparently. Won a couple of awards."

"What breed?" asked Hamish. "No, let me guess—North Country Cheviot."

"Spot on."

"In that case," said Hamish, running his fingers through his red hair, "there are two houses in the glen we need to call on where I don't think people have been entirely honest wi' me about Kate Hibbert. The first is the Mackenzies' place."

The Land Rover rumbled easily down the smoother stretch of the track, then started bucking and rolling when Hamish guided it down the top part of the more rutted section. He turned off to the left and revved the engine to take them up to Gregor and Clara Mackenzie's cottage. Clara was standing at the door to welcome them, wiping her hands on a tea towel. Hamish introduced Davey.

"Nice to meet you," said Clara. "Come away in. Gregor's just down off the hill having a cup o' tea. Would you like some?"

"No, thanks," Hamish replied. Clara gave him a look of surprise. It was not like Hamish Macbeth to refuse tea, coffee, cake, sandwiches or anything else that was on offer when he came to call. He smiled, reassuring her that all was well. "We're a bit pushed for time. We just need a quick word."

The front door opened directly into the living room where Gregor stood to greet them, then resumed his seat at the small dining table by the window, offering them the other dining chairs. As they sat, Davey glanced round the room. There was a door at the back of the room which, he presumed, led to the rest of the house. In a corner away from the window, to avoid light reflections, there was a TV screen and on the other side of a small fireplace, again in a corner out of sunlight, a large, well-polished silver trophy sat on a display table. The figure of a ram sporting impressive, curled horns stood proudly on the lid. Gregor watched Davey studying the trophy.

"That's the Strathbiggie Breeders' Cup," Gregor explained, as proud as the silver ram. "I won it outright for the third time last year."

"Aye," said Hamish, "and against stiff competition as I recall. Actually, Gregor, it's one of the things we need to have a wee word about."

He slid the Lothian Livestock receipt across the table to Gregor. Clara took in a sharp breath.

"Where did you get that?" Gregor asked.

"Let's no' play games," Hamish said. "You know where I got it. Kate Hibbert stole it from you, didn't she?"

"She took it from our accounts book," Clara wailed. "If only folk knew what that woman was really like! She was evil! I told you this would happen, Gregor! I told you this would all come out in the end!"

"Nothing's come out, Clara," Hamish assured her, calmly, "but I need to know the truth. Why did you buy a prize ram, Gregor? You were the bookies' favourite to win that trophy with your own, home-bred beast."

"Aye, I had a grand buck, Hercules. Raised him myself from a lamb. He'd have taken the top prize, no bother at all," Gregor agreed.

"If the trophy is for a ram you bred yourself," Davey asked, "why did you have to buy one from down south? What happened to Hercules?"

"I found him one morning at the bottom o' the bluff further up the hill," Gregor admitted, his voice wavering. "He was lying on the rocks, all battered and broken." He choked back a tear. "I can't bear to think of it even now. There was nothing I could do. He was dead."

"He fell off a cliff?" asked Davey.

"He never fell!" Gregor growled. "He was stronger and more sure-footed than any beast I've ever seen! He was flung off that crag. Somebody killed him to stop me winning!"

"It wouldn't be the first time rival breeders have turned to dirty tricks," said Hamish, nodding in sympathy. "So you decided to replace Hercules."

"No," Gregor said, defensively. "I didn't set out to do that. I had given up hope of winning at Strathbiggie, but when I travelled down to talk to Lothian about other things, I saw a ram that was the spitting image of Hercules. Nobody—nobody except the bastard that killed him—knew what had happened, so I brought the new Hercules back up to Sutherland wi' me."

"You have to understand," Clara said, looking at Davey, "this is our livelihood. We breed champion animals that fetch the top prices when they go to auction."

"And Kate Hibbert found out what you had done," said Davey.

"She was ay hanging around, watching, listening, interfering, eavesdropping," Gregor said. "She heard us arguing about it."

"And when she found the receipt," Clara added, "she

threatened to tell everyone, starting wi' the Strathbiggie committee. We'd have been humiliated...and the business ruined."

"She damned near ruined us anyhow," Gregor cursed. "She was ay at us for another few quid to keep her mouth shut."

"You must have been relieved when she disappeared," Davey said.

"Aye, that was a day I'll never forget," Gregor admitted.

"You drank that much whisky, I'm amazed you can remember it at all," Clara chided him.

"Seeing the back of her was something worth celebrating," her husband replied.

"But that doesn't mean we killed her!" Clara said quickly, a look of alarm spreading across her face. "We hated her, right enough, but murder..."

"Don't worry about that, Clara," Hamish said, gently raising a hand to calm her. "I've known you both for years and I know fine that you're no' capable of...what happened to Kate Hibbert." He stopped himself from revealing any details of Hibbert's grisly demise.

"Now that the whole world knows," Gregor said softly, reaching out to hold Clara's hand, "we're sunk anyway."

"But the whole world doesn't know," said Hamish. "Only us. I think you probably know who killed Hercules, Gregor..."

Gregor nodded.

"Well," Hamish continued, "whoever that was got his comeuppance when you won the trophy wi' the Hercules lookalike, and he's no' going to say a thing. Otherwise, he'd have to admit what he did."

He retrieved the receipt from the table, tucking it into his pocket.

"We have no interest in telling anyone about this, do we Davey?" he said.

"As far as I'm concerned," Davey responded with a shake of his head, "this conversation never happened."

"You'll no' be seeing this again," Hamish said, patting the receipt pocket. "It will go on my fire once we catch Hibbert's murderer."

They took their leave, again spinning the story about the murderer possibly suspecting that a friend of Hibbert's might be a witness and warning them to be on their guard. Clambering into the Land Rover once more, Davey slapped the dashboard in a display of temper that took Hamish by surprise.

"I can't believe Hibbert was prepared to wheedle her way into so many people's lives and then cause so much stress and misery!" he said. "These people trusted her and she was a monster!"

"No' such a monster as those that tortured and murdered her," Hamish pointed out. "Just an extortionist on the make. There's some see money in other folks' misery. There's some will do anything for money. Hibbert's cousin's no' much different—ay thinking about money."

"Diane's nothing like that," Davey argued. "She didn't know anything about what Hibbert was up to."

"We can't be sure about that," Hamish said. "Blair

might be right to have her on his list o' suspects. No' everyone is what they appear to be. We've already seen plenty wi' secrets to hide."

"Aye, I suppose you're right," Davey admitted. "Who else was it that you wanted to visit in the glen?"

"In the time that she was here, Hibbert made sure of getting to know practically everyone that lives in Hurdy's Glen, and more besides. Seems like the ones where she 'wheedled her way in' were the ones where she saw an opportunity. She helped Fiona Duncan make a bonny wee garden out o' a patch o' gorse and heather—spent quite a bit o' time wi' her. I don't know Fiona and her husband, Ian, as well as the Mackenzies, but Fiona seemed right nervous when I spoke to her about Hibbert. That's our next visit, but we have to plan ahead. I need to get up to The Corloch to talk to Sally Paterson."

"She's not a suspect, is she?"

"No, but she found the body. The murderers might also think she found whatever it is they're looking for."

"That sounds like a pretty weak excuse to me, Sergeant Macbeth," Davey said, teasing Hamish with a smile. "Are you sure that's all you want to talk to her about?" He wiggled his eyebrows suggestively.

"Is that all you ever think about?" Hamish frowned at Davey, then stared out the windscreen down towards the loch. A leaden ball of guilt dropped into his stomach. Did he really need to talk to Sally Paterson? It seemed he'd been thinking more about her over the last couple of days than he had about Dorothy. He felt disloyal, yet could you really be disloyal to a woman who was lying in her grave? He shook his head to clear his thoughts. "Let's just keep our minds on the job. We also need to get over to Braikie to see my friend Dick Fraser. He's a master at quizzes and suchlike. He might be able to help us wi' the jumble o' numbers and names on Hibbert's spreadsheet."

"We'll never get up to The Corloch or over to Braikie in this car without being spotted by someone who'll report us back to Blair."

"You're right. We need another car. My pal Dougie Tennant might be able to help us wi' that. He runs a garage on the Scourie road."

Hamish hit a contact number on his phone and exchanged a few brief pleasantries with Dougie Tennant before explaining that he needed to borrow a car for a few days.

"What kind o' car?" asked Dougie.

"Anything that goes and doesn't look like a police Land Rover," Hamish replied.

"Then I've got just the thing," Dougie said. "I'll bring it down to you."

Hamish agreed to meet Dougie where the Hurdy's Glen track joined the main road.

"Right," he said to Davey, starting up the Land Rover. "Let's pay Fiona and Ian Duncan a wee visit."

The Duncans lived further down the glen, close to the spot where Hibbert had disappeared. Their home was a long, low building comprising two small cottages that had been knocked into one. Hamish's bold knock on the front door was answered by Fiona. In her early fifties, she had dark hair with just a hint of grey, dark eyes and a pale face drawn long by a look of heavy worry that bordered on dread.

"Good afternoon, Mrs. Duncan," said Hamish, removing his cap and introducing Davey. Fiona Duncan simply nodded. "Could we come in for a quick chat, do you think?" Hamish went on, no invitation having come from Fiona.

"If you must," was all she said, showing them into her neat front room where she stood stiffly by the mantelpiece, her left hand nervously clutching her right wrist.

"Is Mr. Duncan not around today?" Hamish asked.

"No."

"Where is he?"

"Cromish."

"Is he working up there?"

"Aye."

"When will he be back?"

"Saturday."

"What does your husband do, Mrs. Duncan?" Davey asked.

"Um...all sorts," came the curt reply.

"Mr. Duncan is well known around Lochdubh for being able to turn his hand to just about anything," Hamish said, filling the awkward silence. "This cottage was little more than two tumbledown ruins afore he set about rebuilding them, isn't that right, Mrs. Duncan?"

"Aye."

"He's done a fantastic job," said Davey, looking around. "You have a very nice home, Mrs. Duncan, and that's a lovely old clock on your mantelpiece." Davey stooped to take a closer look at the clock's dark wood cabinet and stark white face. "Have you had it long?"

"It was my grandmother's," said Fiona, protectively setting her right hand on the mantelpiece by the clock as though poised to prevent Davey from running off with it. "Ian keeps it running perfect."

"Is Ian working on a boat in Cromish, Mrs. Duncan?"

"Aye."

"Well, it would be good to talk to him as well," Hamish said, "but in the meantime, I'd like to ask you a bit more about Kate Hibbert."

"No." Fiona Duncan shook her head. "No, I'll no' talk to you about her. You must speak to Ian."

She shielded her face with her free hand and stared at the floor to avoid any kind of eye contact.

"We'll do that," Davey said, tipping his head towards the door in a signal to Hamish that they should leave. "Don't fret, Mrs. Duncan. There's nothing for you to worry about."

Trying not to make it sound like she really *did* have something to worry about, Hamish paused on his way out, gently explaining about Hibbert's murderer perhaps believing there had been a witness and advising her to lock her doors at night. No sooner had they left the cottage than they heard the front door being bolted behind them. Once they were sitting in the Land Rover, Davey retrieved the black parcel from under his seat.

"What's up?" Hamish asked. "Why did you want us out of there?"

"This is why," Davey explained, rifling through the photographs of the superhero couple. He showed Hamish one, pointing to an object in the background.

"Crivens!" Hamish gasped. "That's the clock on the mantelpiece. That picture's right dark, but it's the Duncans' front room!"

"And when you look at Catwoman," added Davey, unable to prevent a smile creeping onto his face, "once you *know* it's her, you can see it's Fiona."

"The poor devils," said Hamish with a groan of sympathy. "Hibbert must have threatened to make sure everyone in the area saw these. The shame would have devastated them. They'd never have been able to show their faces anywhere in Lochdubh ever again."

"On the other hand, they might have made some interesting new friends." Davey grinned. "Maybe there's a Spider-Man or Supergirl lurking somewhere nearby."

"Davey, this isn't funny."

"Och, come on, Hamish." Davey laughed. "It is a wee bit."

"Aye, okay," said Hamish, allowing himself a smile and starting the engine. "Maybe a wee bit. And you must be right about the Duncans having friends. Somebody took those photos. Whoever it was could also be Hibbert's victim, or Hibbert's murderer. We'll away up to Cromish tomorrow and talk to Ian Duncan. In the meantime, we need to find Dougie."

* * *

"It's a bit flash, is it no'?" Hamish was standing beside a sleek, sky-blue sports car. The dark blue soft-top was lowered and Dougie Tennant was climbing out of the driving seat. He removed a protective plastic cover from the seat, revealing pale-cream leather untainted by the oil and grease on his overalls.

"You wanted something that didn't look like a police car," he said, "and this surely fits the bill—a Jaguar XK8. I bought it off a woman in Dunfermline. It's over twenty years old but it's as good as the day it left the factory. Probably better—I've done a lot o' work fixing it up."

"It's a bonny motor, right enough, Dougie," Hamish agreed. "Are you sure we're all right to borrow it for a few days?"

"Aye, just make sure you bring it back in one piece," Dougie replied, handing Hamish the keys.

"Cruising in a Jag in the sunshine with the roof down," Davey cooed, opening the passenger door. "This will be fun."

"Aye, but no' for you just yet," said Hamish, closing the door and handing Davey the Land Rover keys. "I need you to give Dougie a lift back to his garage. I'm off up to The Corloch. Meet me at the Tommel Castle later. We can park the Jag there—we don't want anyone seeing it outside the station."

Davey headed for the Land Rover with Dougie, then turned to Hamish and grinned. "Good luck!" he called, with a wink of his eye. He popped a stick of gum in his mouth and climbed into the car.

Hamish tutted and shook his head before easing his lanky frame into the Jag's sumptuous cockpit. There was a surprising amount of space, even for someone who needed as much legroom as he did, and most of the space seemed to be clad in leather and polished wood. The car started with a rumble of power from the engine that settled to a comforting purr. It took only moments to familiarise himself with the controls before he set off for The Corloch, the wind ruffling his red hair.

"Young Davey might be right," he said to himself, smiling. "This could be fun. Aye, well maybe you're overdue a wee bit o' fun, Hamish."

Arriving at The Corloch Lodge, Hamish parked by the main entrance and was heading into the hotel reception when he heard what sounded like a scream. He paused, and it came again—definitely a scream and a splashing sound. Someone was in trouble down by the water! He sprinted across the hotel lawn, burst through the hedge that bordered the road, and immediately saw Sally Paterson struggling in the loch a few yards from the shore. Dashing across the beach of pebbles and rocks created by the low water level, he plunged into the loch and waded towards her. When he was within touching distance, she threw her arms around his neck and he lifted her easily out of the water.

"Oh, thank you! Thank you, Hamish!" she said over and over again, clinging to him like a limpet.

"Don't worry," he reassured her, taking a step towards the beach. "You're fine now. Look—the water only comes up to my waist."

"I can't..." she said, struggling to pull her face away from where she had buried it in his neck. "Does it...? I can't look. I'm so frightened of the water..."

"Frightened of the...?" Hamish stopped and looked over his shoulder to where Sharon Nolan was dragging a listing boat towards the shore. "So why were you...?"

"I'm fine," Sharon called. "Best get her back on dry land."

Once she heard the crunch of Hamish's boots on the pebble beach, Sally finally looked down and allowed her feet to be lowered to the ground.

"Oh, thank goodness," she breathed. She moved her hands from Hamish's neck to his face, drawing his head towards her and kissing him. "I was in a complete panic," she said, hugging him tightly. "I don't know what would have happened if you hadn't shown up."

"You'd...you'd chust have, well...here iss 'no'," he said slowly, still recovering from the unexpected kiss, his Highland tone singing through the words. "Here iss no' ass deep ass it seems. You'd have found your feet."

He took a step back, then tried to shrug off the awkwardness of the moment by helping Sharon haul the small aluminium rowing boat out of the water. He examined a gash in its floor. Blue paint was flaking off around the tear in the metal.

"Why did you take this boat out if you're feared o' the water?" Hamish asked, turning to the shivering Sally.

"That was my fault," Sharon admitted. "We had a couple of glasses of wine this afternoon and decided to cure Sally's fear by going for a row on the loch."

"It...it seemed like a good idea at the time," said Sally.

"No doubt." Hamish smiled. "Whose boat is it?"

"We don't know," said Sharon. "It was tied to a tree by the water's edge over there."

"We just sort of...borrowed it," Sally confessed, looking shamefaced. "Then when we got out a bit, we saw water coming in through that hole and we tried to push the metal closed but that only made things worse..."

"And because we were both leaning over to one side," Sharon explained, "and water was coming in, the thing tipped over and we both ended up in the drink."

"I think maybe the drink in you was the start o' the problem," Hamish said. "We'll leave the boat here. You two had better go back to the lodge and get changed out o' those wet things."

"What about you?" Sally asked. "You're just as wet as us."

"I'll be fine," Hamish told her. "I'll dry off standing in the sunshine. I'd like a wee word wi' you once you've changed."

"A wee word about borrowing boats that don't belong to us?"

"No, something else," said Hamish. "Come away up to the lodge now."

Once the two women had gone up to their rooms,

Hamish sat on a garden bench in the sunshine, took off his boots, and squeezed water out of his socks. What had just happened? What was that kiss all about? Was she just relieved and grateful, or was there something more? He wasn't sure he was ready for anything more. He wasn't sure he would ever be ready, yet the kiss had felt... good. He shook his head and laid his socks on the bench beside him, then took his phone out of his pocket and wiped it on a dry patch on his shirtsleeve. Even thinking about a romantic entanglement seemed cruelly disloyal to Dorothy. In any case, there were important things to be done. Being waterproof, the phone worked perfectly when he went to his list of contacts and called Jimmy Anderson, who answered on the second ring. He immediately started firing questions at Hamish for a progress report.

"Jimmy, Jimmy... wheesht for just a minute. I've no' got much time," Hamish said. "Can you get a message to one o' your people on Blair's team?"

He paused as Jimmy demanded to know why, loading another stream of questions into the same breath.

"Listen, Jimmy," Hamish said quickly, cutting off the flow of queries. "I'm up at The Corloch Lodge. I shouldn't really be here and if Blair finds out, I'll be for the high jump. Can you let your people know that there's a boat beached in front o' the lodge. It's damaged and there's flaking blue paint..." He paused as Jimmy broke in, then resumed as quickly as he could. "Aye, so I'm thinking it's worth checking out. Somebody must know who owns it.

Charlie Stuart, the bailiff who issues the fishing permits, would be a good bet. If the paint matches the traces found on Hibbert's coat, then this is the boat used to dump the body. I'll get over to see you tomorrow morning so we can talk properly."

He fended off another barrage of questions, then hung up and turned his face to the sun. His damp trousers were clinging to his legs in a very uncomfortable way, although his shirt hadn't suffered too much of a drenching. He decided that his socks would take too long to dry and he'd be more comfortable without them. He plucked them from the bench, hauled on his boots, and squelched over to the Jag, where he tossed the socks behind the driver's seat.

"Is that your car?" came Sally's voice. She was strolling towards him, dressed in a fresh white T-shirt, jeans, and flip-flops. "That's your cap on the passenger seat. It *is* your car!"

"Aye, well, no' really," Hamish confessed. "I've borrowed it for a few days."

"It's really pretty." Sally smiled. "A perfect car for a sunny day like this. So what did you want to talk to me about? I know—maybe you could take me for a spin round the loch and we can talk on the way."

"Go for a wee drive?" Hamish pondered the idea. "Aye, why not?"

He reached a hand into a soggy pocket to find the car key and was relieved when it started the engine first time. They set off on the road that looped round The Corloch, enjoying the fresh air, the sunshine and the scent of pine from the forest that cloaked the hillside. Eventually he broke the silence, feeding her the story about Hibbert's murderer suspecting there might be a witness.

"Have you noticed anyone strange hanging around the lodge?" he asked.

"Only the anglers." She laughed. "They're all pretty strange! I mean, they're strange in a nice way—adorably eccentric, rather than dangerous."

"I know what you mean," he said, smiling, "but if you do see anyone, you must call me straight away."

"What about the other police officers who've been talking to me? Shouldn't I tell them?"

"Well...no." Hamish hesitated, then decided to garnish his lies about the murderer with a pinch of the truth. "Probably best if you don't mention talking to me. Maybe you could say the same to Sharon. I'm no' really meant to be up here today."

"It's just as well for me that you were," she said. "You were my knight in shining armour."

Hamish guided the car through the bends that snaked around The Corloch and they chatted about the trees, the mountains, The Corloch and Sally's fear of the water. Her hair, at first damp from her dip in the water, dried in the sun and the breeze, billowing around her head. She pulled it back from her face, winding it into a knot at the back of her neck.

"Thank you," she said when they finally arrived back at the lodge. "That was a very relaxing way to get over my little upset earlier. And thank you for being my hero—I'm so sorry you ended up drenched."

"Och, that's nothing," Hamish replied. "It's just the sort of thing I have to put up with in this job."

"You're very sweet," she said, leaning over to kiss him on the cheek. Before he could say another word, she had stepped out of the car and was waving him goodbye. "See you again soon," she called, strolling over to where Sharon was sitting in the sunshine on the terrace with a pot of tea on the table in front of her.

Hamish drove back down to Lochdubh with a comforting, warm feeling inside from his latest encounter with the archaeologist from Turn-bridge-wherever helping to offset the distinctly uncomfortable, chilly feeling from the damp trouser legs clinging to his thighs.

CHAPTER EIGHT

Sometimes the smallest things take up the
most room in your heart.
A. A. Milne, *Winnie the Pooh*

"So we will definitely have a choice of Tommel Castle special Cullen skink or warm tattie scones with pine-smoked salmon to start with, then a rack of venison with a haggis crust or a roast rib of dry-aged Aberdeen Angus beef, or pan-fried sea trout with a seaweed hollanda-ise..." Freddy Ross paused for breath only for Priscilla Halburton-Smythe to interject.

"Freddy, you promised me those heather-scented honey-roast carrots. He let me taste one when he was experimenting yesterday," she admitted, rolling her eyes. "They were divine!"

"I've never seen someone get so excited about carrots," said Freddy with a laugh that chased the serious expression from his face. He was as tall as Hamish and awkwardly thin with the gangly legs of a young giraffe and a severe, bony face. Hamish was pleased to see him laughing. When Freddy had been his constable in Lochdubh, he had been far from happy. He had been a good policeman, but he had real talent in the kitchen. "But if you want them," Freddy added, "you shall have them. You're the boss."

"Not quite," said Priscilla, turning to Davey, her smooth bell of blonde hair shimmering in the sunshine. She wore a cool blue silk top with a plunging V-neck that showed off her slim figure and white, three-quarter-length linen trousers with high-heeled sandals that accentuated the length of her legs. "My parents own the hotel. I live and work most of the time in London, but I like to come up and lend a hand whenever I can." Her smile showed her perfect white teeth, and her dazzling blue eyes held Davey in their spell for a brief moment before she looked away towards the Jaguar. Hamish was intrigued. Was she flirting with Davey? She certainly had every ounce of his attention. He looked mesmerised.

"It's Dougie Tennant's car," Hamish explained. "He's loaned it to me for a few days. Will it be all right to leave it here now and again?"

"On one condition," Priscilla said, teasing him with a raised eyebrow. "You must both come to the Grand Gourmet Night on Saturday. No, actually, two conditions—you must both come *and* you must both bring partners."

"No problem," Davey said, grinning. "Sounds like a grand night out."

"Good," Priscilla chirped, then frowned at Hamish. "You don't look so sure, Hamish."

"No, no..." Hamish said, shaking his head. "I'm sure that will be fine."

From the window of the lounge in the Tommel Castle's private, family wing, Colonel George Halburton-Smythe looked down on the four figures in the car park. He decided to have a word with his daughter to find out what was going on. Macbeth was, in his opinion, a lazy scrounger who was always hanging around the hotel drinking free coffee and eating whatever he could mooch from the kitchen. He had never understood why his daughter had become engaged to a mere police officer. She could certainly have done far better for herself and the ignominy of her choosing Macbeth had turned to utter mortification when *he* chose to reject *her* by calling the whole thing off. He shook his head, as if it might help to rid himself of all thoughts of the humiliation.

Still, he mused, Macbeth had shown a good deal of intuition as a policeman, helped, on a number of occasions, by the colonel himself bringing some military discipline to the Highlander's shambolic efforts. Then there was that dreadful business with bride-to-be—Dorothy, wasn't it? She had been a fine-looking young woman. Priscilla was to have been one of their matrons of honour. Then poor Dorothy was murdered on the morning of the wedding—ghastly. Macbeth seemed to have come through it, though. He'd shown some real backbone there.

Now, who was the young man with Macbeth? He must be the new constable everyone had been talking about. A detective, apparently—never wears a uniform. That was a shoddy state of affairs. He should be proud to wear a uniform, proud to serve his country, even if it was only as a police officer. Priscilla seemed to be paying him rather a lot of attention. Surely she wasn't contemplating another dalliance with a policeman? That was something he definitely had to nip in the bud. The moment he saw Macbeth and the other policeman climb into the Land Rover, he marched downstairs double-time to intercept his daughter.

"What was all that about?" Hamish asked Davey once they were clear of the hotel. "Where are we going to find dates for Saturday night? It's only the day after tomorrow."

Davey was in the driving seat but, keeping his eyes on the road, still managed to lift his hips enough to manipulate his phone out of his trouser pocket. He waggled it at Hamish.

"I had a text from Diane," he said. "They'll be back at the hotel sometime tomorrow. We can go with them on Saturday—me with Diane, you with Elspeth."

"Och, no, Davey," Hamish said slowly, with more than a tinge of exasperation. "Elspeth and I are friends but..."

"I know you're just friends," said Davey, "but friends can still enjoy an evening together. Anyway, it will be a good chance for us to find out more about what's happened down in Edinburgh."

"Did she say anything about that?"

"Only that her flat had been turned upside down. The fingerprint guys did their thing but the only prints they were able to get were Diane's. When they were finished, she and Elspeth tidied up and it didn't look like anything had actually been taken."

"That's maybe because *we* have what the burglar was looking for. We need to take a look at the blackmail package again. Put your foot down, Davey, I need to get out o' these wet breeks."

Back at the police station, Hamish left Davey to feed Lugs and Sonsie while he went upstairs to shower and change. When he came back down, he put the black parcel on the kitchen table and poured glasses of whisky for Davey and himself.

"I suppose we can count ourselves off duty now," he said, and they clinked glasses.

"Except we're still going to talk about this, right?" said Davey, watching Hamish empty the contents of the package onto the table.

"Aye, we are," Hamish agreed, sorting the items into two separate piles. "We know who the earrings belonged to," he said, "and there's no' much we can do for poor auld Hannah now."

"Except find her killer," said Davey.

"Chances are she died of a heart attack," Hamish pointed out.

"Aye, but I don't think you believe it was entirely from natural causes," said Davey.

"No," Hamish agreed, taking a sip from his glass. "I

think somebody walked in through her front door and gave her such a fright that she had a heart attack."

"So she was frightened to death."

"Aye, and we're going to find who did it," Hamish said, a grimly determined look on his face. "We also know about the Lothian Livestock receipt and the love letters." He set those envelopes aside.

"And we know about the photographs," Davey added.

"But we don't know who took them. The spreadsheet wi' the jumbled numbers is also still a mystery, so let's take a closer look at these."

"How about something to eat, though?" Davey suggested. "My stomach thinks my throat's been cut. I'd think better with some food inside me."

"Good idea," Hamish said, gathering up the envelopes. He took the three he had set aside through to the office and slipped them into his desk drawer. "Let's away down to the Italian. Willie Lamont was another one o' my constables. He married Lucia, the owner's daughter, and works there now. He'll give us a nice table tucked away in the corner where we can talk about these things in peace. We'll get a good plate o' pasta—my treat."

"Really? I was hoping the tickets for Saturday would be your treat."

"Aye, right," said Hamish, shrugging on a jacket, folding the two remaining envelopes and tucking them into an inside pocket. "Dream on."

They walked briskly along the pavement by the seawall to what Willie Lamont always described as

Lochdubh's finest Italian restaurant. The fact that it was Lochdubh's *only* Italian restaurant never seemed to matter much to him.

"Willie!" Hamish called, shrugging off his jacket as soon as they entered and heading for a discreet corner table. "A bottle of your Valpolicella, please!"

"Hamish!" Willie looked up from polishing cutlery at the restaurant's long wooden bar. "Bentomato!"

Hamish and Davey both looked at him quizzically.

"Does he mean 'bentornato'?" Davey asked. "That's 'welcome back.' I remember it from a rugby trip to Rome."

"Probably," Hamish replied. "Willie's an awful one for getting his words mixed up."

"Good to see you again, Hamish," Willie said, walking towards them, wiping his hands on a tea towel, a welcoming smile on his face. "You must be Davey," he added, shaking hands. "I've heard all about you. Welcome to Lochdubh. Are you sure you want the Valpolicella, Hamish? I have an Amarone that is absolutely exquisive."

"Is that exquisite, exclusive or expensive?"

"All o' those."

"We'll stick wi' the Valpolicella."

Hamish hung his jacket on the back of his chair and they settled themselves in the quietest corner of the room, studying the menu. Willie arrived, fussing over opening the wine and insisting that Hamish taste it before he poured.

"Tonight, gentlemen," he said, "I can recommend the lasagne al porno."

"Willie," sighed Hamish, "even I know that should be 'al forno.'"

They both asked for spaghetti with meatballs in tomato sauce and, once Willie had bustled off to relay their order to the kitchen, Hamish took the envelopes from his pocket. The restaurant was far from full and the other occupied tables were too far away for anyone to overhear them above the selection of pan-pipe interpretations of Barry Manilow hits being played on the sound system.

"We'll be safe enough to take a look at the photos here," Hamish said. "Nobody else can see us in this corner."

"What exactly are we looking for?" Davey asked.

"Any clue about who might have taken them. You spotted the clock, well now we're looking for a figure in the background, a reflection in a mirror, somebody else's hand wi' a distinctive ring or a watch— anything."

They looked, swapping the photographs between them so that each had the chance to examine all of them, but they found nothing.

"We need to visit Ian Duncan first thing tomorrow morning," Hamish said, dropping the photos back into their envelope. "Maybe there are more photos. Maybe whoever was behind the camera is so desperate to get them back that they'll stop at nothing."

"That would have to be someone very important,"

Davey said, nodding. "The stakes have got to be pretty high if you're prepared to resort to torture and murder. This would have to be someone with a lot to lose if the photos became public."

"Aye, and that really doesn't sound like Fiona or Ian Duncan. That's why we need to know who else was involved in their wee games. What about this?" he added, laying the spreadsheet on the table. "It just looks like a jumble o' numbers and foreign names to me."

They both stared at it. Davey shrugged.

"That's what it looks like to me, too," he admitted. "It could be a set of accounts in some sort of code."

"Who do we know that would keep a set o' accounts? These could be Hibbert's own accounts—her keeping track o' the people she swindled."

"Aye," Davey agreed, "and then there's Morgan Mackay, who was a banker, but why would a retired banker be keeping coded accounts? Is that something Hibbert could have found out about?"

"Maybe, and what about Tom Simpson—Jean's husband? He's an accountant. Could Hibbert have discovered he was keeping secret accounts for some reason?"

"I suppose it's possible, but putting the squeeze on the husband *and* the wife would be dangerous. They might talk to each other when they realised that each of them was paying out money from savings, or wherever they were getting it. From what we've found out, it doesn't seem like any of the folk she was blackmailing knew about any of the others."

"That's the way she'd want to keep it. When too many people know a secret, it's no' a secret any more and it's no' worth paying a blackmailer to keep it quiet."

"I get the feeling that this spreadsheet may be the thing that Hibbert was murdered for."

"We need to know what it all means," Hamish said, slipping the document back into its envelope when he saw Willie approaching with their pasta. "Then we'll know if it's important or not. My friend Dick in Braikie is yet another o' my ex-constables. He now runs a bakery wi' his wife, Anka. We can show this to him tomorrow once we've been up to Cromish."

"Wow!" was Davey's reaction when the plate was set in front of him. "That's quite a plateful there, Willie."

"I asked the chef to ladle on a wee bit extra," said Willie, placing Hamish's plate carefully on the table. "I told him you two looked ravishing."

"That would be 'ravenous,' Willie," Hamish corrected him, "but you're right, and this looks great."

They were tucking into their food when Davey's phone lit up, buzzing and vibrating on the table.

"That's a message from Diane," he said, grinning. "We're on for Saturday night."

"I don't know why I'm letting you drag me into this," Hamish said, shaking his head.

"It's because, Hamish Macbeth, you secretly want to have a wee bit of fun!" Davey shovelled a twisted forkful of pasta into his mouth, sucking in the tail end of the spaghetti, which promptly lashed the side of his face with a smear of tomato sauce. He laughed and wiped his face with his napkin.

Hamish watched him and smiled. Perhaps he did need to be a bit more like Davey—more willing to get out there and enjoy himself. On the other hand, the reason that he so loved Lochdubh was because he could enjoy a quiet, peaceful life here. Wasn't that why he and Elspeth had grown apart? She loved the bright lights and glamour of being a TV presenter among the bustle of a busy city like Glasgow. He liked staring out across the loch and watching the rain roll in from the Atlantic, then seeing the sunlit mountaintops appear in blue sky while the clouds still crept eastwards along their lower slopes. Nothing, of course, could compare with standing in his own back garden late on a clear winter's night with frost sparkling on the roof of his chicken shed. On nights like that, with so little light pollution from street-lamps or other buildings, he could see more stars than a lifetime of counting could ever tally and, on the most magical of nights, great swathes of stars were washed away by waves of green and mauve when the aurora borealis staged its northern lights display. He had watched the lights playing in the heavens with Dorothy at his side. That was how he had planned to spend the rest of his days—here, in Lochdubh, with Dorothy. She had understood. She had wanted to build a life with him surrounded by all the things he most loved—but it was not to be. How could a gourmet evening at the Tommel Castle ever hope to fill the void she had left?

"Cheer up, Hamish!" Davey grinned. "Saturday night's

something to look forward to, eh? It will take our minds off all this blackmail and murder!"

"Aye," Hamish agreed. "Taking our minds off other things...that's no' a bad idea."

It was late when they left the restaurant but the lingering dusk still held Lochdubh in its half-light, calming the waters of the loch and softening the crags on the mountain tops. They strolled along the seawall, breathing in the cool air and exchanging a few words until they neared the police station and Hamish spotted a chicken standing on the low fence that surrounded his small front garden.

"Look, Davey—that's Myrtle. What's she doing out of the shed?"

He quickened his pace, with Davey at his heels, and spotted that the back door was wide open. He dashed down the short garden path then froze when he looked into the kitchen. The place looked like a bomb had gone off. Every cupboard door was open and its contents— food, pots, pans and crockery—strewn on the floor; every drawer was turned out with tea towels, cutlery and condiments scattered everywhere; the fridge and cooker doors stood open and even the washing machine had been hauled out from its place under the sink.

"Shit!" breathed Davey, arriving at Hamish's shoulder. "We've been done over!"

"Never mind that," growled Hamish. "Where are Lugs and Sonsie?"

He turned towards the back garden, then paused by

the corner of the building before bounding towards the small lawn where Lugs lay on his side, his eyes closed.

"Lugs!" he called, kneeling by his dog. "What's happened to you, boy? What's happened?"

Lugs's ears pricked up when he heard Hamish's voice, his eyes opened to narrow slits and his tail twitched, attempting a forlorn wag.

"He's alive!" Hamish yelled to Davey, reaching out to lift Lugs. "We have to get him to the vet."

"Don't try to lift him, Hamish," Davey said, appearing from the chicken shed with two large pieces of hardboard. "You might make things worse. I spotted these in the shed. We can use them like a scoop stretcher."

He gently slid the boards underneath Lugs until they overlapped and they were able to lift the dog carefully, carrying him to the Land Rover. It was then that they spotted Sonsie on the roof of the car, licking cuts on her shoulder and flank.

"Leave her there," said Hamish, climbing into the back of the car beside Lugs. "You drive. It's no' far. I'll phone Peter."

The vet's surgery was a small, modern, purpose-built bungalow at the end of a narrow lane off Lochdubh's main street. Davey drove at little more than walking pace while Hamish spoke to the vet, Peter Abraham, who was waiting for them in the three-car parking space outside his premises. Sonsie glowered defiantly down at him from the roof of the Land Rover, daring him even to attempt to lay a hand on her.

"I can see she's got some quite deep cuts, Hamish," Peter said as Hamish stepped out of the back of the car, "but she doesn't seem to be bleeding too badly. I doubt she'll let me near her. In any case, you need a special licence to treat wildcats, or even to keep one for that matter."

"Let's worry about Sonsie later," Hamish said, bluntly. "Lugs looks like he's in a far worse state."

The vet examined Lugs on the floor of the Land Rover, gently running his hands over his limbs and torso, using a stethoscope to listen to his heart and breathing, all the while talking in soothing tones, repeating Lugs's name, to reassure his patient.

"My nurse is on her way in," Peter said, backing out of the Land Rover to join Davey and Hamish. "Let's get Lugs inside where I can do some X-rays."

"How bad is it, Peter?" Hamish asked, his voice strained. "Will he..."

"The only time I've seen injuries like this on a dog before is when one's been hit by a car," Peter admitted, giving Hamish a sombre look. "He's taken a lot of punishment, Hamish."

Peter's veterinary nurse arrived while he and Hamish were carrying Lugs inside. She looked up at Sonsie, who narrowed her yellow eyes, bared her teeth and hissed. The nurse hurried inside. Davey sat on the front wing of the car, keeping an eye on Sonsie.

A few minutes passed before Hamish came back out. At first Davey thought he looked utterly despondent, his head bowed, his shoulders hunched. Then he could see Hamish's fists were clenched and, when he looked up, his hazel eyes were blazing with fury.

"I need to get Sonsie," he said, through clenched teeth.

"Let me help," said Davey, stepping towards him. "I can—"

"No!" Hamish snapped, pointing to the front of the car, sending Davey back again. "You bide where you are."

He walked to the rear of the Land Rover where there was a ladder that allowed access to the roof. Climbing the ladder, he called softly to Sonsie.

"Careful, Hamish," Davey warned, watching the powerful wildcat react. "She looks really angry."

"No' wi' me, she's no'," said Hamish, reaching his arms out to Sonsie. "Come to me, my poor wee lamb."

The big cat dragged herself to her feet, limped along the roof and, with a kitten-like meow, collapsed into Hamish's arms. He carried her carefully down the ladder and into the vet's surgery. Davey waited just as he'd been told, chewing nervously on a stick of gum. The night was still and calm. The only sound Davey could hear above that of his own chewing was the rhythmic pulse of the waves chasing pebbles up the beach.

Then came another faint noise—the scrape and rustle of shuffling footsteps. Davey looked towards the end of the lane, where the road petered out into a rough path leading off into a shadowy area of bushes and trees. Suddenly a figure emerged from the shadows. It was a man with long, straggly grey hair and a grey beard. He was wearing a long, white robe with strings of black beads around his neck. Davey looked on, spellbound, as the man drew closer, emitting an eerie, high-pitched, keening lament.

"Heed me well," trilled the old man, walking past Davey, staring straight ahead. "Death stalks Lochdubh and his work is not yet done."

Davey watched the old man make his way down the lane to the shore road.

"Was that old Angus Macdonald?" The nurse had emerged from the surgery.

"No idea," said Davey, relieved to see another person. "Creepy as hell is what it was."

"That's Angus." The nurse smiled. "Some say he has the second sight. They even believe he's a 'seer,' able to predict the future and see things that the rest of us can't. Others say he's just an old eccentric—some are no' so kind. Hamish asked me to tell you he'll be out as soon as he can. We've not much room inside. He wants you to wait here."

"Aye, fine," Davey said, nodding. "I'll be here."

Half an hour later, Hamish walked out of the surgery, the same angry fire in his eyes.

"Hamish." Davey stepped towards him. "How is... I mean what... what's happening in there?"

"Sonsie's been sedated," Hamish replied, coldly. "They've stitched her wounds and she's sleeping it off. Lugs... Lugs took a real battering. He might no' make it. They say it's touch and go..."

"No..." breathed Davey. "Hamish, is there anything I can do?"

"Aye, there is. Get back to the station and put everything back as it was, as best you can. See if they took any o' the other blackmail items."

"But what about fingerprints? The place will have to be dusted and—"

"There will be no fingerprints. Whoever turned over the station also did Diane Spears's flat and Kate Hibbert's cottage. They put the cottage back together nice and neatly because they had plenty o' time. They knew exactly where Hibbert was because they'd abducted her and were holding her prisoner. She might even have been dead by that point. They knew she wasn't coming home. At the flat and the police station, they would have been up against it. They didn't know how much time they had so they did it the quick and messy way."

"I suppose that Lugs and Sonsie must have got in their way."

"I suppose you're right, but they're no' going to get away wi' this, Davey. We're going to find them, and they're going to pay."

Hamish gave Davey a look that left him in no doubt he intended to exact his revenge, whether within the law or by any other means necessary.

"Okay, Hamish," Davey said with a curt nod. "You can count on me."

By the time Davey had finished tidying the police station, the night had grown as dark as it could manage and dawn was threatening to inflict another sunny morning on the Highlands. Not having lived in the station for very long, he had to guess where some of the things he cleared from the floor rightfully belonged. He was congratulating himself on having done a pretty good job when he suddenly realised why he was doing it. They'd been burgled. Lugs and Sonsie were at the vet's and Hamish had not yet returned. He realised that he'd been concentrating so hard on the tedious chore of tidying up that he hadn't spared a thought for Lugs and Sonsie, or Hamish. He felt a twinge of guilt followed by a surge of sympathy for the big Highlander, which left him suddenly very tired, and he sat at Hamish's desk perusing the earrings, the receipt and the letters. None had been taken. They had been left on the floor along with their respective envelopes.

"A tidy job, Davey," came Hamish's voice from the kitchen. "It's almost like the bastards never wrecked the place."

"Hamish! How are Lugs and Sonsie?"

"Sonsie's no' going to be quite herself for the next wee while," Hamish admitted, "and Lugs... well, he's still alive. Peter says if he makes it through the next twenty-four hours, he might stand a chance but..."

"I'm sorry, Hamish. This must be a nightmare for you."

"We've no time for nightmares or daydreams or any o' that kind o' nonsense," Hamish said, looking down at the desk. "Left those behind, did they? Then it was one o' these two envelopes they were after." He slapped the envelopes with the photographs and the spreadsheet down on the desk. "Best try to get a couple of hours' sleep, Davey. We're off to Cromish bright and early."

Curtains and windows were being flung open in Lochdubh to let in the fresh, early morning air as Hamish and Davey drove along the waterfront in the Jaguar, heading for the humpbacked bridge leading to the road that would take them northeast towards Assynt. There, they skirted the loch before turning left where the road climbed to cross high moorland with the craggy shoulder of Quinag in the distance to their left and the gentler slopes of Glas Bheinn to their right. They then began the long descent towards Newton and Unapool, where they rounded a bend that brought them alongside the still, glassy waters of Loch Glencoul before they climbed away again to round the headland where the road finally dropped down to Kylesku. Just before they arrived there, they passed a sign on the right for the Kylesku Hotel.

"That's a grand wee place," Hamish told Davey. "We should go there some time. They have all kinds o' seafood in their restaurant. The hotel's been there forever but it was all modernised nicely no' so long ago. It's where the ferry used to run across Loch Glendhu to Kylestrome. During the Second World War, they trained on top-secret midget submarines in the loch there."

Davey watched Hamish concentrating on the road ahead and decided that he was doing precisely what he had done earlier when tidying up the mess in the station—allowing his mind to focus on other things so that he didn't have to think about what was happening in Peter Abraham's surgery back in Lochdubh.

"I remember this bit from giving Dougie Tennant a lift up here," Davey said. "There's a little bridge."

"Aye, it's the reason there's no' a ferry any more," Hamish explained. "It's the Kylesku Bridge. Certainly no' Scotland's longest bridge, but it's a bonny view you have from here."

They motored up to Scourie, where they passed Dougie Tennant's garage and caught their first real glimpse of the Atlantic way off to the west, then pressed on to where the road touched the head of Loch Inchard. Here they turned left, taking an even narrower road that wriggled along the northern shore of the loch towards Kinlochbervie and, a little way beyond it, Cromish. The far north-west of Sutherland is the most sparsely populated place in Scotland, and Cromish does little to boost any census figures. The village came into existence during the Highland Clearances that spread to Sutherland in the early nineteenth century, when farmers were evicted from their smallholdings by landowners to make way for larger, more profitable sheep farming. Coastal crofting communities like Cromish were established to provide some of the farmers with alternative housing and work in the fishing and kelp industries. The harsh environment, tough work, widespread famine, and the collapse in demand for kelp meant that most of these communities struggled. Many crofters were left with no choice but to emigrate to Canada or the United States. Hamish and

Davey drove past a small cemetery on the outskirts of Cromish.

"There's no' much here in Cromish, and that place," Hamish said, nodding towards the cemetery, "has ay meant that the dead outnumber the living. There's only a few cottages down near the wee harbour, and a general store."

To their left was Cromish Bay, a small tidal inlet shaped like a spoon, the low headland to the west protecting the harbour that was the head of the spoon from the worst ravages of the mighty Atlantic. The sunshine on the calm water made it look as flat and pale as blue ice, reflecting the pale hue of the early morning sky. To their right, a little higher than the road, was the first of the village houses, a small, low, stone-built affair, standing alone, isolated from the huddle of harbour cottages by a wide meadow where sheep were grazing. The cottage looked down over a sloping front garden stocked with a colourful display of hydrangea, delphinium and foxglove. A small, bulky, elderly woman struggling to bend and pull weeds looked up as the Jaguar approached.

"Och, no," Hamish groaned, recognising the address and slowing the car to a halt. "That must be Moira Stephenson and she's spotted us. Bide here, Davey, I need to do a bit o' . . . community relations."

Hamish knew that his "community relations" might well involve an apology and some light grovelling, given his previous conversation with the woman who was scared of spiders. That wasn't something he wanted Davey to witness.

"Mrs. Stephenson," he called, giving her a friendly wave. "Hamish Macbeth from Lochdubh—we spoke on the phone the other day."

"Aye, I mind o' that," said the woman.

"I'm sorry if I was a wee bit short wi' you . . ."

"Short? Bloody rude is what I'd call it."

"Aye, well, I was under a wee bit o' pressure wi' the body having been found in The Corloch."

"You might be under a lot more pressure when two are found in Cromish Bay," Mrs. Stephenson said, stony faced. She looked down towards the water's edge where two small boys were foraging on a thin stretch of pebbly beach beside a tumbledown jetty.

"Would you care to explain?" asked Hamish.

"Those two wee laddies are ay wanting to play on the jetty, and I'm ay raging at them to stay off it. The jetty's mine, but it's no' safe. I want to get it rebuilt so I can have a seat out there when the weather's fine like this, but I can't get anyone to come up here and do the work. I'm terrified those two are going to fall through it into the deep water there."

"Don't worry, Mrs. Stephenson, I'll have a word wi' them. How is your spider problem?"

"I'm still plagued wi' them." The old woman shuddered. "I have to ask neighbours to come in when I spot them, but the neighbours are no' always around."

"There's no' much I can help you with there, I'm afraid," Hamish apologised, "but I can deal with those two rascals for you."

Hamish crossed the road to the beach where he found Davey already chatting with the boys. Each of the boys had an old jam jar with a screw-on lid, and each of the jam jars contained several spiders.

"Look at this, Sergeant Macbeth," said Davey, grinning. "The lads have captured some real monsters by the jetty."

"Aye," said Hamish, folding his arms and staring down at the boys, "and I think I know what they've been doing wi' them!"

"It was his idea!" said the smaller of the two boys.

"No it wasn't!" came the other's wide-eyed denial.

"Aye it was! He said the auld witch was scared o' them and if we put them through her letterbox, she would die wi' a heart attack and then we could go on the jetty whenever we wanted."

"Names!" Hamish said, sternly, scowling at the boys with exaggerated anger and taking out his notebook.

"Billy Stuart," said the bigger boy, hanging his head.

"John Hogg," said the other. "You'll no' tell my mum, will you?"

"Tell your mum?" Hamish boomed, writing the names in his book. "By rights I should arrest the pair o' you for attempted murder and throw you both in the jail! You've just one chance. It's called community service..."

Davey was struggling not to laugh, resorting to chewing gum, as Hamish outlined the terms of the deal before taking the boys across the road to talk to Mrs. Stephenson.

"These two," he told the old lady, "would like to help with your spider problem. Tell Mrs. Stephenson, lads."

"We'll come by every day and check your shed and your peat store," said the first offender.

"And we'll check under your sink or anywhere else you want us to, and we'll catch all the spiders," said his accomplice.

"We're really good at catching spiders," the first boy boasted, holding up his jam jar to show off the specimens. The old lady caught her breath and took a step back.

"I'd be very grateful for that, boys," she said. "In return, when I get the jetty rebuilt, you can use it whenever you like."

"That was a job well done," Davey congratulated Hamish back in the car. "Would that be our next stop?" He pointed to the tiny harbour where a small yacht had been hauled out of the water and was standing on the dockside, supported by scaffolding props and substantial timber posts. A heavily built, dark-haired man was painting the hull. He looked up from his work, eyeing the car as Hamish drew up on the dock.

"Mr. Duncan," Hamish said, striding towards him. "We were hoping to have a wee word with you."

"What do you want, Macbeth?" he grunted. "I'm right busy, as you can well see."

"We'll no' keep you long," Hamish said, smiling and introducing Davey.

"I need to keep on working," Duncan said. "The

owner wants this back in the water next week. What's this about?"

"You know fine what it's about," Hamish said, watching Duncan recharge his paint roller. "We've just dealt wi' a problem where the culprits had found out a secret about someone else—a secret fear in this case. I see it a lot in my job. I think it's human nature—people find out secrets and use them to get what they want. I think you've been a victim o' someone who did exactly that."

Duncan sighed and put down his roller.

"Fiona told me you'd probably be up here to see me," he said, wiping his hands on a cloth. "It's about the Hibbert woman, is it?"

"It is," Davey confirmed. "She was blackmailing you, wasn't she?"

"Blackmail?" Duncan muttered, looking shiftily from Davey to Hamish. "What do you mean?"

Hamish reached into his pocket and produced one of the photographs.

"I have another half-dozen o' these, Ian," he said. "That's you and Fiona, isn't it?"

Duncan nodded, shamefaced, looking down as if to concentrate on wiping his hands.

"So Hibbert found the photographs and started blackmailing you," Davey said.

"No' straight away," Duncan said, looking Davey in the eye. "At first she wanted to join in. She said she could be Wonder Woman, but that was out o' the question."

"You didn't fancy her, then," Davey prompted.

"It wasn't just that," Duncan explained. "Sheena was ay Wonder Woman when we played these wee games."

"So there were others involved," said Hamish.

"Eric and Sheena," Duncan said, looking up at him. "A couple we know in Nairn. They took the pictures. This all started out as kind o' a dare after a few drinks, but it was just for a laugh. We weren't hurting anyone."

"Was there anyone else involved apart from them?" Hamish asked.

"No, just them," Duncan admitted.

"Are there any more photographs?" asked Davey.

"Eric and Sheena have the ones we took o' them."

"Was Hibbert squeezing them for cash, too?" Hamish asked.

"No, she knew nothing about them. It was just us she was into. She took near all our savings, but we had to pay, otherwise she said we'd be exposed..."

Davey covered a snigger with a gentle cough.

"Fiona could never have shown her face in Patel's supermarket ever again," Duncan said quietly. "But nobody has to know now, do they? Eric and Sheena don't have to find out. Nobody has to find out—not now that she's gone."

"Aye, that must come as quite a relief to you..." Hamish said, slowly, "...Hibbert being gone."

"Well, we can get back to normal now, so we're glad she's gone," Duncan agreed, then a look of panic crossed his face and he held up a hand as though calling a halt to whatever Hamish was thinking, stopping whatever he might have been about to say. "That doesn't mean we killed her, though! I'm no murderer!"

"Maybe no'," said Hamish, "but we think whoever killed her believes a friend o' Hibbert's saw him take her, so keep your wits about you for any strangers lurking around."

Duncan nodded and his eyes flitted to the photograph Hamish was tucking back in his pocket.

"I'll hang on to the photos until we find the murderer," Hamish explained. "Then you can either have them back, or..."

"Burn them," Duncan said. "I never want to see the things again."

"Fair enough," said Hamish, casting an eye over the fresh paint on the yacht's hull. "You're doing a fine job on this boat, Ian. When you're finished wi' it, you should have a word wi' Mrs. Stephenson just down the road there. She needs someone to rebuild her jetty."

With that, Hamish and Davey got back in the car, leaving the Atlantic behind them, the rugged peaks of Foinaven and Arkle looming large on the horizon as they headed for Braikie.

CHAPTER NINE

I'd be glad of a retaliation that wouldn't recoil on myself; but treachery and violence are spears pointed at both ends: they wound those who resort to them, worse than their enemies.
Emily Brontë, *Wuthering Heights*

Compared to Cromish, Braikie was a positive metropolis. The old market town boasted a wide range of shops lining its main street and some very grand Victorian buildings, the most prominent being Braikie Library, in front of which stood a statue of George Granville Leveson-Gower, the first Duke of Sutherland, who instituted the Highland Clearances in the region, destroying the livelihoods of countless farmers. Known as "Glaikit Geordie" to the Braikie locals, the statue was regularly decorated with a traffic cone on its head, courtesy of the Saturday-night pub crowd. The following morning it was always a point of interest, in a "will he, won't he?" sort of way, for churchgoers on their way to the nearby Braikie Cathedral.

It took Hamish and Davey almost two hours to reach Braikie from Cromish. Hamish chose a familiar route to the hospital, leaving the car in the car park there before he and Davey walked the short distance to the small side street where Dick and Anka had their bakery. A substantial queue of locals and office workers on their lunch breaks stretched out of the shop and along the pavement. Dick, having been alerted by phone to their imminent arrival, ushered them in past the queue.

"Come away in, lads!" he called, leading them towards the stairs to the flat above the shop. Dick's two shop staff, a cheerful youth and a pretty young woman, smiled and waved before returning to the throng of customers. "Anka's waiting upstairs, Hamish. We've got a couple of new treats for you to try."

No sooner had Dick settled them on a comfortable sofa, in front of which was a coffee table bearing a tray with colourful mugs and a tall coffee pot, than Anka appeared from the kitchen. She looked as glamorous as ever, tall and slim with long, auburn hair and the beautifully sculpted cheekbones of a Polish model. Hamish had once lusted after Anka himself but she had lost her heart to the portly Dick Fraser with his twinkling eyes and grey moustache.

As a police constable, Dick had been, at best, disinterested. He had always, however, been a voracious reader, gifted with an amazing memory, making him an absolute champion when it came to puzzles and quizzes. He had won a whole host of prizes from televisions and microwave ovens to garden tools and sheepskin coats, but the biggest prize of all had been Anka. They had bonded over a love of baking and now, with Anka setting a three-tiered cake stand on the table, Hamish noticed a new roundness to her figure. He looked towards Dick, sitting in an armchair to his left, to find Dick watching him, a proud smile on his face and his eyes twinkling more joyously than ever.

"Aye, Hamish," he said, his smile broadening into a grin, "I'm going to be a daddy!"

Hamish stood to greet Anka, offering his congratulations, and she kissed him on the cheek three times, right, left and right again, as is the Polish way with those dearest to them.

"And you," she said, "will be Uncle Hamish." She then kissed Davey twice, he not yet being a close friend or family member.

"Now, Hamish," Dick said, rubbing his hands and loading slices of cake onto a plate, "we can celebrate by trying some new twists on a few old Polish favourites."

"We have marcinek," Anka explained, "which you might say is more of a dessert, really. It is layers of dough with vanilla cream but we have kept it very light. I think you will like that one. Then there is wuzetka, a kind of chocolate cake with homemade plum jam and rum, and finally piernik, a honey and spice cake, also with the plum jam."

"We went a wee bit over the top making the plum jam this year!" Dick laughed, pouring them all coffee. "Tuck in, Hamish—you too, Davey. We want to know what you both think."

What they both thought was that every mouthful was sublime. They complimented their hosts, then Dick took a sip of coffee, giving Hamish a serious look.

"So what is it you want to talk to us about?" he asked. "Is it the body in The Corloch?"

"In a roundabout sort of way," Hamish said, handing Dick the spreadsheet. "What do you make o' this, Dick?"

"At first glance," said Dick, "I'd say it was a number code. You'd need a lot more information about what had been encoded before you could crack this thing, but by the way it's all laid out in columns, it looks like some kind of payment record. I could see how this might be names, followed by account numbers, followed by dates, with amounts at the far right. It just has the feel of a bank statement about it."

"Like a bank statement…" Hamish pondered, turning to Davey. "Mackay?"

"Is he a suspect?" Dick asked.

"He's certainly what you might call a person of interest," said Davey.

"Hibbert—the murder victim—was a blackmailer," Hamish explained. "Mackay's tangled up in it. He has a big house in Hurdy's Glen no' far from where the victim lived. He lives wi' a Polish servant called Bogdan."

"Ha!" Anka exclaimed. "I know them. They have

been in the shop a few times and this Bogdan has spoken to me in Polish but his Polish is really bad. He has a heavy accent. He is a Russian, not a Pole."

"Russian?" Davey frowned. "Why would he pretend to be Polish?"

"Why indeed?" Hamish said, deep in thought. "There were a lot of Polish folk working in Scotland afore the UK left the European Union."

"Many Polish people were allowed to remain," Anka said, then added with a laugh, "some of us even married Scotsmen! So a Pole would attract less attention than a Russian."

"Aye, that would help if he wanted to keep a low profile," Hamish agreed, explaining a little more about Hibbert's blackmail activities. "Now, as far as we know, none o' the blackmail victims knew about each other. None o' them knew that we had all those things in the envelopes."

"Aye," Davey agreed and, being careful not to name names, he went on, "the couple in the photos didn't know about the letters, the farmer wi' the receipt didn't know about the earrings, and so forth…"

"So who would know to search my police station for this?" Hamish asked, tapping the spreadsheet. "Mackay knew we had the letters. I'm thinking he's our man—him and Bogdan."

"There's more, Hamish," Dick said, examining the names at the bottom of the sheet. "These names—they're anagrams. Rearrange the letters and you get three other names...Ralbi is Blair; Serdonna is Anderson; Vadoit is Daviot."

"What?" Davey almost choked on a mouthful of wuzetka. "How did they get mixed up in this?"

"Anagrams, you say?" Hamish's hazel eyes flashed towards Dick. "They're the sort o' thing you might find in a newspaper crossword, aren't they, Dick?"

"Aye, they're fairly common in crosswords."

"Mackay was doing the *Scotsman* crossword when we chatted wi' him," said Hamish, getting to his feet. "He's our man, Davey, but we need to check in wi' Jimmy afore we nail him. We need to know why three senior police officers have their names at the bottom o' a murderer's coded list o' payments."

On their short walk to the hospital, Hamish phoned Peter Abraham's surgery for an update. The nurse answered.

"We tried to put one of those plastic funnel collars on Sonsie," she explained, "to stop her in case she tried to bite her stitches. We managed it while she was still dopey from the anaesthetic, but she woke up looking like an angry daffodil and ripped it off. Now she won't let us near her."

"Sounds like she's on the mend," Hamish said. "What about Lugs?"

"There's no change, really, Hamish. We'll just have to wait."

He thanked her, then hung up with a heavy sigh and trudged up the stairs outside the hospital. Detective

Chief Inspector Jimmy Anderson was on the phone when Hamish and Davey walked into his room. His iPad was on the bed beside him along with a couple of newspapers and a notepad. He motioned them to wait while he finished his call.

"Blair is organising a press conference to declare Hannah Thomson died from natural causes," he said, talking quickly, his mind clearly agile even if the rest of him was temporarily immobile. "He's saying it's nothing to do wi' the Hibbert murder, even though his team went door-to-door and discovered that two men may have knocked on her front door the day she died. There are no reliable descriptions. He says they were probably either travelling salesmen or Jehovah's Witnesses."

"We're no' really used to seeing either o' those in Lochdubh," Hamish said, shaking his head. "I bet I can get a description if I talk to the right folk."

"That would be useful," said Jimmy. "After his wee starring role wi' the press, Blair has called a strategy meeting for his lot in the pub in Lochdubh."

"Sounds like an excuse for a Friday-afternoon booze-up to me," Hamish replied. "Have you got anything for us on that boat up on The Corloch?"

"Aye, it belongs to someone who keeps it there from time to time for the fishing," Jimmy said. "His name's Morgan Mackay."

Hamish and Davey exchanged a glance.

"Bogdan and Mackay could easily lug a body around," said Davey, "and take it out in a boat to dump it."

"But if the water level was lower than they were used to," Hamish went on, "they could have torn open the bottom of the boat on rocks they would normally have glided over, panicked and ended up dumping the body in shallower water than they intended."

"Do you know Morgan Mackay?" Davey asked Jimmy.

"Well...I...what makes you think..." Jimmy stumbled over his words, looking down at the papers on his bed, seeming a little lost for words, evading the question.

"Come on, Jimmy," Hamish said, a sharp impatience in his voice. "Why can you no' tell us if you know him?"

"Because, Sergeant Macbeth, he was sworn to secrecy," came the voice of Superintendent Daviot. He stood in the doorway wearing a black, zip-neck top that had the words "POLICE" in small letters halfway up each sleeve and his star-and-crown rank badges on black epaulettes clinging to his shoulders. It looked to Hamish like a sports shirt and was entirely at odds with Daviot's elaborate uniform cap, its peak resplendent with two crescents of silver oak leaves. "Why are you asking DCI Anderson about Morgan Mackay, and what are you two doing here?"

"We're asking because it's...um...pertinent to our enquiries..." Hamish said, glancing at Davey and recalling his last meeting with Daviot, "...sir."

Daviot removed his cap and seated himself in the chair beside Jimmy's bed.

"I thought I would pay DCI Anderson a visit," Daviot said, looking sternly at Hamish, "to see how he was doing. I suppose you've been keeping him up to date with the Hibbert case. That's not exactly what we agreed, Macbeth, is it?"

"Well, we didn't agree that I wouldn't do that either, you know..." Hamish said with a shrug.

"I see," Daviot said, pursing his lips with annoyance. "Now tell me why you are asking about Mackay."

"Actually we're looking into..." Hamish began, but he was caught short by Davey.

"Hamish, we might save a lot of time if we come clean here," he said. "We believe that Kate Hibbert had a spreadsheet in her possession that may have belonged to Mackay."

"Aye," Hamish agreed, handing the spreadsheet to Daviot and Jimmy. "We think she was blackmailing him. The numbers are clearly a code but there are three anagram names at the bottom o' this sheet—Blair, Anderson and Daviot."

"Hibbert couldn't have known what she was looking at," Daviot muttered, studying the numbers.

"No," said Jimmy, "and neither do I. What's this all about?"

"Hibbert must have found it hidden somewhere in Mackay's house," Hamish said, tactfully avoiding mentioning that was her modus operandi with her other victims. "If it was hidden, she'd have reckoned it was important, so she stole it and was trying to extort money out of him for its return."

"We think the number code is a list of payments,"

Davey said. "What we don't know is why your names are on there."

"I hope you're not suggesting that we've been receiving illicit payments!" Daviot snapped.

"Not at all, sir," Hamish assured him, although it had been the first thought that had popped into his head, "but we want to avoid any embarrassment for you when we go after Mackay. This," he added, taking back the spreadsheet, "will be evidence in our case against him."

"I'm as mystified as you are about why Mackay has our names on there," Daviot said, shaking his head, "but we *do* know who he is."

"He was manager o' the Strathbane Savings Bank," said Jimmy. "About thirty years ago one o' the bank staff, a young guy called Carter, went missing. A large amount o' money also went missing."

"Over two hundred thousand pounds as I recall." Daviot took over the story. "I was the senior investigating officer on the case. DCI Anderson and Blair were both sergeants on my team."

"We never found any trace o' Carter or the money. We had a few leads we were following," said Jimmy, "but then we were told to wind up the investigation and get on wi' other things."

"Wind it up?" said Hamish, looking puzzled. "Why? Who told you to do that?"

"The order came from on high," Daviot said, shifting uncomfortably in his chair. "Two men flew in from London and turned up in our office with the Chief Constable.

They took all our files and we were ordered not to talk about the case."

"From London?" Davey asked, frowning. "Who were they?"

"The cloak-and-dagger mob," said Jimmy. "MI5. The Chief Constable waved a copy o' the Official Secrets Act under our noses and threatened us wi' loss o' rank, loss o' our pensions and even the jail if we didn't keep our traps shut. The secret boys said it was a 'matter of national security.' "

"That being the case," Daviot said, holding out his hand for the return of the spreadsheet, "the document you have must now be passed on to the security services. They will want to deal with Mackay and his accomplice."

"No!" said Hamish bluntly. "That's no' the way this is going to work. Those two are responsible for the deaths o' two women on my patch. They raided my station, they damn near killed my cat and they've left Lugs at death's door because they were defending my home. I'm hanging on to this piece of paper, and I'm going after Mackay and his sidekick."

"You'll do no such thing!" Daviot blustered. "You will *not* turn this investigation into some kind of personal vendetta! Sergeant Macbeth, I am ordering you to—"

"Loss o' rank? Loss o' pension?" said Hamish, holding up the folded spreadsheet. "This could go badly for you if anyone finds out about this conversation, or if anyone finds out that your names are on here, for whatever reason. We do this my way, and I'll make sure you're kept out o' it."

Daviot looked at Jimmy. Jimmy nodded and grunted.

"Very well," said Daviot, stiffly. "Just keep us informed."

Back in Lochdubh, Hamish and Davey exchanged the Jaguar for the Land Rover and were heading for Morgan Mackay's house in Hurdy's Glen when a silver car fell in behind them. Hamish wrinkled his brow, studying the car in the rearview mirror.

"He's a bit close, is he no'?" he said, and Davey turned round to look just as concealed blue lights behind the car's radiator grille began to flash. Hamish muttered a curse under his breath and slowed to a halt at the side of the road.

"Who pulls over a police car?" Davey wondered.

"Only one numpty I can think o'!" snarled Hamish, stepping out of the Land Rover. "Blair!"

He looked through the windscreen to the car's driver. The detective behind the wheel gave him an apologetic shrug.

"Macbeth!" roared Blair, struggling out of the rear seat to heave his bulky frame onto the road.

"What do you want?" asked Hamish.

"Where have you been? Why have you no' been doing what I told you?" Blair demanded, strutting towards Hamish.

"I have," said Hamish, "and where I've been is none o' your business."

"None of my...?" Blair's jowly face flushed red and quivered with anger. "As long as I'm assigned to this God-forsaken hellhole, *everything* you do is my business! You need to learn your place in this..."

As Blair continued his rant, Hamish plucked his phone from his pocket and pressed a contact speed-dial number.

"...and another thing!" Blair paused for breath when he saw what Hamish was doing. "Put that away when I'm talking to you! You need to show some respect. You can start by calling me 'sir'! Need I remind you that I am a chief inspector? That's two full ranks above you!"

"Aye, well, I'm under orders from Superintendent Daviot," Hamish said, then spoke quickly into the phone. "Blair's holding me up." There was a short pause before he handed the phone to Blair. "The boss would like a word wi' you. Mind you call him 'sir' now—he's one full rank above you..."

Blair spluttered and stammered into the phone in response to the lambasting Hamish could hear from Daviot. After only a few seconds, he slapped the phone into Hamish's outstretched hand.

"I warned you to stay out o' my way," Hamish snarled. "I'll no' tell you again."

"You can't talk to me like..." Blair began, but then saw the fire in Hamish's eyes and backed away. "You've no' heard the last o' this! I've got a strategy meeting to get to but—"

"Bugger off," Hamish growled, and climbed back into the Land Rover.

"What did you tell him?" asked Davey once they were on their way again.

"Nothing," said Hamish. "I'll bet he's been lurking

around waiting to spot us so that he could pump us for information before he goes back to his 'strategy meeting' and claims credit for anything we might have discovered in order to look like a big man in front o' his team."

"Sounds a bit desperate."

"Aye, well, that's Blair for you."

"So what's our plan for Mackay and Bogdan?"

"We go up to the house and arrest them."

"It might not be that simple, Hamish. I could see us slapping the cuffs on Mackay easy enough, but I reckon Bogdan will put up a bit of a fight."

"That's what I'm counting on," Hamish said, looking over at Davey. "Mackay's too soft to have got the better o' Lugs and Sonsie. Bogdan's the one that gave Lugs a kicking."

"Right," said Davey, nodding slowly, "then he's got it coming to him."

The Land Rover rattled up the rougher stretch of the track in Hurdy's Glen, then settled into the smoother, steady climb towards Mackay's house. Hamish pulled up at the bottom of the drive.

"It all looks quiet," Davey said.

"It will ay look quiet up here," Hamish pointed out. "There's no car outside, though. It was a grey thing, was it no'?"

"Aye," said Davey, "a big BMW X6. They'd need four-wheel drive to get up the track."

"They would," Hamish agreed, "but wi' a powerful car like that they could have drifted down the easy stretch o' track, abducted Hibbert and made their way back up here without Gregor Mackenzie having seen or heard them."

"So they kept her here," Davey said, popping a stick of gum in his mouth and scanning the house, his eyes searching every window. "I can't see anyone watching us."

"Good," said Hamish. "You make your way round the back. I'll go in the front."

They slipped quietly out of the car, Hamish waiting a few seconds to give Davey a chance to circle round behind the garage before walking swiftly up the drive to the front door. He tried the handle and the door opened easily. Treading carefully and moving silently, he checked the front room to find only the *Monarch of the Glen* staring back at him. The smaller study on the other side of the hall was also empty. He crept forward to the dining room where he found Davey, who had entered from a door leading to the kitchen. Davey shook his head. He had found no one. They made their way upstairs but the bedrooms and the bathroom were equally empty.

"Nobody's home," said Davey.

"Let's check the outbuildings and the garage," Hamish said, loping downstairs, abandoning any attempts at stealth.

The kitchen had a back door out to the garden, which was the door Davey had used, and another leading directly to the garage. Davey tried the handle of the second door and pushed it open.

Morgan Mackay sat slumped against the opposite wall, the handle of a large knife protruding from his belly and a vast, glistening pool of dark red blood spreading off to his left, across the concrete floor almost to the front doors. His face was deathly pale. He smiled weakly at them.

"I wondered if it would be you," he said softly.

Davey grabbed towels from the kitchen and rushed towards Mackay.

"We need to put pressure on the wound," he said. "We have to stop the bleeding and ..."

"It's too late for all that," Mackay said, managing to raise his right arm enough to brush Davey's hands aside. "It's stopped hurting now. Don't touch me. Don't make the pain start again."

"Was this Bogdan?" Hamish asked, taking Davey's place at Mackay's side.

"If that's his real name." Mackay nodded, his voice little more than a whisper.

"Why?" asked Davey. "Why did he do this?"

"You have my spreadsheet," Mackay said. "That has kept me alive for years. Once he knew that you had it, the game was up, and I could be ... eliminated."

"What does the spreadsheet mean?" Hamish asked. "The number code—what's it all about?"

"Ah, the code." Mackay smiled again. "I devised my own code. The entries show names, payments and dates."

"Who were the payments to?" Hamish asked. "What were they for?"

"Information," Mackay explained. "We had people in various places—the nuclear facility at Dounreay, the military range at Cape Wrath, the submarine base at Faslane, even at the Holy Loch when the Americans had their nuclear submarine base there. We had quite a network."

"You were spying?" Davey said, astounded. "For the Russians? Why would you do that?"

"Because I have the courage of my convictions, my boy," Mackay said, his voice momentarily gaining strength. "There were those of us who believed we were doing the right thing in helping the Soviets, as they were then, to keep up with the West. We were helping to maintain the balance of power, helping to prevent the war that would destroy the planet."

"What has this got to do with the disappearance of Carter from your bank?" Hamish asked.

"He found out I was passing money through the bank." Mackay's eyelids closed. "The Soviets killed him and I made it look like he ran off with a small fortune. The three detectives started to get close to the truth but MI5 shut them down. They suspected I was the paymaster for a network and thought they could use me to track the others down. The Soviets discovered MI5 were on to me and decided I was no longer any use to them."

"I'm guessing you let your Russian friends know about the spreadsheet to make sure they wouldn't do to you what they did to Carter," Hamish said.

"I gave a copy of the spreadsheet to a friend in Glasgow for safekeeping." Mackay opened his eyes again and sucked in a gulp of air. "I put the list in code so that if he looked at it, he wouldn't know what it was. He was to hand it to the security services if anything happened to me. They'd have been able to work out my code."

"What about the anagrams?" Davey asked. "Why were Blair, Anderson and Daviot on there?"

"Kept a note of their names..." Mackay let out a wheezing breath and his chin dropped onto his chest. "When they were getting close, thought I could pay them, buy them off...but...the case was dropped."

"Why is all this so important now? Why are the Russians bothered about a thirty-year-old list?" said Davey.

"Because..." Mackay mumbled, "the network still... exists..."

"Mackay!" Hamish called, forcefully lifting the man's head to look him in the face. "Where is Bogdan? Where has he gone?"

But Morgan Mackay was dead.

"It must have taken him a good while to die," Davey said, staring down at the body and the slick of blood. "If Bogdan wanted him dead, why do it like this?"

"This is his warning to others," Hamish said solemnly, standing by Davey's side. "Anyone who crosses him will suffer a slow, painful death."

"What do we do now?" Davey asked.

"We need to call this in," said Hamish, "but no' in the usual way. We'll phone Daviot. He'll get people up here and he'll be able to put out an alert for Bogdan at ports and airports. He can also get every patrol car between here and the English border looking out for that BMW."

Hamish had his phone in his hand, about to call Daviot, when it started to ring. It was Peter Abraham.

"Hamish," he said, "I think you should get down to the surgery as soon as you can. Lugs..."

"I'll be right there," Hamish said, cutting Peter off and making for the door. "Davey, you bide here and call Daviot!"

He sped down the track to the main road where he flicked the switch to turn on the Land Rover's blue lights. It was a short drive to Peter's surgery but he wasn't going to let anyone slow him up. He needed to be there with Lugs. Peter was waiting when he burst through the surgery door.

"How's Lugs?" he said. "Is he..."

"Take a look," said Peter, waving Hamish towards a table where Lugs lay on a blanket.

"Lugs, my poor boy," Hamish said, crouching by the table. At the sound of his voice, the dog's eyes flicked open, his tail began beating a tattoo on the table and he stretched his neck, trying to reach far enough forward to lick Hamish's face. His eyes were full of light and life and he was overjoyed to see Hamish. "Lugs!" Hamish cried. "You're all right!"

"It will be a few weeks before he's bouncing around again like he used to," Peter said, watching Hamish gently hug the dog, "and I want to keep him here for a few more days, but I think he's out of the woods now, Hamish."

"Peter, I can't thank you enough," Hamish said, shaking the vet's hand.

"Lugs did all the hard work." Peter grinned. "We just did our jobs."

"Aye, well now I'm going to do mine," Hamish said, "and find the man who did this."

Hamish made his way back to the station and sat monitoring the radio, listening for any reports of the BMW being sighted. At the same time, he called every other cop he knew, passing on a description of Bogdan and urging them to let him know if they spotted the Russian or his car. Then he thought of the one person he knew who was always watching the road. On a fine day like this, Dougie Tennant would be out on his forecourt, helping tourists fill their tanks, listening to Biffy Clyro on his headphones and keeping an eye on the traffic. Dougie was car-mad and hated the thought of missing anything unusual or exotic passing by.

"Dougie," Hamish said when the mechanic eventually tore himself away from his music to answer the phone. "I need you to keep an eye out for a grey BMW X6 wi' a male driver. Let me know straight away if one comes in for fuel or drives by the garage."

"Funny you should ask," Dougie said. "One flew by here no' so long ago. Must have been doing over ninety. Near took the front off a wee Peugeot that was trying to pull out onto the road."

"Thanks, Dougie!" Hamish yelled, dashing outside to the Land Rover.

He had the blue lights on, the siren wailing and was racing along the shore road through Lochdubh when he got Davey on the phone.

"Davey, get your running legs on and get down the track to the main road!" he yelled above the howl of the engine. "I'll meet you there!"

"Hamish, nobody else has got here yet," Davey objected. "I can't abandon a crime scene."

"Of course you can!" Hamish shouted. "Daviot will have folk there soon enough, and Mackay's no' going anywhere, is he? I need you wi' me!"

Davey was waiting, breathless and sweating, when Hamish slithered to a halt at Hurdy's Glen. He heaved himself into the Land Rover and Hamish sped off.

"Get on the radio, Davey," Hamish instructed him. "Sounds like Bogdan was heading north, so he's no' likely to turn down the road to Lairg, but let's get a car on that road anyway. We need a car up by Durness on the north coast road, too, and…" Hamish's phone rang. He handed it to Davey so that he could concentrate on the road. Davey switched on the phone's speaker so they could both listen.

"Is that Sergeant Hamish?" came a child's voice.

"No, this is Detective Davey," Davey answered, recognising the voice of Billy Stuart.

"It's Billy here," said Billy.

"And John Hogg," came John's voice in the background.

"Lads, we're a bit busy right now," said Davey. "What's this about?"

"Well, we went back to our house because my mum had our dinner ready," said Billy.

"Only she calls it 'lunch' because she's English," added John.

"And when we came back to catch spiders for Mrs. Stephenson, she didn't answer the door," Billy explained.

"Maybe she was just out," said Davey, about to cut them off.

"No, no, she was in there all right," John said, "and she had someone else in there wi' her."

"Aye, and round the back o' the house there's a big grey BMW," Billy added. "So she's no' keeping her part o' the bargain and..."

"Stay away from the house, boys!" Davey shouted, casting an anxious glance towards Hamish. "Go straight home right now, you hear? Go home! We'll be there soon!"

"What the hell is he doing in an auld woman's house in Cromish?" Hamish muttered.

"Who knows?" said Davey. "But we do know what he's capable of doing to women. Step on it, Hamish!"

CHAPTER TEN

When our actions do not,
Our fears do make us traitors.
William Shakespeare, *Macbeth*

Apart from the distant figure of Ian Duncan labouring on the boat propped up on the dock, Cromish was as still and silent as its graveyard when Hamish's Land Rover rolled quietly to a halt just short of Moira Stephenson's cottage.

"The car's out o' sight o' the cottage here," Hamish said. "Let's check the place out nice and quietly—we don't want to panic him if he's holding her hostage."

"Okay," Davey agreed. "How do you want to play this?"

"Same as the Mackay place," said Hamish, picking up his mobile phone. "You go round the back, I'll take the front. Set your phone to silent alert, so that it will vibrate in your pocket. That way if either of us spots anything and wants the other to back off, we might be able to do it without even letting him know we're here."

"Right," said Davey, tapping at his phone. "Give me thirty seconds to get across the corner of that field and round the back of the house."

Once Davey had gone, Hamish waited for half a minute, then crept up to the front of the house, hugging a hedge that ran up the side of the front path, his eyes constantly scanning the windows of the cottage for any sign of movement. He flattened himself against the front wall of the cottage and risked a quick peek in through the window. The room was clear. Two strides took him to the front door which, like the front door of Mackay's house, opened easily when he turned the handle. Pushing the door slowly open, he looked into the small hall. He could see no one.

"Hamish!" Davey yelled from the rear of the house. Hamish dashed down the hall into the kitchen, where Moira Stephenson sat on a kitchen chair, sucking in long gulps of air. Round her neck was a tea towel that had been used to gag her, but loosened by Davey, who was now working on the tape used to fasten her wrists and ankles to the wooden chair. She looked pale and frightened, but she was alive.

"His car's still out the back of the house," Davey reported. "Wherever he's gone, he went on foot."

"Mrs. Stephenson," Hamish said, crouching beside the old lady. "Are you all right? Did he hurt you?"

"I'll be fine," she said, still breathing heavily. "I was so scared...I thought I'd be left here for days..."

"Davey, put the kettle on," Hamish said, using his

pocket knife to cut the tape at Mrs. Stephenson's ankles. "You've had a real shock, Mrs. Stephenson. We'll get you an ambulance."

"It's bad enough having your police car outside," she tutted. "An ambulance would only give folk even more to gossip about, and I'll no' have them saying I'm so frail I needed an ambulance."

"That's the spirit," said Davey. "We'll let everyone know that you stood up for yourself against that man."

"Aye, well, when he drove up the side o' the house and dumped his car in my back garden, I went out to tell him to get lost," the old lady explained. "I was right shocked at the sight o' him. He had on a white T-shirt and there were awful bad, deep scratches across his face and his neck, like he'd been attacked by a tiger. One o' his trouser legs was cut off at the knee so he could bandage wounds there, too, but there was blood seeping through the bandages.

"Before I could say a word, he clapped his hand over my mouth and twisted my arm up my back. He had the strength o' the devil in him. My feet hardly touched the ground afore he dragged me inside and had one o' my very own kitchen knives under my chin. Said he would cut my throat if I made a sound."

The old lady paused, her bottom lip trembling.

"He got me to clean up the wound on his leg—there were teeth marks and a big chunk o' flesh missing—then he strapped me in this chair."

"Did he give you any idea where he might be going?" Hamish asked.

"When he left, he took the path out the back that goes down to the village," she said. "He was on his phone awhile afore he went."

"What was he talking about?" Davey asked.

"I've no idea," replied the old lady, "it was all in foreign. Then he put the knife to my throat again afore he gagged me. He said the only reason I was still alive was because I minded him o' his granny!" Mrs. Stephenson paused, took a deep breath, and burst into tears.

"Is there someone we can call to come and be with you?" Hamish said, gently.

"What's going on?" Billy Stuart appeared at the back door with John Hogg in tow.

"Billy, do you know how to make a cup of tea?" asked Davey.

"Aye," Billy replied.

"Good," said Davey. "Mrs. Stephenson has had a bad shock. Make her some hot, sweet tea."

"Maybe she should have a biscuit, too," said John, picking up a tin of shortbread with a poor version of *The Monarch of the Glen* on the lid.

"The boys will look after me," Mrs. Stephenson said, dabbing her eyes with a tissue. "Then I can phone a friend in the village. You two must go, Sergeant Macbeth. You'll catch him, won't you? You'll get him…"

"We'll get him all right," said Hamish, standing to leave.

They cruised the road into the village, studying every window of every cottage, every hedgerow and garden shed for any sign of anything out of the ordinary. At the dock, they questioned Ian Duncan, but he hadn't seen any trace of the man they described. Turning right at the harbour, they headed inland. Beyond the last cottage, the road became no more than a farm track that ran up to a viewpoint from where you could see down across Cromish Bay, with a glimpse of the Atlantic beyond, as well as east over a seemingly endless mountain landscape. A young couple wearing shorts and hiking boots were sitting eating sandwiches at the viewpoint's picnic table. The man flagged down the police car.

"There's a maniac up there on the Sandwood Bay trail!" he said angrily, pointing to where the track narrowed to a path. "He looked in a bit of a state but when we asked him if he was all right, he pulled a knife on us!"

"Are you both okay?" asked Davey.

"Aye, we kept well away from him," the man replied.

"How long ago?" Hamish demanded.

"About an hour, I suppose," said the man.

Hamish gunned the engine and the Land Rover shot forward, lurching onto the path. Ahead of them was a wooden fence with a stile for hikers to climb over. Hamish accelerated towards the fence.

"Hamish, is there a gate we . . . ?" Davey said, gripping the edges of his seat. "Hamish, there isn't a gate . . ."

The Land Rover smashed through the fence with a boom that reverberated through the bodywork and a clattering crack of splintering wood. Davey reached out of his window to drag some debris off the windscreen, including an official notice that said, "Walkers Welcome."

"No cars allowed at Sandwood," Hamish shouted above the roar of the engine.

"What's at Sandwood Bay?" Davey yelled, hanging on to a grab handle above his door to steady himself against the jolting and lurching of the car.

"The most beautiful beach you've ever seen," Hamish called, raising his voice above the hammer and crash of the car's suspension. "No' many people, just a mile o' sand. He must be getting picked up by boat."

The car bounced off boulders and at one point almost turned over, the wheels on Hamish's side slithering into a ditch, but somehow he kept it thundering forward at breakneck speed until the path approached an array of sand dunes. He aimed the car at a gap between two of the tallest dunes and the car shot into the gully of soft sand, twisting right and left until the dunes opened out, a vista of sand and sea filling the windscreen. They immediately found themselves airborne, the engine racing with all four wheels clear of the ground, and the car plunged down a drop of several feet, hitting the beach with such force that the front suspension collapsed. They struggled forward for a few yards before the Land Rover shuddered to a halt. Hamish looked across at Davey, who let out a long breath of relief.

The car had ended up pointing along the beach, rather than towards the sea. A small group of walkers, who had been heading for a barefoot paddle in the sea, stood staring at the car. Then Hamish spotted a figure emerging from the dunes a few yards ahead of them, wearing a white T-shirt and one-legged trousers, walking with a pronounced limp.

"There he is!" he cried, leaping out of the car. "Davey, keep those people back!"

Hamish loped along the beach, his long legs closing the distance between himself and Bogdan in just a few seconds. The Russian turned to see Hamish launch himself through the air, cannoning into him, knocking him to the ground. Both men rolled over in the sand and were on their feet again in a heartbeat. Hamish saw the livid red welts and scars running across Bogdan's face from his nose to his left ear, where Sonsie had slashed him with her claws. He pushed himself forward, landing a vicious punch in the middle of the mess Sonsie had made. The Russian staggered backwards and fell over, but rolled onto his feet again before Hamish could reach him. The largest of Mrs. Stephenson's kitchen knives was in his hand. He waved it left and right, advancing towards Hamish, his right leg dragging slightly, its fresh dressing already oozing blood. Hamish jerked his upper body away from the knife, swinging his left boot to plant a bone-crunching kick on the wound Lugs had made. Bogdan screeched with pain, dropping onto his right knee, although he was upright and ready again in the instant that it took Hamish to regain his balance.

Hamish could hear only their laboured breathing over the constant wash of the waves breaking on the beach. Then came a sharp crack. Bogdan paused, an expression of utter surprise on his face, and he looked down to see a red stain spreading across his chest. Then there was a second crack and a gout of blood erupted from the side of his head.

Hamish threw himself to the sand, turning to look down towards the sea where a speedboat was approaching the beach, a gunman with a sniper's rifle lying prone on the deck. He flinched as a third shot kicked up a spout of sand a couple of feet in front of him. The sniper was joined by another man with a machine gun and Hamish scrambled to his feet, pounding towards the Land Rover as fast as he could.

He could hear the crackle of automatic fire and see more sand fountains spurting to his right. Diving behind the disabled Land Rover, he crouched, curling himself up as small as he could. Hamish had never regretted being tall. He had always been pleased with himself for being the tallest in his class at school and was proud to be the tallest recruit in his year at the police training college, but now he was desperately wishing himself smaller. He wanted to shrink himself so that he could curl up behind the engine to put as much protective metal between him and the chattering machine gun as possible.

Bullets whipped up the sand in front of the Land Rover and slammed into the bodywork, tearing through metal and shattering glass. Some passed straight through the car to bury themselves in the dunes behind him. The noise was deafening and he found himself holding his breath, praying it would all stop. And then it did. The din of the barrage ended, there came the deep throb of a marine diesel engine and Hamish risked a peek out from behind the car. The speedboat had wheeled round and was surging out to sea trailing a foaming white wake.

"Hamish!" Davey's voice came from a low mound of sand, behind which he had shepherded the walkers. "Get over here! Get away from the car—it's on fire!"

Hamish glanced over his shoulder to see black smoke billowing from the Land Rover's front widows, accompanied by a lick of orange flame. He checked that the boat was really gone, then sprinted over to take cover with Davey. He watched the flames leap higher, at any moment expecting the Land Rover to blow itself to bits. Yet there was no thunderous explosion, no shower of flaming debris and shrapnel, just a gradual increase in the height and strength of the flames until the whole car was engulfed, slowly turning into a charred black skeleton, disfigured and deformed by the heat of the blaze. At first, Hamish watched the car burn with an anger as intense as the inferno itself, but once the level of adrenalin pumping through his system began to subside, he was overcome with a feeling of sadness. Losing his old car was a bit like losing an old friend.

For a while no one spoke, Hamish, Davey and the walkers all lying behind the hump of sand, stunned. Then Davey broke the silence, his voice full of bewilderment: "They shot him…They shot their own man. Why did they kill him?"

"He'd become a liability," said Hamish. "They couldn't get him off the beach here and get away clean with us around and they didn't want us taking him prisoner, so they murdered him. Dead men tell no tales, after all."

"Ruthless," Davey mumbled, slowly sliding a comforting stick of gum into his mouth. "Absolutely ruthless."

"Aye," said Hamish, hauling himself to his feet and pulling his phone from his pocket, "but they're no' our problem any more, Davey. You talk to these people and make sure they stay around. We'll need statements from them. Somebody has to explain to the outside world what happened here, and I reckon Daviot is just the man."

Hamish and Davey spent the rest of the day taking statements, bringing officers arriving from Strathbane up to speed with what had happened and waiting for Blair and Daviot to arrive. Blair looked bewildered and began to berate Hamish for not having kept him properly informed, but Daviot cut him short, ordering him off the beach and instructing him to return to Lochdubh to supervise the crime scene in Hurdy's Glen. Daviot then strolled along the beach with Hamish and Davey, allowing gentle trickles of receding waves to lap at the soles of his walking boots.

They paused once they were out of earshot of the other officers and the forensics team, all of whom had hiked with their gear from the viewpoint and were now methodically photographing and cataloguing everything they could find around the burned-out Land Rover and Bogdan's body. A metal detector was being used to find bullets in the sand.

"They'll find more than they bargained for wi' that thing," Hamish said. "There's countless shipwrecks under the sand here. Somewhere on the beach there's even what's left o' a Spitfire that crashed in 1941."

"I'm sure they will be thorough and professional," said Daviot, gazing south towards a distant finger of rock, a 200-foot tall sandstone sea stack known as "The Shepherd." "I wanted to remind you both that some of what you discovered during this investigation may still be highly sensitive. You are both bound by the Official Secrets Act. The document you discovered that led to Hibbert's murder and today's..."—he looked back along the beach to where smoke was still rising from the Land Rover—"...carnage must not be discussed with anyone."

"Would that be the document with your name at the bottom, sir?" Davey asked.

"Don't be flippant, Constable," said Daviot, and he turned to Hamish. "That's a bad habit he's picked up from you, Macbeth."

"We'll still have to put something in our reports," Hamish pointed out.

"Your reports will come directly to me," Daviot instructed them. "The official version of events is to be that Hibbert was blackmailing Mackay over the murder of Carter and the theft of the money from the bank. We are saying he brought in Bogdan to get rid of her."

"It's no' that far from the truth." Hamish nodded. "All the best lies ay need a wee bit o' truth in them."

"DCI Anderson has already agreed to this," Daviot continued, "and DCI Blair knows nothing about the spreadsheet. That's the way I want it to stay."

"Fair enough," said Hamish, and they strolled back towards the throng of activity further up the beach.

The following day, Hamish and Davey collaborated on their reports, taking special care to make no mention of the Mackenzies' receipt, the Duncans' photographs, Jean Simpson's letters or Hannah Thomson's jewellery. That evening, the weather remained pleasantly warm and the chimney above the police station in Lochdubh was the only one in the village with a faint trace of smoke drifting up into the sky. Hamish had decided to sneak Hannah's earrings back into her cottage at the earliest opportunity. They would be found by her family in a drawer or on a shelf when they came to sort through her belongings. The other blackmail items all went up in smoke. He looked up from the grate when he heard Davey calling to him.

"Hamish! It's time we were going!" He appeared in the doorway dressed in an electric blue suit which, like the shirt he had worn a few days earlier, seemed to Hamish like it was several sizes too small. Although it was clearly new, it looked like he had outgrown it years ago. The jacket was too short and the trousers too tight. It reminded Hamish of the local fisherman, Archie Maclean, whose wife had regularly boiled all of his clothes in an old copper, shrinking everything, even his jackets. Archie had finally bought her a brand-new washing machine and now he chose to wear everything big and baggy. Most of Archie's clothes, Hamish mused, might better agree with Davey.

"That's your best suit, is it?" Davey said, folding his arms and leaning on the doorpost.

"It's timeless," Hamish said, standing up from the grate, tugging the lapels and sleeves of his jacket, unwilling to admit that, a bit like Lochdubh's Italian restaurant, it wasn't just his best suit—it was his only suit. "A classic."

"An antique, more like." Davey grinned. "You're looking good, though, Macbeth! Now let's get out of here. We'll need to spend some time with Lugs before we get to the Tommel Castle for the gourmet night."

"Aye," Hamish said. "Peter told me on the phone that he's been eating well and should be back on his feet in a couple of days."

"Is he okay with sticking to the story about Lugs being hit by a car?"

"Peter's a grand lad. He knows that everyone in the village will be talking about Lugs, but he'll stick to the car accident story."

"What about Sonsie?"

"Sonsie doesn't let anyone close enough to see she's been hurt," Hamish replied with a laugh, "and she's already down on the beach stalking gulls."

By the time they arrived at the Tommel Castle Hotel, a small gathering of guests was congregating in the main bar, enjoying a pre-dinner drink. The television in the office behind the reception desk was showing the evening news, and they immediately spotted a depressingly familiar face. DCI Blair was holding court at another press conference.

"Have you caught The Corloch murderer, Chief Inspector?" asked one reporter.

"Aye, well we have now…er…concluded our investigation and…" Blair began, hesitating uncertainly, stumbling over his words.

"If I may answer that, Chief Inspector," came Daviot's voice, and the camera panned round until he filled the frame. Gone was the plain black police shirt, to be replaced by a crisp white shirt, black tie and black tunic with shining silver buttons and a thin row of medal ribbons above the left breast pocket. Daviot was playing to the cameras, completely eclipsing Blair in his shabby grey suit. "DCI Blair and his team have been an immense help in tackling some of the more mundane chores connected with the murder at The Corloch. They will now be returning to Glasgow with our blessing. We will be releasing a full statement once we have submitted our report to the Procurator Fiscal but I can tell you that, following a sterling effort by a team from Strathbane under my command and valiantly led by one of my top detectives from his hospital bed, we are confident that the perpetrator of the murders at The Corloch and Hurdy's Glen is no longer at large. The general public, and the many tourists visiting Sutherland at this time of year, are not in any danger."

There was a brief moment when the beginning of a discontented grumble could be heard from Blair, but the news report immediately switched to the football results.

"That's put Blair's nose right out of joint," said Davey, chuckling.

"But he's off back to Glasgow, and good riddance to him," Hamish muttered.

"Don't waste another thought on him," Davey said, looking towards the main staircase. "Here come the ladies."

Elspeth and Diane walked towards them. Both were dressed casually in jeans and T-shirts. Each was also carrying a suitcase. Hamish looked at Elspeth, raising an inquisitive eyebrow.

"I'm really, really sorry," Elspeth said, "but I've been told we have to get down to Glasgow tonight to film an interview in the studio. My bosses want it all done so that it can be slotted into a bigger feature on The Corloch murder."

"So," Davey said quietly, "no Gourmet Night."

"Sorry, Davey," Diane apologised, "but I have to go with Elspeth."

"Not to worry!" Priscilla breezed in from the bar with a cocktail in her hand. "Davey can come with me, as my partner. Sorry, Hamish—it's really a couples' thing. You'd be like a fish out of water on your own."

"Well, I can't…" Davey began, turning to Hamish, but Hamish gripped his arm, guiding him towards Priscilla.

"Yes, you can," Hamish assured him. "You go enjoy yourself. Don't worry about me."

Hamish waved Elspeth and Diane off from the car park, then reached for his phone. An evening with Elspeth might have been a bit awkward but maybe Sally Paterson was free that evening. No sooner had he found her number, than she appeared in front of him, wearing a dark blue evening gown.

"That's amazing," he said, grinning broadly. "I was just thinking about you—just about to call you and..."

"Hello, Hamish." She smiled, a bearded man in a dinner suit joining her. "This is Alan, my husband."

"Husband?" Hamish said, sounding more than a little taken aback and looking down at the rings on Sally's left hand.

"I never wear these when I'm working," she explained, realising that he was staring at the rings. "They're too precious, but I thought you must have known I was married. You are a policeman, after all. You find out things like that, don't you?"

"Aye, aye, we do," Hamish agreed, shaking hands with Alan, a pleasant smile locked on his face. Why hadn't he checked her background properly? Had he been so completely dazzled by the glamorous southerner? By rights, he should have been treating her as a suspect. He scolded himself for not having kept his wits about him. "Welcome to Lochdubh."

Having stumbled through an excuse for not attending the event that evening, Hamish took his leave of the Patersons and sauntered up a short flight of stairs to a raised stone terrace that looked out over the loch to the

Two Sisters beyond. The water was still, hardly a ripple disturbing the surface, and the hillsides were bathed in the soft evening light. He sighed with contentment. He was glad not to have to sit with a whole throng of people, fending off questions all night about murder and the mayhem up at Sandwood. Freddy's food was always fantastic, but who needed to be stuck indoors making polite conversation when there was a view like this to soak in? He heard the click of high heels on the terrace behind him and turned to see a blonde-haired woman in a short black dress walking towards him.

"Been stood up, Sergeant Macbeth?" she asked.

"What? Well...aye, I mean..." Hamish cursed himself for having been caught off guard.

"You don't recognise me without the baggy green overalls and the emergency kit, do you?"

"Claire!" he gasped, trying not to seem too incredulous at her transformation. "You look fantastic. If you're here for the gourmet thing, shouldn't you be inside with the others?"

"I've been stood up, too." She sighed.

"Surely not. Wait a minute...Mike?"

"Aye, Mike," she said with a rueful smile. "Some sort of emergency at the hospital. He's had to pull a double shift."

"You know, if we're both now at a loose end, maybe we could..." He turned towards the hotel, where the dining-room doors opened onto the terrace and a fog of over-lively conversation interspersed with bursts of forced laughter billowed out. "On the other hand, it seems a shame to waste such a bonny evening indoors. How would you like," he went on, his voice sparking with enthusiasm, "a nice evening drive through the mountains up to the Kylesku Hotel to sample their fresh seafood?"

"That sounds tempting," she admitted, "but I heard your car's just a tangle of metal up at Sandwood."

"Aye, but we can take that one," he said, pointing to the blue Jaguar. "We can cruise up there wi' the roof down and the wind in our hair and enjoy the scent o' the heather and the pine forests."

"Now that," she said, beaming and slipping her arm through his, "sounds irresistible."

From the dining room, Davey glanced outside to see Hamish and Claire strolling arm-in-arm towards the Jaguar and shook his head in disbelief. How on earth had he managed to pull such a great-looking girl on the spur of the moment, wearing a suit like that?

A week later, Hamish was standing in his kitchen with a mug of coffee in his hand. Another mug stood ready on the counter for Davey, who was bustling around upstairs, packing his things, getting ready to leave. Hamish looked out the kitchen window across his small back garden to the loch. A few fluffy clouds had begun drifting in from the Atlantic over the past couple of days and the light had changed from the stark brightness of the heatwave to a more mellow, softer glow, a sure sign that the dry spell was about to end.

He was wondering, not for the first time, why anyone would want to leave such a truly beautiful place, when Davey strode in, dumping his bag on the kitchen table.

"Well, that's me all packed," he said, gratefully accepting the coffee mug from Hamish. "I'll be sad to leave, you know. I'm getting used to this place, but Edinburgh is calling."

"It will be like a different world down there in the south," said Hamish.

"Aye, but the new job offer with the CID down there is a good move for me," Davey said. "And then there's the rugby. I'll be able to start training with one of the clubs down there before the season starts in September."

"Will you meet up wi' Diane once you're settled in?"

"I've got her number," Davey said with a shrug, "but who knows? Will she want to see me? I don't know. Women are a bit of a mystery, eh, Hamish?"

"You'll not be the first to have thought that."

"Aye, but last Saturday, when Priscilla took me into the big dinner as her partner, I thought it was all happening that night, you know? But her father was everywhere. He never took his eyes off me and at the end of the night I'm sure he was lurking in the shrubbery when we were in the garden. That was weird. And she seemed to quite fancy me but I was sent home here with no more than a peck on the cheek."

"Davey," Hamish said, sagely, gazing out at Sonsie sunning herself on the roof of the chicken shed, "take it from me, you had a narrow escape."

"Can we drop by Peter's surgery on the way past? I'd like to say goodbye to Lugs."

"No problem. You should come up and see us once he's better. You'll ay be welcome. We'll go for a wander in the hills."

"That would be grand," Davey said and they finished their coffee before strolling outside where a brand new, silver Land Rover was parked. It looked bulkier than the old car and its flanks were decorated with a checked pattern of blue-and-yellow "Battenberg" high-visibility markings.

"It doesn't have the character of the old one, does it?" Davey commented.

"That it doesn't," Hamish agreed, looking up the hill opposite the station to where the Ruby Loch lay, out of sight, beyond the ridge. Maybe he'd be back from Strathbane in time to take a hike up there and make sure Dorothy's grave was neat and tidy. "But everything changes, Davey. Life goes on. Nothing bides still for long and we all have to deal wi' change, even here in Lochdubh. When I drop you in Strathbane, I'll be picking up a new officer. Superintendent Daviot himself, no less, wants to introduce us."

They climbed into the cab. It was more comfortable, better equipped and a far more modern design than the old car's interior.

"You must be pleased with this, Hamish," Davey said, running his hand along the dashboard. "Still, it's not as glamorous as a Jaguar convertible, is it? Not quite so attractive for cruising up to Kylesku of an evening." He grinned at Hamish. "So, will you be seeing your wee paramedic again?"

Hamish paused and looked sideways at Davey.

"None of your business," he said, with a hint of a smile.

"I'll take that as a 'yes'!" said Davey, laughing and slapping his thigh. "Drive on, Macbeth!"

Hamish silently eased open the door to Superintendent Daviot's outer office and squinted inside. Helen had her head down, concentrating on the document on her computer screen, clicking away at the keyboard.

"We'll be needing a cup o' tea, Helen," he boomed, enjoying her startled expression and striding across the room to the inner office door. "You won't forget the garibaldis, now, will you?"

"Wait!" she squeaked. "You can't just..."

But Hamish already had the door open and was stepping inside.

"It is customary to wait, Macbeth," Daviot said, without looking up from the papers on his desk, "until I am ready to see you. This is *my* office, after all, not yours."

"Aye, well, I know your time's precious, *sir*," Hamish said, deciding to temper the intrusion by gracing Daviot with the use of the term, "and you know that I'm..."

"Determined not to spend a second longer than necessary outside of your beloved backwater," Daviot said, reaching across to pick up his desk phone. "Don't bother about tea, thank you, Helen. Sergeant Macbeth is in a hurry..." There was a short pause. "Yes, send him in as soon as he arrives."

Daviot tidied the papers on his desk and motioned Hamish to sit.

"Your new constable is a purely temporary assignment," he explained. "He is coming to us on a kind of 'exchange scheme' from another force in order that he can learn more about how policing works in our area."

"And you're sending him to Lochdubh?" Hamish raised his eyebrows. "It's no' exactly your typical—"

"Ah, here he is now," Daviot interrupted him, standing to greet his new guest. "I believe you already know each other."

Hamish stood and turned to see a tall, slim man enter the room wearing a pale blue shirt with a silver star above the left breast pocket and sergeant chevrons on the sleeves pointing upwards to neat cloth shoulder patches bearing the words "Chicago Police."

"Bland!" Hamish eyed the newcomer suspiciously. They had indeed met before, and Bland had been something of a mystery then—part gambling golfer, part playboy financier, but the largest part a complete enigma. He had saved Hamish's life when Blair had pulled a gun on him and Hamish owed him for that. He didn't like being in debt and he wasn't at all sure if he liked Bland. Having checked him out previously, Hamish knew that Bland was certainly not with the Chicago Police Department.

"Oh, come on, Hamish," Bland said with a wide grin,

holding out his hand, "you know me well enough to call me James, and we are the same rank, after all."

"When we last met," Hamish said, "you said that you sometimes wore a uniform, but you didn't tell me you were a police officer."

"I didn't say that I wasn't a police officer," Bland said in his defence, countering Hamish's suspicious look with a friendly smile. "So I'm here to take a look at policing in your neck of the woods."

"Why would you be interested in the odd burglary, missing cats and bicycle thefts?"

"Because we all have something to learn from the experiences of others," Bland said, "and last time I was here, I figured that you would be an interesting guy to work with."

"We agreed to be friends then," Hamish said, "but friends don't keep secrets the way you seem to."

"Well, I'm happy to share a few secrets with you, Hamish, and maybe you can share a few with me."

"What would I know that could possibly interest you?"

"Quite a bit," Bland said, lowering his voice. "I hear, for example, that you had a run-in with a bunch of Russians..."

So that was it, Hamish thought, running his hand through his hair. Just when he thought he could return to a quiet life in his own wee police station, he gets lumbered with some sort of special agent spy catcher. What on earth were they going to think about their new police officer back in Lochdubh?

Auld Mary's Tale (part two)

Hardly had the echoes of Auld Mary's death cry faded from the hills than there came another heavy, more solid, rhythmic sound—the steady plod of horses' hooves. There was a rustling in the trees and the first horse appeared, its rider easing aside the lower hanging branches. He was tall, an imposing figure in the saddle, and dressed differently than the three kilted men on the beach. Although bare legged, he had leather boots and his kilt was worn with a long tunic of leather armour studded with metal. A sword hung from his waist in a scabbard and in his left hand he held the implement he had used to push aside the foliage—a long, slightly curved bow of pale yew.

He was followed by a second rider mounted on a more elegant horse and dressed in a more elaborate style—the laird, Donald Mackay. His dark bonnet was decorated with a colourful feather, his green jacket was trimmed with black lace and his kilt was of the finest quality. His legs were clad in tartan hose and his feet in leather shoes. The polished brass of the intricately detailed protective basket on his sword hilt gleamed in the moonlight. He glowered at the three men by the water, his mood as black as his long hair and beard.

"We heard a scream," he said.

"It was Auld Mary, my lord," John said. "She killed herself."

"Where is my daughter, John Mackay?" growled the laird.

"*On the water, my lord,*" *replied John,* "*wi' the Gordon laddie. He's taken her in Auld Mary's boat.*"

The laird looked out across the water at the two figures in the small boat and turned to the man carrying the bow.

"*Stop him, Lamont!*" *he ordered.*

With one smooth, swift motion, the archer plucked an arrow from the quiver strapped to his back, slotting the notch at its base onto the bowstring as he raised the weapon, drawing back the string.

"*There's a risk, my lord,*" *said Lamont, squinting along the length of the arrow.* "*The boat sways, the girl moves across the target. At this distance, she is in danger.*"

"*As you were, Lamont,*" *sighed the laird, shaking his head and watching the two figures paddling the boat across the loch grow ever smaller.* "*I'll take no chances wi' my own daughter. How did this happen, John Mackay? How is it that I am losing Malcolm Gordon—a valuable hostage? How is it that my own flesh and blood is being whisked away afore my very eyes? How is it that I am losing my daughter?*"

"*The laddie escaped, my lord, and…and took young Eilidh wi' him,*" *John Mackay attempted to explain.*

"*I can see that quite plainly, you idiot! How could he escape? I put you in charge o' the guards. He's been locked away in yon tower room every night for the past five years and never set foot outside it during the day without one o' your guards watching him. Every night when the door was locked the key was brought to my chambers and kept safe there, while one o' your men was posted outside the tower room. So I'm asking you again—how did this happen?"*

"It would seem, my lord, that your daughter took the key and opened the tower room door."

"Eilidh did what?" roared the laird. "Don't be ridiculous, man! Why would she do such a thing?"

"I understand that they have grown close," John said, quietly. "Despite a watch being kept on him, he has somehow beguiled her. They must have decided to run off together."

The laird's gaze turned once again to the boat. His daughter raised an arm to wave. It was no cry for help, no sign of fear or desperation. It was a sad farewell. The laird lifted his hand to return the gesture, his heart sinking, the anger draining from him like sand from an hourglass.

"In truth, I have seen it," he said, his voice almost a whisper. "I have seen that look pass between them. I thought nothing would come of it. My lovely Eilidh…"

Tearing his eyes from the disappearing boat, he pushed back his shoulders and cursed, rekindling his wrath.

"And the guard? Why did he no' stop her?" he barked.

"Someone gave him a flagon of whisky, my lord," said John. "He drank the lot. He could scarce open an eye when we found him."

"And I will close his eyes forever!" thundered the laird. "Who gave him the whisky? And how is it that my daughter was able to wander the corridors over the length of the castle

without being challenged? She must have had help! Have we a traitor in our midst?"

"Traitor..." said Jamie, turning towards John. "That was Auld Mary's final word—and she pointed at you, John. She said this was all your plan!"

"Seize him!" yelled the laird, and the two men standing with John wrestled the sword from his hand. "Why would you do this thing, John Mackay? Why would you do this to me—to your laird?"

John ceased to struggle when the red-bearded man drew a dirk from his belt, pressing the blade against his throat.

"I have known Eilidh since she was but a bairn," John gasped. "I have watched her grow from being a pretty wee lassie to a beautiful young woman—aye, and I have cared for her as though she were my own. Over the years we have held young Malcolm Gordon, a blind man could have seen how deeply they fell in love. Whenever they were anywhere close, they had eyes only for each other. You would neffer have let them be together. Had she stayed, you would have married her off to another laird for your own benefit in power or profit. I couldn't let that happen to the lassie when there was such a real love between her and Malcolm."

"So you guided her past your own guards, having made sure the one at the tower-room door was in his cups," snarled the laird. "You might have thought that Auld Mary would take some o' the blame, maybe confuse things for long enough for you to disappear afore I could work out that you were the one who helped them escape. Yet I have long arms,

John Mackay, and many friends across the country. How could you have hoped to get away? Search him!"

The red-bearded man held John fast while Jamie ran his hands through the folds of his plaid. In an instant, he produced a soft leather pouch, its contents weighing heavy in his hand. Loosening its drawstring, he spilled a handful of silver coins into his palm. Many more clinked and bulged in the pouch.

"Well, well," breathed the laird. "I'll wager that's Gordon silver. You struck a deal wi' them for the return of Malcolm Gordon. You could run far from The Corloch supported by such a handsome payment for your treachery!"

John swung his right foot, kicking the pouch from Jamie's hand, sending it spinning through the air in a shower of silver. Distracted by the sight of such a fortune, the red-bearded man loosened his grasp and John broke free, sprinting along the path at the water's edge. The laird glanced at Lamont and nodded. The archer raised his bow once more, drew the string taut and sent his arrow streaking through the air. With a dull jolt, it slammed into John's back between his shoulder blades and he pitched forward onto the path, his last breath leaving his body as his face hit the ground.

"Gather up those coins. Bring them to my quarters," the laird ordered the two men, "and heed you both what you have witnessed—the death of a traitor."

About the Authors

M. C. Beaton, hailed as the "Queen of Crime" by the *Globe and Mail*, was the author of the *New York Times* and *USA Today* bestselling Agatha Raisin novels—the basis for the hit series on Acorn TV and public television—as well as the Hamish Macbeth series. Born in Scotland, Beaton started her career writing historical romances under several pseudonyms as well as her maiden name, Marion Chesney. Her books have sold more than 22 million copies worldwide.

A long-time friend of M. C. Beaton's, **R. W. Green** has written numerous works of fiction and nonfiction. He lives in Surrey with his family and a black Labrador named Flynn.

Escape to the Scottish Highlands for More Mystery and Murder in Hamish Macbeth's Next Adventure

Available February 2024

Please turn the page for a preview.

CHAPTER ONE

"Every man at the bottom of his heart believes that he is a born detective."

John Buchan, *The Power House*

He watched the headlights sweep through swathes of darkness as he guided the car along the coast road. On this stretch there were no houses for miles around, no streetlights, and tonight the moon wouldn't put in an appearance until well after midnight. To his right the hillside climbed steeply up towards the craggy peaks and chill waters of the many tarns nestled in the crumpled mountain skirts of the 3,000-foot Beinn Bhan. To his left, the inky waters of the Inner Sound stretched five miles to the island of Raasay, where the hills shielded him from the even more distant lights of Portree on the Isle of Skye.

Tonight, the black night was his friend, and the intrusion of his headlights made him feel almost guilty.

Disturbing the still silence of the dark was not his intention, but it was a necessary transgression. He knew a spot where he could pull off the road just before Applecross Sands and enjoy an uninterrupted view of the clear and cloudless night sky. Glancing down at the binoculars and small telescope in the passenger footwell, he smiled, wondering how many stars he would be able to identify among the thousands he would see. With no competition from man-made, terrestrial light sources, the sky would be a blaze of stars.

His eyes flicked back to the route ahead and he gasped in alarm. There was a body lying in the road. He slammed on the brakes, and the tyres bit into the surface for a moment before the frantic drumming of the anti-lock brakes brought the car to a halt. He peered out through the windscreen and could clearly see a man lying a few feet in front, illuminated in his headlight beams. Beyond the fallen man stood another car, a silver Audi, facing him on the narrow, single-track road, its headlights extinguished and the driver's door open wide.

Flinging open his own door, he rushed over to the prostrate figure, oblivious to a momentary flash of bright light from the darkness up on the hill. He crouched beside the body.

"Are you hurt?" he called, looking for injuries. "Can you hear me?"

Then the body moved, the head turning to stare up at him with vaguely familiar, half-remembered eyes.

"What..." he breathed, then heard a footstep behind

him. He turned in time to see a baseball bat chopping through the air towards his head. He tried to dodge it but the blow caught him on the neck and he collapsed on the ground. The powerful figure wielding the bat took another swing and knocked him senseless.

The man who had been on the ground was quickly on his feet. He rolled the barely conscious driver onto a tarpaulin sheet and dragged him out of the way while the batsman jumped into his victim's car and began manoeuvring it to the edge of the road. The headlights picked out a short stretch of boulder-strewn scrub that fell away towards the edge of a cliff. Leaving the engine running, he leapt out, then sprinted over to the Audi and started it up. With his partner directing him, he positioned the Audi with its rear bumper touching that of the other car. They then bundled the injured driver, tracks of blood now smearing his face and neck, back behind the wheel of his car and slammed the door. A moment later, they had the Audi's engine revving before it shot backwards, launching the injured man's car towards the cliff.

The Audi shuddered to a halt at the roadside while its occupants watched the other car lurch and buck, crashing over boulders hidden in the heather, its headlight beams soaring skywards before plunging back to earth. The car slowed, seemingly desperate to cling to the safety of the slope, and stopped when its front wheels dropped over the precipice, grounding its underside. It perched there for a moment before the weight of its engine and the crumbling of the cliff edge sent it somersaulting out of sight.

The two killers remained sitting in the Audi as another man appeared from the hillside, jogging past them and lighting his way with a flashlight pointed at the ground. He approached the cliff edge and peered over. On the rocks below, the car lay upside down like a dying turtle, its doors closed, only its wheels above the water. The submerged headlights spread an eerie yellow glow around the front of the vehicle for a few moments before they finally faded and died. Satisfied that the job was done, he folded the tarpaulin, taking care that no blood spilled onto the road, and slipped it inside a large black bin liner. He then stowed it in the boot of the Audi before climbing into the back seat. Not a word was spoken as the three men sped off into the night.

***

"This will be some kind o' joke, is it no'?" Sergeant Hamish Macbeth stared Superintendent Daviot straight in the eye. "Have you gone completely doolally?"

"Sergeant Macbeth!" Daviot barked. "You will not use that tone with me! As your senior officer, you will address me with the respect my rank demands!"

"Aye, right," Hamish said, his stare never wavering. "So have you gone completely doolally, *sir*?"

Daviot pursed his lips in anger but he had no time to respond before Macbeth charged ahead.

"You can't seriously expect me to police my beat wi' somebody looking like that!" he growled, pointing at the third man in the superintendent's office. The man was wearing a pale blue shirt with a silver star badge above the left breast pocket and sergeant's chevrons on the sleeves. Above the chevrons were neat octagonal shoulder patches with the words "Chicago Police" embracing a representation of the city's seal. "The folk around Lochdubh will never take me seriously ever again."

"Macbeth, I expect you to follow orders!" Daviot fumed. "I expect you to…"

"Maybe I could jump in at this point, sir," said Chicago Police Sergeant James Bland with a calm, pacifying smile. "Hamish, you know I've been to Lochdubh, so I know a little about your people there, and I don't want to make any waves."

Hamish looked at Bland. The man had always been a mystery—part golfing gambler, part stock market investor, part globetrotting playboy, and now part cop. What else was he into? Why was he now standing beside him in front of Daviot's desk? Why was he back in Scotland?

"How about this?" Bland detached the metal star from his shirt. "I'm happy to wear something less conspicuous—maybe one of your Police Scotland black shirts. I'll just pin my star to it to help explain who I am and why I'm here."

"And just why are you here?" Hamish narrowed his eyes, delivering the question like a challenge.

"Officially, Sergeant Bland is here as part of an

exchange scheme, to learn about the policing methods employed in Scotland," Daviot explained, holding out a document with a Police Scotland letterhead. "Our orders are that he is to be afforded every hospitality and that he is to accompany you as you go about your normal day-to-day duties."

"And unofficially?" Hamish asked, having scanned the document.

"Actually, Hamish," Bland said, still smiling, his American drawl far more relaxed than Daviot's nervous, tense delivery, "the unofficial part's pretty official too."

He offered Hamish a document with a UK Government Home Office heading. Hamish read the text, skipping the preamble to focus on what he immediately recognised as the heart of the matter.

"It says here that you're working 'covertly' and I'm to give you 'every possible assistance in pursuit of the investigation.'" Hamish glowered at Bland. "What investigation?"

"You recognise this?" Bland took back the Home Office document, exchanging it for another piece of paper. It was a printout of a computer spreadsheet showing columns of numbers and, at the bottom of the first column, three names—Vadoit, Serdonna, and Ralbi.

"Aye, I mind o' this," Hamish said with a resigned sigh. He now knew exactly why Bland was back in Scotland. "Four people died on account o' this," he added, shaking the spreadsheet. "It damn near got me killed as well!"

"Then you have a vested interest in finding out what it was all about," Bland reasoned.

"I know fine what it was all about!" Hamish could feel another flush of anger spreading from the back of his neck. He could also feel himself being corralled into a situation that was about as far from the simple, peaceful life he enjoyed in Lochdubh as he could get. Feeling the problems of the world outside his Highland haven weighing heavy on his shoulders, he slumped into a chair, running a hand through his fiery red hair and steadying his temper with a heavy sigh. "It was about secrets, traitors, and spies. A coded list o' names and payments—spies paying for secrets from traitors—and the names Daviot, Anderson, and Blair as anagrams at the bottom."

"I hope you're not suggesting that myself, DCI Anderson, or DCI Blair had anything to do with illicit payments!" spluttered Daviot.

"I don't think that's what Hamish meant at all, sir," said Bland, also taking a seat. "We know the three of you were listed as targets should you have gotten too close to the spy ring. We've no reason to suspect anyone ever paid you a nickel."

"Aye," Hamish agreed. "The traitor Morgan Mackay admitted as much just afore he died."

"I see," Daviot said, stiffly lowering himself into his own chair, slightly galled that, with neither invitation nor permission, two men of inferior rank had seated themselves in his presence—in his own office, for goodness sake!

"But others *were* paid, Hamish," Bland went on, "and some of them are still out there."

"What does it matter?" Hamish argued. "It's all ancient history now."

"That's not entirely true," Bland said, retrieving the spreadsheet from Hamish. "You see, we cracked the code. We turned the numbers into names—the whole spy ring—so we know who they are."

"So why don't you just round them up?"

"It's not that simple. We need help tracking some of them down and we need to do it without anyone knowing we're on to them. You know what these people are capable of when they think they've been cornered."

"That I do." Hamish nodded, thinking of Kate Hibbert, a petty blackmailer who had picked on the wrong victim—Morgan Mackay—and had ended up in a watery grave at the bottom of the Corloch. Then the image of Hannah Thomson ghosted into his mind. The old lady had died of a heart attack—literally frightened to death in her own home by Mackay and a Russian thug. Neither of the women had been involved in the so-called spy ring. "Two women were murdered." Hamish let out a sigh. "I suppose they're what you folk would call 'collateral damage.'"

"Not me, Hamish. I'm not one of them. I'm one of the good guys, remember?"

"Spy or spy catcher, you're all playing the same game, and none o' it is any o' my business."

"Protecting the people on your patch—people who

have faith in you—is your business, though, isn't it? We believe something's happening within the spy ring. We need to find out exactly what's going on to make sure that no more innocent people get hurt."

"I've enough to do as it is without all o' this cloak-and-dagger malarkey."

"We all have our jobs to do, Sergeant," Daviot said, sounding irritated and impatient. "We all have orders to follow. You, more than any other officer under my command, have to make sure that you follow your orders with as little fuss as possible. Need I remind you how precarious your position is in Lochdubh?"

"Precarious?" Hamish raised an eyebrow. "It's the police station closures you're on about, is it? We had a deal…"

"I agreed to do my utmost to keep you and your home in Lochdubh off the list," Daviot said, pointing a finger at Hamish, "and I will continue to do so, but don't imagine the pressure from above to cut costs ever diminishes."

"Are you threatening me?" Hamish bristled.

"It's not a threat, Macbeth," Daviot said, letting his hand fall to the desk. "We're on the same side. You can rely on me to look after your best interests, but if you cause problems you attract the wrong kind of attention from the powers that be. Life then becomes difficult for both of us. Work with Sergeant Bland to resolve his investigation and we can get back to normal again."

"Sergeant Bland," Hamish began slowly, "why you? Why no' a secret service team? Why would a police sergeant be sent all this way to track down a bunch o spies?"

"I'm a cop all right," Bland replied, "or at least it's one of the things I have been. Putting me back in a uniform keeps this all as low key as possible."

Hamish looked from Daviot to Bland before slowly nodding his head. He knew he had no real choice in the matter, but he had at least made his feelings clear. Like it or not, he was now lumbered with a partner he didn't want and an assignment that would doubtless drag on through the autumn and beyond. At least this wasn't happening at his busiest time, the height of the Highland tourist season. He got to his feet.

"Aye, well," he said with a resigned shrug, "I suppose we'd better get on wi' it then."

"We'll need to interview you, sir," said Bland, also standing up, "as well as Mr. Anderson and Mr. Blair."

"DCI Anderson and I will put ourselves at your disposal here in Strathbane," said Daviot. "DCI Blair is down in Glasgow. He will be under orders to do the same."

Hamish and Bland then left Daviot at his desk, Bland picking up a large black hold-all from Daviot's outer office. Helen, Daviot's secretary, looked up from her keyboard as they strode past. She expected some insolent quip from Hamish and had been composing a particularly vicious put-down ever since she'd booked today's appointment with her boss. But he left without a word and, disappointed, she shelved her unused retort in her memory for future use.

Not a word was spoken between Hamish and Bland until they had made their way down into the car park. Hamish pressed a button on his key fob to unlock his Land Rover, then paused, leaning against its side.

"I suppose," he said slowly, "you thought I was being a wee bit unhelpful back there."

"I know you have your reasons," Bland said calmly. "You want a nice quiet life in Lochdubh, and you see me as a threat to that."

"Aye, you're right, but I know you'll do what you have to do whether I'm playing along or not."

"And I know you'll play along because, working alongside me, you can keep an eye on what I'm up to."

"I think we understand each other," Hamish said with a quiet laugh.

"We do," Bland said, smiling and offering Hamish his hand. "When I was last here we parted as friends. Still friends?"

"Still friends," Hamish confirmed, shaking hands. "And I've no' forgotten that I'm in your debt. When Blair went mad and pointed that gun at me, he might have shot me if you'd no' disarmed him."

"Yeah, I reckon you owe me for that, buddy!" Bland grinned, slinging his bag into the back of the car. "But I'm in no hurry to stand in front of any gunmen, so don't expect me to call in that marker any time soon!"

"Aye, but neither will I forget," Hamish assured him, swinging open the driver's door. "Now let's get the hell out of Strathbane and back home to Lochdubh."

***

The route from police headquarters to the Lochdubh road took them out of Strathbane's drab city centre through an area of shabby low-rise factory buildings made to look all the more dilapidated in the flat light, dulled by the heavy grey clouds lumbering in from the Atlantic.

"Strathbane's not exactly the jewel of the Highlands, is it?" commented Bland, staring out the window at the litter-strewn car park of an unused industrial unit, its few windows boarded up and its gate chained shut.

"It's no' all as bad as this," Hamish replied, shaking his head when he heard his own words. Was he really defending Strathbane? He hated the place. He hated the run-down shopping area, the concrete tower blocks, and the seedy backstreets haunted by drug dealers and their prey. Yet it was still part of the Highlands. It was still like a member of the family, and families can bicker, quarrel, and criticise among themselves, with their own—but when anyone from outside the family has a bad word to say, it's a different story. The family stands together. "There are some nice parts. Superintendent Daviot bides here and he has a nice house. Strathbane suffered when the fishing industry collapsed, and nothing they've tried to get up and running here has ever really worked."

"So, ripe for regeneration, eh? But never a patch on Lochdubh."

"That it's not," Hamish agreed, "and never will be."

The road climbed up out of the town and through a

belt of pine trees, emerging onto an area of high moorland, where Hamish turned onto the A835 heading towards Inchnadamph.

"This is more the kind of scenery I remember from my last trip to Scotland," Bland said, waving a hand at the steep rocky hillside on their right and the boggy ground on their left that rose more slowly through countless ponds and lochans to mountain peaks smothered with cloud. The sinister dark blues and greys of the clouds made it look as though scraping the summits had bruised their underbellies. "What's over there, Hamish?"

"That's the Drumrunie Forest wi' the twin peaks o' Cul Mor yonder. It's no' the highest hereabouts, under three thousand feet, but on a good day you can see all the way out to the Isle of Lewis from the top, and Lewis is near forty miles offshore."

"Did you say Drumrunie *Forest*? I'm not seeing a whole lot of trees out there, bud."

"Aye, well at one time—and we're talking about thousands of years ago—the whole o' Scotland was one massive forest. Here in the northwest there were oak, birch, rowan—all sorts, including the Scots Pine, of course."

"Really? The only trees we've come through looked like well-managed forest, like the countryside had been tamed. Up here it's really dramatic—really wild."

"It's wild, right enough, but there are still plenty who live here, crofters and the like. When this was all forest it was properly wild. There were wolves, bears, elk, boar, and even big cats like lynx. All o' those are long gone."

"What happened?"

"People. Around six thousand years ago people began burning the forests to create grazing land. Then there was a spot o' what's nowadays called climate change that didn't fare well for some o' the trees. What was left was hacked down over the next three thousand years to build houses and ships, and for fuel."

"All of the original forest is gone?"

"There are massive areas o' new forest, but only patches o' the ancient Caledonian Forest still exist. Down south in Fortingall there's a yew tree they say is over five thousand years old."

"Wow. I'd like to go take a look at that."

"Fortingall's down near Aberfeldy," Hamish said, shooting a glance at Bland. "That's near a four-hour drive from here. I thought you were here to catch spies, no' to hit the tourist trail."

"I've never been against combining business with pleasure," Bland said, grinning, "but the old yew tree might have to wait a while longer. I need to fill you in on what we now know about the guys we're looking for."

"Aye, and maybe we can try a bit o' business and pleasure on that front," Hamish responded, peering out through a windscreen now spattered with raindrops at an ever-darkening sky threatening to deliver a deluge. "Once we're back in Lochdubh this evening and I've fed my dog and cat, we can head out to the Italian for a bite to eat. The food there's top notch."

"Sounds good to me," said Bland as the automatic

windscreen wipers kicked in, working desperately to clear the mix of giant raindrops and hailstones now battering the car.

***

By the time they reached Lochdubh, dense curtains of rain were scouring the road, and crossing the stone humpbacked bridge that was the only way into the village, Hamish could see the waters of the River Anstey running fast and black down to the loch. The rocks over which the river usually tumbled, creating lacy white frills, were now completely submerged, and the Anstey was threatening to burst its banks.

"River's running pretty high," said Bland, peering down through the gloom.

"Aye," Hamish agreed. "I've no' seen it swell so quickly in a long while."

They drove on into the village, the whitewashed cottages on the lochside road looming like ghosts in the gloom. When they reached the police station, they made a dash through the rain to the side of the building and the kitchen door. Hamish's dog, Lugs, a large joyous creature of several colours and numerous breeds, provided his usual manically enthusiastic welcome, tail waving like a flag, ears flapping like wings, as he bounced around their legs. He seemed every bit as happy to welcome Bland, a stranger, as he was to see Hamish. Sonsie, Hamish's cat, was far less generous with her affection. She rubbed herself against Hamish's legs, her purring rumbling like pebbles on a drum. Then she gave Bland a look of pure disdain, turning her back on him with divine indifference and strutting over to sit by her food bowl. She stared at Hamish, blinking twice as though issuing an instruction for him to do his duty.

"I've a bit o' pollock for you, Sonsie, and some venison sausages for you, Lugs," Hamish said, opening the fridge. Lugs barked joyously on hearing the words "venison sausages."

"That's a real big cat," Bland said, leaning against the kitchen sink. "I can understand why there are rumours about her."

"Rumours?" Hamish raised an eyebrow. "Those would be rumours about her being a wild cat, would they?"

"Just what I heard." Bland shrugged.

"It would be illegal to keep a wild cat without a special license, and in any case, no wild cat has ever been tamed." Hamish offered the two undeniable facts to smooth the way for something that was much farther from the truth. "Sonsie's just a big tabby."

"Whatever you say, Hamish." Bland grinned, picking up his bag. "Can I stow this somewhere, then maybe we can grab that bite to eat at your Italian place."

"Upstairs on the left. We'll drive to the restaurant. Willie will have a table for us." He glanced out the window. "Any table we like, I should think. Nobody else will be out on a night like this."

***

Half an hour later they burst in through the door of The Napoli restaurant, shaking rainwater from their fluorescent, hi-vis Police Scotland rain jackets, although both had changed into casual clothes rather than their uniforms. Willie Lamont looked up from where he was polishing one of the establishment's complement of empty tables.

"Hamish, come away in. Good to see you!" Willie called cheerfully.

"Willie, this is Sergeant James Bland from Chicago," Hamish said, hanging his jacket on a coat stand near the door. "He's going to be working wi' me for a bit."

"*Benvenuto*," Willie said, shaking Bland's hand.

"*Piacere di conoscere,*" Bland replied smoothly in Italian. Momentarily paralysed by a mix of panic and confusion, Willie gave him the fixed, frozen smile of a cartoon character who's just been whacked with a frying pan but isn't yet feeling the effect.

"Okay if we sit here?" Hamish said, parking himself at a table by the window.

"I'll bring you the menu," Willie said, recovering sufficiently to scurry off to the bar area.

"Willie's no' very good at talking Italian," Hamish said in a low voice. "In fact, he gets his English words mixed up as well, but he tries hard."

"I can help him practice a bit," Bland said, smiling. "I've spent some time in Italy."

Willie returned and offered Hamish a menu, recommending the starter of "Proscoosho di Parma."

"I think that's *Proscuito di Parma,*" Bland pointed out.

"Aye, that'll be it," Willie agreed, handing Bland a menu.

"We'll have a bottle o' your Valpolicella, Willie," Hamish said, looking to Bland, who gave an approving nod.

"Excellent choice!" Willie congratulated Hamish on choosing exactly the same wine that he always chose, while scribbling unnecessarily on a pad. "Una bottickleyo."

"A bottle is *una bottligia,*" said Bland, and Willie nodded an acknowledgment, although looking slightly peeved at having been corrected again.

"And I'll have the spaghetti wi' meatballs," Hamish announced, once again ordering his usual. Bland opted for that as well, holding out his menu for Willie to take.

"*Grazie,*" said Bland.

"Pricko," Willie responded.

"I think you mean *prego,*" said Bland.

"Of course," Willie said, smiling politely, then hurrying to the kitchen muttering softly to himself. "I ken fine what I meant…pricko."

"Willie used to be my constable," Hamish said. "Then he married Lucia, whose parents own this place, and came to work here."

"She must be quite a woman for him to give up his career."

"She is that." Hamish nodded. "But, truth be told, Willie's heart was never in being a police officer. He's far happier here."

"I seem to recall that another two of your guys work at the big hotel that I stayed in on the edge of the village."

"Aye, Freddy's the chef at the Tommel Castle and Silas works security. Both o' them were my constables at one time. I've another one, Dick Fraser, now runs a bakery business in Braikie wi' his wife, Anka."

"Yeah, I met Dick on my last visit too. It's good to know that you have people in the area that you can trust. We might need them."

"No!" Hamish waved a hand across the table as though pushing that thought straight through the window and out into the storm. "I've seen what these people you're after are like, and there's no way I'm putting any of my friends in any kind o' danger."

"I'm with you there, buddy. We don't want that. All I meant was that it will be useful to have eyes and ears around the area while we're tracking down the bad guys. You know people around here. They trust you. That's why I need you to help me find the men on our list."

"So who are they?"

Bland fell silent as Willie appeared with the wine and made a show of opening the bottle and offering a taste before pouring two glasses.

"*Grazie,* Willie," said Bland, smiling.

Willie looked at him for an instant, finally deciding that Bland was trying to be friendly rather than patronising, and gave a slight nod.

"*Prego,*" he said, taking care to pronounce the word just as Bland had done before returning to the kitchen.

"We've identified a dozen names on the spread-sheet," Bland explained. "Over the years, four have died of natural causes—some of these people are getting on a bit, you know. Of the remaining eight, two have died very recently—quite soon after you got your hands on the spreadsheet—in circumstances that can only be described as highly suspicious. I think it's a bit of a coincidence to have two such deaths just when it looked like the spy ring was about to be exposed."

"The only really believable thing I ever heard any TV detective say was that when it comes to murder, there's no such thing as coincidence."

"Too true," Bland said, laughing. "Proving they were murdered isn't really what I'm here for, but taking a look at the deaths, talking to known associates, might help us to track down the rest of the outfit."

"Who were the dead pair?"

"The guy down in Glasgow was Edward Chalmers. He used to work at the Royal Navy's submarine base at Faslane. He apparently committed suicide at his home in Glasgow by setting fire to himself."

"That's a hellish way to die," Hamish said with a grimace. "No' the way most folk would choose to end their lives, but a braw way to destroy any evidence of foul play."

"Exactly. The second dead guy was Callum Forbes, who seems to have driven his car off a cliff somewhere south of here, near Lochcarron."

"Aye, I heard about that," Hamish said, rubbing his chin. "It was at Applecross only a few days ago, was it no'? I've a pal, Lachlan, works at the police station in Lochcarron. We can ask him about yon car crash."

"That could be a good place to start."

Willie arrived bearing two huge plates piled high with steaming pasta, glistening in a rich tomato sauce, with tempting meatballs peeking out from behind a veil of spaghetti strands. He made a great show of offering them grated "*parmigiano*" from a small bowl and "*pepe nero*" from a large, phallic-looking pepper grinder, then retreated to the kitchen again, pleased that Bland appeared to approve of his pronunciation.

"So, what about the final six?" Hamish asked once they were alone. "Surely they're no' that hard to find if you have their names."

"I think I've traced one of them," Bland said, tucking into his meal. "Hey, this is real good…But we need to approach him in a way that won't alert the others. Trouble is, I don't really know who the others are. I have names, but that's about it. One of them has gone to ground—dropped off the radar completely. The others—well, the names we have could be phony because there's no trace of them at all."

"I can probably come up wi' some way o' getting to talk to the one you've traced," Hamish said, twirling pasta on his fork. "I'll see if I recognise any o' the others. You can show me the list when we're back at the station."

"Your station's also your home," Bland said, and Hamish nodded, his cheek bulging with a mouthful of meatball. "What was all that between you and Daviot about stations being shut down?"

"There's ay a list sitting on somebody's desk," Hamish said, having swallowed hard to clear his mouth. "There's ay somebody wi' one o' the top police jobs trying to balance his books. There's ay a plan to save money by shutting down what some see as wasteful rural stations. No' so long ago there were police stations all around the north coast. Folk could go there when they had a problem and somebody was ay there for them—they could rely on their local police. Now a police station's a rare sight, heading for extinction like the lynx and the elk, and those that are left aren't all permanently manned. Ower at Dornoch, the police station used to have an inspector, a sergeant, and a dozen constables. Now it's gone."

"So you do whatever you must to keep Lochdubh open and keep policing at the heart of your community."

"I suppose so," Hamish agreed, "but more than anything, it's my home."

They ate in silence for a few minutes before Hamish reached for the bottle to top them up with a second glass of wine. Suddenly his phone rang.

"Hamish! We're on the bridge!" a voice cried through the thrash of torrential rain and the heavy boom of fast-moving water. "It's broke! The bridge is broke!"

"Mrs. Patel?" Hamish said, getting to his feet. "You mean the bridge over the Anstey?"

"Aye, the van's stuck and the bridge is going!"

"We'll be right there!" Hamish called, reaching for his jacket and heading for the door.

"I'll keep this warm for you!" Willie shouted, appearing

as if by magic to spirit their plates away just as his only two customers ran out into the rain.

They raced along the lochside road in the Land Rover, blue lights flashing and siren wailing.

"Had trouble with the bridge before?" Bland asked.

"No' as far as I can remember, but there's no' been any kind o' maintenance on that auld bridge for years, so maybe this was just a matter o' time."

They slammed to a halt just short of the bridge where Mrs. Patel stood at the side of the road, waving and pointing. Somewhere behind the dazzling glare of its headlights, Hamish could make out the shape of a van slouched sideways at an unnatural angle. He jumped out and strode over to Mrs. Patel.

"Mrs. Patel—is Mr. Patel in the van?" he said, raising his voice above the howl of the storm.

"Aye! Please get him out o' there, Hamish!" she wailed. "The van's stuck but he won't leave it. We've been to the cash-and-carry in Strathbane and we've near a fortnight's worth o' stock in it!"

"Get in the Land Rover, Mrs. Patel," Hamish said. "We'll get him off the bridge."

With Bland at his side, he ran the few short yards to the bridge, hauling a flashlight from the pocket of his rain jacket. He could hear the frantic revving of the van's engine accompanied by the useless spinning of its rear wheels.

"Take it easy, Mr. Patel!" Hamish yelled through the driver's window. "Let us have a wee look!"

Bland was already at the rear of the van with his own flashlight, and he grabbed Hamish's arm as he approached to stop him going any farther.

"Half the middle section of the bridge has vanished!" he shouted above the noise of the rain and the rushing water. He played his torch beam across a dark gap below which they could see a massive tree trunk wedged under the bridge. "That thing must have hit the bridge like a battering ram!"

The van's rear wheels were floundering in the gap, spinning in the air. A couple of stones from the side wall detached themselves and disappeared into the water.

"The whole bridge is starting to crumble under its own weight!" Hamish shouted, turning towards the van again. He yanked open the door and dragged a protesting Mr. Patel out into the rain. "It's no' safe here!" Then, each taking an arm, he and Bland half-ran, half-carried Mr. Patel down to the Land Rover, bundling him into the back seat, where his wife threw her arms around him.

"We can use the Land Rover's winch to haul the van clear o' the bridge," Hamish said, grabbing a remote-control handset from the glove box. "James, stay here wi' the car just in case."

Moving to the front of the car, he released the winch hook, using the handset to start the motor reeling out the cable. Carrying the cable back through the rain towards the bridge, he hooked it securely to a towing point beneath the van's front bumper. He then pressed a button on the handset to reverse the winch motor, and it began slowly dragging the van forwards, heaving its rear wheels out of the gap. With the wheels back on a solid surface, the van began slithering towards the bridge's side wall. Hamish jumped into the cab. He tried starting the engine but it wouldn't fire. Then, coming from behind him, he heard the ominous rumble of falling masonry.

"Hamish!" Bland roared. "Get out of there! The whole bridge is going!"